# BLACKBOX

# BLACKBOX

Nick Walker

review

First published in Great Britain in 2002
by Review

An imprint of Headline Book Publishing

10 9 8 7 6 5 4 3 2 1

ISBN 0 7472 6876 2

Typeset by
Letterpart Limited, Reigate, Surrey

Printed and bound in Great Britain by
Mackays of Chatham plc, Chatham, Kent

HEADLINE BOOK PUBLISHING
A division of Hodder Headline
338 Euston Road
LONDON NW1 3BH

www.headline.co.uk
www.hodderheadline.com

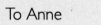

To Anne

# THE TROPOSPHERE

Five miles high, over the Atlantic. The jet stream pushing east, atmosphere thin, pressure low, the world spinning counter-clockwise.

A plane finds a swift westerly and hitches a ride. Five hundred knots. Crossing time zones.

Its name is SA109. Its tail fin is green and so are its passengers. The cabin crew smile but unconvincingly.

The sea, the sky, and the spirit are all black.

Not the flight recorder though. That's orange. There are arrows on the wings pointing to its location. Recording now. One, two, one two.

It is a decisive journey. For me, at least.

I have a little radio with me. I twist the dial trying to find a Phone-In, Flight Fright, or Funny Phobias. Or even Tommy Tempo's Nite Moods Orchestra. He's a catchy arranger. You can dance all night long with Tommy Tempo. He does a smooth *Don't Fence Me In* by Bing Crosby using a tenor sax for Bing's voice and some clarinets for the Andrews Sisters.

It would be good to have some music now. It's good for keeping the spirits up.

But the plane flies through frequencies so fast I can't find any stations. Either that or it's broken. Or there's something wrong with my ears.

And I am freezing.

And I am light-headed.

And it is very hard to keep a train of thought.

There are stewardesses aboard this plane, and a flight engineer, and a co-pilot and a pilot with good teeth and a deep voice.

He is in the toilet. Washing his face, looking at himself in the mirror, he feels old, muttering his thoughts: not everyone so well. Not everyone so happy. Not everyone so glad.

He feels a sense of relief now and he's counting down the seconds and there are not so many of them now and they get shorter and shorter and he tries to remember, but it's all too late and his uniform's too tight and he smells of sweat, and in his dream he's on his best behaviour and he's dancing in a little white suit by a river where it's muddy and he's singing for his parents the song they want to hear and he's not swearing like a cunt now because he doesn't want to upset them and he's trying to make friends with all the other children and he's covering his toys in shit because he's starting to lose hope and it better come soon because he's not as patient as he hoped he was and he's older now and he can't remember numbers and he's frightened that it's going to hurt and so if it isn't quick he may start crying and he's got to stay calm and he's got to bite his tongue and grip his wrist and he's got to remember to smile.

He dries off his face and rejoins his colleagues in the cockpit. And they ask him how he is and he says he's fine. He says he's good.

And there's a passenger on this plane who thinks of herself as a flower on a cherry tree, opening her petals and falling through the sky. Scattering her sweet blossom bravely and beautifully on the ground. She thinks about writing a little poem about it on her drinks serviette, but she hasn't got a pen.

And I thump out a little rhythm. Bump bump bump. Bump bump bump.

But it is an erratic beat. Like my heart. And my head is full of distracting questions. I am wondering how much physical hardship a human body can endure. I am wondering about the effects of oxygen on the function of memory. I'm wondering what sort of lard sea swimmers use to keep warm and where they get it from. I'm wondering if these are really the best circumstances under which to be telling a story.

And we are higher than a mountain and there's no air above us. It's all below us, at ground level, and it's compressed by the atmosphere. And the pressure's one kilo on a square centimetre, but it doesn't bother them there as the blood is thick and it can stand it just fine.

And breathing this air is an air traffic controller who looks at blips. And the blips swim in front of him because he's tired and unhealthy and when he shuts his eyes they're still there, expanding and shrinking and pirouetting under his lids.

But today he's not at his screen. He's not in the tower. He's in a field and his feet are wet and there's sick on his shirt and his breath is frosting and he's looking up and waiting and wishing things were different.

And his breath floats upwards and he's wondering what has happened to the trade winds. Perhaps they've died. Perhaps he's in the doldrums. He's thinking of dead calm and slow moving surface winds, Horse Latitudes, above and below the equator, where sailing boats flounder and had to throw precious cargo overboard in an effort to lighten the load. Horses were discarded. Valuable but heavy.

He wonders how they got them over the side. Did they make them jump? Perhaps they were made to walk the plank. Blindfolded. He imagines a slow drifting vessel in a sea of thrashing horses. Crew praying for a wind. Water screeching. Perhaps some of the horses swam after the crawling ship, hoping to get pulled back on board.

He thinks of tragic cargo as he waits and waits.

No light breeze here though. No need to jump ship unless I make the choice myself. I'm in a jet stream. The wind is at my back. And Solomon said, 'Around and around goes the wind, and from its circuits returns again.' And he was right and if you're facing the wrong way it can hit you square in the face and knock you off your feet. He should have pointed that out.

I say Solomon; in fact it was someone pretending to be Solomon, writing Ecclesiastes and calling himself the son of David. High risk. You're bound to get found out sooner or later. You've just got to hope it's after you're dead.

But I am real. I'm pinching myself and though my fingers are numb and the thing I'm pinching is numb, and though I can't see myself because it's so dark and I can't hear myself speak because it's so loud, I know I exist. *Cogito ergo sum.* And the story is mine and this plane is its end.

Another plane is its start.

And its arrival is the point of departure.

Its name is SA841 and it took off from New York City and landed six and a half hours later at Birmingham International Airport, UK, at 7.05 GMT. The day is yesterday.

I don't know how they number planes. Were there eight hundred and forty planes before SA841? Eight hundred and forty pitiful journeys where the reading lights cast their limp beams over damaged cargo and the safety film stars Kurt Cobain. And what is SA? Sorry Ass? I don't know the answer so I shall tap my feet and rock to and fro and I will count them all. From SA841 to nothing. Each one a little dedication. A little disappointment. A little journey to the here and now and when I reach nothing, I will be nothing, and all will be well and all will be over.

Wings level, the hover over, friction howl and reverse thrust. The plane touches down. In the control tower it is the last plane of Michael Davies's shift.

This is the start of my countdown.

## 840

Another black scar on the runway.

## 839

Michael guided the plane to its gate, clocked off and an hour later pulled onto the A45 and put his foot down hard. Reaching into his breast pocket he fished out the cassette that Rose had given him. Rose was a cleaner at the airport. He put the tape into the machine and a rich Welsh voice greeted him.

'Hello, I'm Dr Frankburg PhD. Before we proceed I should tell you that there will be times during this tape when I will be encouraging you to concentrate soley on my voice. This is to draw you into a state of deep relaxation. So I'm asking you now to put yourself in an environment which is free from distraction. One where it is safe to close your eyes.'

Michael Davies hit seventy.

'This tape is designed for you to overcome your fears and become a more confident and relaxed person.'

## 838

Rose said the tape was a head-cleaner of sorts.

## 837

A piano played gently in the background.

'It may be that you are listening to this tape because you are feeling unhappy with life's pressures. It may be that you are finding things more difficult to cope with. You have become more tense recently. Perhaps you are having problems in a relationship. You may have a big decision pending, or perhaps you have a stressful job...'

A speed camera flashed in his rear-view mirror.

He cursed Dr Frankburg PhD and hoped for his sake the camera was out of film. This relaxation tape was having the opposite effect to the one intended.

## 836

According to *Aviation World*, the ten most stressful jobs ranked:

1. US President
2. Firemen
3. Chief executive officers
4. Undercover Agents
5. Taxi drivers
6. Surgeons
7. Policemen
8. Astronauts
9. Football players
10. Air traffic controllers

## 835

Michael thought it was nice to get into the top ten of anything. Even bad things.

And he was in pretty glamorous company. Except taxi drivers.

'...find you are talking to yourself...'

Michael Davis had missed a bit of tape. He rewound.

'...are listening to this tape because you are feeling unhappy...'

Too far, he skipped on.

'...sexual impotence...'

He rewound again.

'...listening to this tape because you are feeling unhappy...'

He turned the cassette off. He would arrive home pent up. He'd argue with his wife.

## 834

Michael's wife is called Beth.

She is agoraphobic and won't have left the house. She listened to world events on the radio. Trying to get her mind outside, even if her body couldn't.

As Michael drove towards home, she was sitting on the stairs and a World Service newsreader was telling her that a group of people had set fire to themselves in China. They had emptied plastic bottles of fizzy pop, filled them with petrol, taken them into a public square, drenched themselves and lit their clothes with cigarette lighters. It took three minutes from when the fire was first set to the time it was extinguished. Two out of the eight lived, but only just. Beth hoped that the next day's delivery of the newspapers would print photographs of the event and perhaps include a picture of the survivors. Then she could cut it out and put it into her scrapbook. Alongside the others.

She thought about ringing her newsagent to ask him to add *The South China Morning Post* to her paper delivery but suspected he wouldn't have it. He already went out of his way to get her a dozen internationals. The paper delivery boy was only twelve but had a hernia coming.

Beth has other phobias too. And she has phobophobia: fear of one's own fears.

## 833

Michael assumed that Beth would prefer a familiar row to an unfamiliar calm brought about by a self-help tape. He assumed she'd get suspicious that he was having an affair or hadn't gone to work at all.

Beth, in fact, couldn't give a shit one way or the other. Wouldn't mind if he got pissed and crashed his car. It would serve him right for pretending to recycle her newspapers but actually fly-tipping them on the A45.

## 832

Beth's favourite cutting is a picture of Thich Quang Duc who immolated himself on a busy crossroads in Saigon in 1963. He'd remained seated in the lotus position and hadn't moved a muscle or uttered a sound. It was the crowd surrounding him who had wailed and sobbed.

Beth had also been burned in 1963, almost on the same day, and almost as badly. She was fourteen, but unlike Thich Quang Duc her picture hadn't made *Life Magazine*. Not even the *Surrey Gazetteer*.

## 831

Michael let the car be silent. The day's anxieties stayed crackling below the surface like static on a muggy day. The road slipped under him. A page from *The New York Times* blew onto his windscreen. Michael flicked it away with his wipers.

He is an unhappy man but would hate anyone to think so.

## 830

In the back room of the Wellington Arms in the same city and at the same time, a man calling himself Unfunny John paced behind a damp curtain.

The cigarette smoke made him wheeze. The temperature in the room made his face flush red and his ruffled shirt stick to his body. There was a patch of eczema on his chest which had flared up. He resisted the urge to scratch it. If he scratched it he would get blood underneath his fingernails and it would make him hate himself.

## 829

John has a wife too. She is called Emma, he hasn't seen her for ten days and if he's not careful he'll never see her again. Emma worked at a morgue and thought about death, on average, every moment of her working day. She thought about it in her leisure hours too but she kept it hidden. Like people do.

Ten days ago she asked John if he knew what the 'divine wind' was. John felt a gag about indigestion coming, but swallowed it. Emma got withdrawn if he didn't take her seriously. So withdrawn she looked like she was on the slab herself and John thought the look unflattering.

## 828

Unfunny John worried about his stage name. Was it ironic or was it true? Perhaps he should change it to Suicide John.

No, who'd laugh at that?

He used to be a magician. Old school, despite being a young man. Sleight of hand. Illusions. Escapology.

Emma had been his assistant. She didn't want to be, she said she was already an assistant. He said a morgue assistant was no kind of assistant so he'd put her on stage, locked her in boxes and put swords through her. He'd made her cap her teeth, lose weight, and wear body stockings. She was better than this, she told him, she saw real men cut real people in two and magic didn't come close.

So Emma went back to the morgue and John became Johnny John, a knowing, politically conversant wisecracker doing open slots. Then he became the Mysterious Monsieur Jay, stream of consciousness observations on life which went down badly in working men's clubs. Then Screaming Johan, Political Fury. It was too hard to sustain and he'd croaked off stage after only half a set. He tried to be Comic John Heron but that was too exposing because John Heron was his actual name.

Ah, what the hell. Names were for tombstones.

He gouged a small hole in the black backcloth. Front side, the backcloth supported a banner reading 'Wellington Comedy Night'. Back side he was using the hole to scope the crowd. Looking for troublemakers. Looking for goofy laughers. Looking for psychos who might glass him.

In order to get a panoramic view he had to twist the curtain round, making the banner crumple and read 'Wellington Cody Night'.

One audience member laughed at this, but her name was Cody so she was the only one.

## 827

Cody Jameson was a writer. She was roughing it because she was blocked. She'd dyed her hair and was wearing tinted contact lenses to stay incognito. She was sitting at the back and thinking about Crime and Nerve.

## 826

From the hole John didn't spot a single familiar face. Not Benny. Not the hen party of stewardesses the manager had promised. Not no one.

He went back to pacing.

## 825

Today Michael Davies had had no panics, no complicated vectoring. The weather had been decent. His coffee hot. His new shirt complimented. His chair refurbished.

But there had been more traffic than normal. A couple of planes diverting from East Midlands. A light aircraft was off course. Nothing you'd call an emergency, just a little more concentration needed, and he felt he was running short.

He wondered if his mind was losing its sharpness. He did mental arithmetic: forty-five times thirty-seven. He timed himself.

## 824

*You Too Can Fly*. Rose the cleaner said it wasn't really about flying, it was about fear. She'd found the tape in a bin at the airport and had listened to it on her headphones. She gave it to Michael as he left the tower.

He insisted he didn't need it. Rose said course he didn't and patted him on the shoulder.

## 823

One thousand four hundred and eighty. Twenty-four seconds. Mind razor sharp. Michael Davies overtook and undertook and cut people up.

He would give *You Too Can Fly* to Beth.

Beth could only manage very short flights to Europe and only if she was dosed up with drink and tranquillisers. Aerophobia. Or pteromerhanophobia, depending on which sort of flying one was afraid of. Beth believed she had both.

She thought she'd try boring herself out of the problem. Skipping the Channel was never going to give her long enough to exhaust the phobia but if she flew to another continent her body might run out of energy to worry any more.

Tomorrow she'd fly to New York City. There and back, first class.

It would cost her more money than she could afford, but if it worked, money well spent.

It might not, of course. She could have ten of the most hellish hours of her life. But no one said busting a phobia would be a walk in the park.

Not that Beth found a walk in the park a walk in the park.

Michael wasn't going with her. He made things much worse on the whole.

She stared at her suitcase, packed and ready, and felt pin pricks of sweat pop out over her scalp. She turned the news up louder.

A tennis star had tested positive for drugs, a shuttle had successfully repaired a space station, and in New York City a crude explosive device had been discovered under the car of the CEO of a pharmaceutical company.

## 822

In New York, the police told the CEO off the record that the device was so badly made that it wouldn't have done more than scratch the paintwork. Even so he should remain vigilant. And so should his family. The CEO asked for round-the-clock protection but was refused. Not that politely, he thought.

## 821

The man responsible for making and planting the device was a fireman living in Brooklyn. He was at that point standing in the middle of Central Park, Manhattan, taking deep, deep breaths, getting the smell of car oil out of his nostrils and calming himself down. He waits for the boom. He thinks it is LOVE which is making him do these things but what does he know? I'll tell you he knows crap.

This man is my youngest brother. I wish I could say a few positive things about him. He calls himself 'the fireman', though he isn't part of any official firefighting unit. Indeed, if he ever saw a fire he would just stare at it, hypnotised. Or throw wood on it. His name's Edward but the name sticks in my throat.

## 820

The boom didn't come. No bangs or screams or fire engines or helicopters. Edward the Fireman let his breath billow dragon-like in the cold air.

He must have got his wires crossed, he thought. Or had a loose connection. He'd need to get some technical training if his GREAT ACTS were ever going to impress anyone.

# 819

Unfunny John wished backstage was more roomy. It was cramped and no good for pacing. He had been edgy all evening. Nameless, elusive edginess.

It started as he ate his TV dinner. He thought it might be food poisoning.

It wasn't though. He jittered. Coughing became gagging.

It stayed with him through his taxi journey back to the Wellington Arms and through the small tour of the backstage area. It eased off during the introductions to the bar staff but intensified during his pint of lime and soda and peaked at the arrival of his fellow performers (all strangers). Up and down, up and down.

Whatever was going on, he knew it was auxiliary nerves and not stage nerves. He'd dealt with those a long time ago.

His wife, Emma, was returning home that evening. Ten day trip away. New York City. Visiting a friend. She'd accumalated up ten days leave by working late. Tagging feet and cleaning scalpels. Before she left she said she'd tagged someone with her own name, Emma Heron, how about that? John said it was a common name. She said she'd painted the corpse's toenails. John said nice touch. She said she thought about sending a big dose of electricity through her and sending her home to John in her stead. John said he probably wouldn't notice. She said no he probably bloody wouldn't and stalked out. John said he was joking. She said he wasn't funny. He said he was Unfunny John, what did she expect? She said she expected something much, much, much, much, much, much, much, much, much, much, much, much, much, much better than this.

Perhaps she'd left for good. Perhaps this was why he was edgy.

He'd been told by someone, a therapist on a phone-in maybe, that correctly identifying a fear made the physical symptoms go away. Bringing it to the conscious mind, expressing it verbally, stopped the shakes. Or might.

'My wife's coming home today,' he said out loud.

The three other stand-ups looked up from their papers.

'What?' said one. Shelley.

'My wife. Emma. She's coming home today after a short trip abroad.'

There was a small pause.

'Jamaica?' asked Shelly.

'No. New York.'

There was another pause.

'I don't get it,' said a thin pale man.

He still shook. The phone-in must have got a B-list therapist.

Could be this club, thought John. It's new, I don't know anyone.

## 818

The 'divine wind' that John's wife referred to was a tempest that saved Japan from Mongol invaders in the thirteenth century when Kubla Khan dispatched an immense armada to conquer it. Realising that they were outflanked and outnumbered, all the shrines in Japan prayed to the sun goddess Amaterasu. Suddenly a typhoon appeared out of nowhere and struck the Mongol fleet, sinking or beaching most of the ships and killing over one hundred thousand of the Mongol troops. The resident pathologist at Emma's morgue was Japanese and talked to her about his native land whilst removing spleens and weighing brains.

'I think I am dead,' Emma told him once.

'Do you want me to feel your pulse?' he replied.

'That won't tell you anything.'

'Divine Wind', or Kamikaze, Emma wanted John to have it in his mind as she boarded her plane. Though John also thought a lot about death, Emma didn't think he thought about it seriously enough.

## 817

Beth Davies was sick on the floor. She hadn't been able to make it to the supermarket to buy proper food so she'd eaten old lentils and dried fruit. It'd been coming out of both ends.

She wouldn't mind diarrhoea on the plane though. The toilet was the best place anyway.

## 816

'Why is this curtain damp?' John asked.

'Sweat?'

'Right.'

On the stage, the manager of the Wellington Arms was trying to get the ball rolling. There was an amplified thump as he tapped the mike.

Unfunny John checked his appearance in the mirror. A dated dinner suit with the arms and legs just a bit too short. 'The suit's been hired,' went one of his jokes, 'I mean I own it's just been highered.'

The manager was getting front-line experience.

'Is this working?'

John couldn't remember the manager's name.

'Um hi, hello, hi.'

'Yeah it's on, you prick,' someone shouted.

'No, I know it's on, I'm saying, hi. I'm starting. I'm welcoming you to tonight...'

John had met this manager twice. Once on the phone the day before yesterday, once in the flesh twenty minutes ago.

What the hell was his name? Miles? Something like that.

On the phone, Miles had said he'd had a last-minute drop-out for his inaugural comedy night at the Wellington and could Unlucky John fill in.

'Unfunny John, the act's name is Unfunny John.'

Miles apologised. He was new to the game, didn't have a full grasp of who was who. But he'd made inquiries and was sure that Unfunny John was a who. A bona fide who.

John asked who had recommended him.

Miles said one of the other acts had tipped him off.

John asked who the other acts were.

Miles said they hadn't exactly been confirmed but they were very, very good. Big names.

John asked Miles to name them.

Miles claimed he didn't have the list in front of him.

John said he had a reputation to maintain and asked again who were the names.

Miles said they were pretty damn respected in the comedy community.

John had a bad vibe so made himself unavailable for the night in question.

Miles said he hadn't told John when the night was.

John lied and said he was in a sitcom which was taking up all his time so it didn't matter which date it was.

Miles asked which sitcom this was.

John's mind went blank and he didn't answer.

Miles said if he was in a sitcom then it would really bring the punters in.

John was still groping for the name of a sitcom.

Miles said if the opening night could have a sitcom star in it he'd be prepared to offer John two hundred pounds cash for a twenty-minute slot.

John immediately accepted the sum.

Miles said at least it would help him get other comedians in.

John pointed out that Miles said he already had other comedians, big name comedians.

Miles floundered but by this time both of them had lost their enthusiasm and were more than pleased to get off the phone to each other.

When John met Miles at the Wellington twenty minutes before curtain up, Miles asked John about the sitcom so that he could weave it into his introduction.

John said the sitcom had been temporarily cancelled because one of the actresses had died on set and he'd be grateful if Miles didn't bring it up. Miles had said oh bollocks and walked off, only later worrying that he might have been tactless.

It didn't matter to John, he'd made the story up. Though there was some spark of recognition. Perhaps he'd read about something similar in a paper.

## 815

As Michael Davies approached the city, he gave Frankburg another try.

'...as well as alcohol, prescription drugs, or massage. You have probably found that these are temporary measures, outside stimulants which give short-term relief but which leave you with a sense of emptiness, depression and feelings of inadequacy...'

He switched it off again.

## 814

John watched Miles's build up.

Miles was dealing badly with a nasty wail of feedback. He'd barely started but his face was already drenched in sweat.

The audience were finding it trying. He made a joke about it.

'Do you know what? That wailing sounds just like…' Miles's mind went blank.

## 813

John had left Emma's name with the doorman so she could get in free. She'd left New York at seven o'clock in the morning on SA841. Seven hours' travel time took you to two o'clock US time, add on the time difference, five hours, touch down at seven UK time, give her an hour to get through passports, pick up luggage, meet Benny, Benny explains about the Wellington show, half an hour for Benny to drive her home, half hour for a bath, something to eat, make some calls. What time now? He'd lost track. He started again. Left New York at seven…

## 812

'I'm saying the wail, it's…'

The crowd helpfully let the silence grow.

'Um…'

Miles had prompt cards. They were getting clammy in his breast pocket. He was going to use them to introduce the acts. He had a good joke about getting the cards muddled up and welcoming Frank Sinatra to the stage. But he was only going to get to the cards later, he'd learned the opening by heart. A snappy intro followed by a general housekeeping notice about being careful with the glasses.

Perhaps the crowd would let it go. After all, they were quite drunk and boorish, and they weren't here to see him anyway. He'd just move on.

'Sounds like what, you prick?'

## 811

Emma wouldn't come. Why should she? She'd seen the damn act a million times before. She hated it. He knew that. He wasn't blind. The last thing she'd need after jet lag was a couple of hours with a hostile crowd at the Wellington Arms watching his lame act go badly and have to spend the rest of the night going through the whys and wherefores.

How would she get to the Wellington Arms anyway? Benny wasn't going to hang around while she had a bath, was he? At least he hoped he wasn't. An unwelcome image popped into his head. He shook it away. Get a grip. He looked through the hole again.

No wife. No Benny.

## 810

'That sounds like a nasty bit of feedback there. Might have to watch that.'

## 809

John's confidence drained away.

His act was that of a nervous performer making a farcical mess of his performance. He'd bound on, all smiles and savoir-faire, clock the crowd, freeze, gulp, tug at his too tight collar, smile nervously, try to speak, croak 'Good evening', cough to clear it, sweat. His voice would break, he'd drop the microphone, get caught up in the lead, pick it up, electrocute himself, pretend his brain had short-circuited, deliver a stream of rubbish jokes with forgotten punchlines or no punchlines at all.

It had been hit and miss in the past and it needed a showbiz build-up to give a good contrast.

Miles was supplying no such contrast. His intro lacked showbiz.

'You don't want to go on first, do you, Shelley?' asked John.

'No.'

John heard the sound of smashing glass.

'Now that reminds me,' said Miles. 'I have got something I want to say about glasses, as it happens, and I don't want to get heavy or anything, we're here to have a good time after all, but those glasses need to be returned to the bar...'

There was another smash.

'...OK, there goes another one, and as yet it's not serious, but I will say, and

I think I'm being fair, that if there are any more breakages, I'll have to operate a sort of deposit scheme whereby—'

He was drowned out by the sound of smashing glass.

## 808

Michael Davies hit eighty-five and hummed Sinatra to unwind.

## 807

Did he give the doorman Benny's name? John couldn't remember. Benny would get pretty pissed off if he had to pay.

## 806

Michael overtook a family car with a MIND MY CHILD sticker in the back window. The kid inside gave him the V. Michael stuck his fingers up back and the dad saw him. The dad mouthed 'Fuck you' at him. Michael mouthed 'Fuck you' back. He saw the kid ask the dad what was being said.

Michael accelerated to ninety to get away from it all and sang Sinatra loudly. Not very tunefully though.

## 805

'OK, on with the fun, ladies and gents, and for our very first act, I'd like you to give a very warm Birmingham welcome...'

John shook out his hands and jumped up and down like a sprinter. It's two hundred quid, you'll be home in an hour.

'Who's getting two hundred quid?' said Shelley

'What?' said John, unaware he'd been speaking aloud.

'To Frank Sinatra!' said Miles.

'What did he say?' said John.

'It's an open slot, we're not getting paid,' said Shelley.

'Oh, sorry, that's next week. Got my cards muddled up there.' Miles's cards were like pulp in his hands.

'Frank Sinatra, is that your act's name, Shelley?'

'No.'

'What's he talking about then?'

Someone called Miles a wanker.

'John here's getting two hundred pounds. Anyone else here getting two hundred pounds?'

'Unfunny John, ladies and gentlemen!'

John bounded out onto the stage.

The spotlight hit him like a Colditz escapee. He was glad to be blinded. It stopped him from seeing the hostility in the eyes before him.

## 804

...and my name is Stephanie Wiltshire. Stephanie. Born in 1949. Hair greying. Skin greying too. Eyes brown but shut. Pinch, pinch, pinching hard. Nails unpainted and digging into my palms.

## 803

...and my teeth are straight but chattering, and my mouth is numb but counting down, eight hundred and t-t-t-...

## 802

...and here's something for you.

Any one of us is only six acquaintances away from anyone else. In 1960 Stanley Milgram, Harvard social psychologist, sent letters to randomly chosen residents of Omaha, Nebraska, and asked them to deliver the letters to a Mr Smith in Massachusetts. If they didn't know Mr Smith, they had to send it to someone else with the same instructions until someone who genuinely knew Mr Smith could post it to him. The average number of steps before Mr Smith received his letters was six.

## 801

So, if you gave me a celebrity, any celebrity, Frank Sinatra for example, if I had enough information about him I think I could find a link from me to him in six. Or less. After all, I'm a well-travelled girl.

## 800

I was once a stewardess and they go all over. I like to think I am the hero of this story because I'm telling it. Though, if asked, I don't believe many of the people in it would've said I'd been very heroic.

## 799

...and the Hs are stuttering out. N-n-n-n-nines are n-n-nightmare.

## 798

Frank Sinatra was helpful to Michael Davies on his journeys home.

He'd once found himself stranded with a broken clutch on the outskirts of Birmingham and had accepted a lift from a table tennis player returning to the city following a disappointing competition in Barnsley.

She'd had Sinatra on the stereo and had picked up Michael Davies because he looked even more disappointed with his luck than herself. They'd spent a while sitting silently together, driver and passenger, brooding on their bad fortune, till a muttered obscenity from one of them initiated a conversation based on the theme of keeping one's eye on the ball.

'Where's the risk?' Michael had asked. 'No risk, no stress. Take your eye off the ball for a second and a point's lost, a game. But no one's going to die as a result of an off backhand. Now take air traffic...'

She'd said it wasn't just about the death quotient. It was about shattered egos.

He'd said air traffic control had shattered ego plus the innocent lives of hundreds of people.

She'd asked what made him so sure they were innocent. Who was innocent?

He'd said all right not innocent, strangers then.

She'd said statistically many of them wouldn't be strangers either.

He'd asked her why couldn't she let him make his bloody point?

She'd said strangers was a relative term. He had some connection with someone on that plane, any plane, however slight. She'd said get talking to anyone, on a plane, on a bus, and he'd find that the school he went to was the same school as that attended by the girlfriend of the other one's cousin.

He'd said what?

She'd said for example.

She'd said it would be far more weird if one *didn't* find anything. She'd said the point was, each plane he'd guided in that night, and every night, would've been full of people he had some connection to. However slight. So technically they weren't strangers.

## 797

And she was right, too.

## 796

He'd said that made it worse. The lives of hundreds of friends and relatives were at stake. Whichever way she looked at it, he had a higher level of stress than a table tennis player.

Though not football players. He respected those.

She'd asked why. He didn't know exactly.

She'd said the issue was public failure. She'd had twenty thousand people watching her that night.

He'd said twenty thousand? For table tennis?

She'd said perhaps not twenty thousand.

In Barnsley?

She'd said all right, not twenty thousand.

He'd asked if her opponent had been Frank Sinatra.

She'd got irritated at his tone and threatened to kick him out.

He'd changed the subject by singing along to 'My Way' and saying he'd forgotten what a good voice Sinatra had.

## 795

Michael Davies thought *You Too Can Fly* by Dr Frankburg didn't compare to Sinatra, didn't even come close.

He overtook a transit and wondered what had happened to the table tennis player. They'd endeavoured to find a connection between them in six stages or less. They'd gone through everything. Childhoods, friends, schools, relations, holidays. They'd taken a long detour to prolong the game. Nothing had come up, to their disappointment.

It wasn't an exact science, she had said, and wrote her phone number on the Sinatra cassette cover. She'd given him the tape as well.

## 794

Unfunny John's hands were shaking. He still couldn't see his audience. Why didn't they turn the lights down? Sweat poured into his eyes and dislodged a contact lens. It fell out. John tried to catch it in his hands but failed. One eye went blind.

## 793

Michael drove through one of the city's long and satisfying underpasses thinking about the table tennis player. Even if she'd quit sport, she'd still be quite firm, unlike his wife. And he'd bet she was phobia free. He bet she flew, bet she was adventurous.

He felt in the glove compartment for the cassette cover to find out if her telephone number was still legible.

It had been a year ago, it might have faded.

In the flashing lights of the underpass he was just able to decipher it. Well, no harm in giving...

## 792

Another insult hit Unfunny John in the face and the corner of his eye ticked nervously. 'Tosser yourself,' he said feebly.

'Who booked this arsehole?' said someone.

Miles fidgeted nervously at the back. This isn't how he thought the evening would go.

'You can't make me leave,' said John. 'I have things to say.'

'Piss off!'

'Please listen.'

'Piss off!'

Everyone was saying piss off. Fuck off.

John began to tremble.

'Get this twat off the stage.'

John twitched in the spotlight. He took out a handkerchief and mopped his brow.

'I'm not a twat,' he muttered weakly.

'Bollocks!' shouted someone else.

A cunt hit him. And another, a left and a right. Both flanks. There was a lot of overlapping, he couldn't distinguish individual attacks.

Backstage a big bearded comic was looking from the wings slack-jawed. This was as bad as he'd seen it.

Shelley too. She left. She grabbed her stuff and went down the fire escape. The other comic had already gone: he heard the first 'wanker' and called a cab from his mobile.

Someone flicked a lit cigarette onto the stage. The burning end hit John's lapel and bounced off. Unfunny John's eyes glazed. He was rooted to the spot like a man who'd been hit hard on the head but hadn't yet gone down.

Miles was agitated. He considered his emergency options. Pulling the electricity would only plunge everything in darkness and that was the last thing he needed. He thought about setting off the fire alarm, but who'd hear it over the noise? What was this guy doing? Where was his sitcom material?

A glass hit the back curtain and smashed on the floor.

'Move on to the plastic glasses!' Miles shouted to his bar staff. He'd lost too many this evening.

From the back, working its way forward, a chant of 'You're shit!' was building into an organised rhythm.

John's eyes filled with tears.

'I'm not ... I'm not shit.' Trembling. Horrible.

The chanting grew louder. The room pulsed.

The mob stamped their feet and banged their glasses. Urgent beats reverberated round the room. Tribal. Baying.

More cigarette butts were flicked. A beer mat was lit and spun onto the stage. Cheap indoor pyrotechnics pleased the crowd. Another followed, and another.

Miles wished he had a sprinkler system. The noise crescendoed.

Unfunny John was besieged.

Two more glasses landed near his feet.

Tears streamed down John's face.

Anything said over the mike would be lost in the mêlée.

John felt like a child caught too far out to sea, facing an enormous wave with a tiny wooden surfboard.

Miles again turned to his bar.

'Pull the shutters down!' he shouted. 'Secure the bar! Where's the doorman I asked for?'

The storm intensified, the wave grew as if created by an earthquake out at sea. Sending a monumental breaker towards the city. Destroying all in its path.

When it seemed that it had reached the Wellington and would break over the stage, Unfunny John took a gun from his breast pocket.

He looked at it. Almost as if he was surprised that it was there. It was an army service revolver. Polished to a rare sheen.

Those at the front fell instantly silent.

John turned the gun over in his hands and then checked the barrel. Everything seemed to be in order.

John lifted the gun and put it inside his mouth.

The wave died. A silence broke.

Unfunny John looked around at the audience in front of him. The woman to his left, who twenty seconds ago had called him a 'fuckwit arsehole', now stood open-mouthed, as if the words had petrified on her tongue. An empty glass poised. Frozen like Lot's wife.

Many of the rest of the audience were in the same state.

Miles was no less immobilised. He'd never seen a firearm of any description before. He dreamt about getting shot with one. Many times. It was a recurring theme.

John stood to attention, gun in mouth.

A glob of dribble ran down the barrel.

John raised his free hand in a waving salute.

In his head John counted slowly to ten.

Miles was one big heartbeat.

1.2.3.4.5.6.7.

John started waving. A little wave, a small wiggling of his fingers.

Bye bye. 8.

Bye bye. 9.

At ten the shot was fired.

BANG!

## 791

BANG! John felt blood in his ears.

## 790

BANG! Cody felt a jolt of adrenaline burst through her body.

## 789

...SHIT!

Michael Davies swerved violently.

Brakes and tyres screeching. The sound bouncing off the walls of the tunnel. The underpass lights disorientating him completely.

Wheels mounting the kerb. Passenger door scraping the central wall. Sparks.

Avoiding the figure standing in the middle of the underpass.

A big sway to the right, the car almost tipping onto two wheels.

Back down. Fighting with the steering. More skidding. But past her. Didn't hit her.

'What the hell...'

In control of the car and out of the tunnel, Michael pulled over to the side of the road. Jumping out of the car, he looked back.

A figure. A woman. Dressed in a dark coat and carrying a suitcase (A suitcase? The police would ask, not a briefcase? So, a Samsonite, big, silver) was walking down the underpass away from him.

'Hey!' Michael shouted.

The woman stopped.

'Fucking idiot!' Michael shouted.

The woman looked around her, she appeared dazed, unsure.

She noticed Michael at the exit to the tunnel. For a moment the two looked at each other.

The woman took a pace towards him.

'Would you...?' She started saying.

But the moment passed, the woman turned back and seconds later went through a service door.

Michael waited till the thumping in his chest had calmed and his breathing had evened out, then he got back into the car and drove the rest of the way home.


## 788

BANG! A man was hit by a train and a woman puked on the platform.


## 787

BANG!

Blood and God knows what else exploded over the back curtain and John fell to the floor.

There was chaos again.

A woman collapsed. No one caught her. Strong men turned white or were sick on the floor, or both. Some screamed and screamed.

Miles, standing at the back, his hands on the bar shutters, started trembling so hard that it made the shutters rattle like hail on a tin roof. The big bearded comic hyperventilated, puffing out 'Oh Gods' with each shallow breath.

Somewhere in Miles's brain came the instruction to take control of the situation.

He turned to catch the eye of a young bartender who he'd hired the day before to cope with the comedy night rush. She had her hands over her ears and her eyes screwed shut. Miles remembered telling her that the pub was busy but friendly. He hadn't mentioned the possibility of someone shooting themselves in front of her.

Miles turned back. The room resembled a road disaster. He felt his life dismantling around him. Never had he seen such a distraught collection of people. Stumbling and confused, holding on to each other, recoiling from the stage. Sickened by the horrible guilt. We've driven this poor man to such an act.

We're animals.

## 786

John lay still. His eyes had stayed open. He could see his contact lens on the floor in front of him. A drop of sweat from his forehead dropped onto it and John watched it clean it and make a little prism, refracting the stage lights into a tiny rainbow. Red, green, violet.

He was glad he couldn't see his wife. Glad she hadn't made it. He thought, on this occasion, she wouldn't feel inclined to clap.

He remembered hearing of a man who'd hanged himself in his bedroom and had stuck a note on the door saying, 'Happy birthday, darling. Wait till you see this!'

The gun was still in John's limp and clammy hand. Emma's gun. She'd been given it by her father. He was old now. He'd been in the war. It had once killed someone. A German, Emma assumed, but it had been an English soldier. Friendly fire. Her father had kept that quiet.

## 785

Michael Davies pulled over and was sick in a layby.

## 784

Edward the Fireman walked out of Central Park with a stone and threw it through the window of a company which made painkillers. Then he ran away. Not as destructive as a bomb but a protest all the same. He disappeared into the subway, breathing heavily, thinking he wasn't as young as he used to be.

## 783

John put out a finger and touched the tiny rainbow and let his contact lens curl round his fingertip.

Then he slowly rose to his feet.

Again the chaos died and silence rippled through the room. John felt in control of a highly disciplined orchestra, well-drilled and responsive, capable of moving effortlessly from fortissimo to pianissimo.

Now, in the hush, he brushed himself down and straightened his bow tie. He took his handkerchief and dabbed the corners of his mouth as one would after eating a messy pear. He approached the microphone.

He coughed.

## 782

To Miles, the amplified sound was so otherworldly that he thought God himself had paused creation to speak to him directly.

Miles mouthed, 'Yes, Lord?'

## 781

'Ladies and gentlemen,' said Unfunny John. 'My name's John Heron. You've been a wonderful audience. Remember, comedy nights are here every Friday at the Wellington Arms. Goodnight and enjoy the next act.'

John left the stage.

'You're on,' he said to the big bearded comic.

## 780

Cody ran out of the Wellington Arms and onto the street where she breathed the air. She stopped a stranger and asked him for a cigarette. She smoked it and let the night dry the sweat from her face. Though she was trembling, she felt more relieved than she had done in months.

## 779

Beth let Michael Davies into the house because his shaking hands wouldn't let him get the key into the lock.

Oikophobia, she thought. Fear of the home.

## 778

In New York City, Edward the Fireman emerged from the subway into a high-class part of town. He thought about some more rock throwing, or a car-jacking. After all, if he did some time in the clink SHE might visit him. Kiss him through the bars. Write him dirty letters.

Every car seemed to be a cab though, and cabbies could get violent. And he'd left his gun at home.

Instead, he put a tape in his Walkman and walked into a fancy department store and started telling a sales assistant just what she could do with her so called in-store credit card.

## 777

The New York police visited the daughter of the pharmaceuticals CEO and told her it might be a good idea to vary the journey she took to work each day. Tamy said she would do. She always did. She was disappointed that the police didn't need to ask why anyone should want to kill her father.

## 776

Miles burst into the cramped dressing room.

'What the hell was that?' He was flustered from dealing with traumatised customers, many of whom had muttered darkly about suing him.

'It was my act.'

'You shot yourself.'

In one of his leisure moments John had found an obscure little course, run for theatre professionals, which in a week taught him how to rig up stage pyrotechnics, fireworks and small explosions. It taught him about wiring and timing devices and suppliers of small incendiaries. It gave him a certificate at the end.

Working tirelessly in the rented house he shared with Emma, John had created a gory package consisting of stage blood, chopped liver, and lubricant jelly contained in a polythene bag. A number of small detonators were attached which, when triggered, would cause the package to explode. It sounded like gunshot.

He'd experimented with various strengths of explosions and positionings, and various consistencies of gore, using many different ingredients. He'd pestered Emma for titbits from work.

'No,' she'd said.

'Just a few leftovers,' he'd asked, 'a bit of gristle, or an eyeball – an eyeball would be perfect.'

'STOP ASKING,' she'd shouted.

Quite a lot of money had been spent and his flat had looked like an abattoir by the end of the process, but the perfected effect, John believed, exactly duplicated the appearance of someone shooting their head off at close range.

He'd never seen anyone actually shoot their head off, of course, but he imagined if he did, it would look like this.

'Who's going to pay for that backcloth? It's ruined.'

'The jelly's water-based. It'll wipe off.'

Automatic learned response on hearing the words 'You're on' meant the big bearded comic had wandered dazed onto the stage. He hadn't started his routine, he'd just managed to pick a bit of liver off the microphone.

'They'll be all right. It'll just take them half an hour or so to get over it. Shock works like that. Now they know it wasn't real they'll have a new outlook on life. They'll cherish each moment much more. They'll start laughing again soon, I should think.'

John and Miles listened. There was nothing as yet.

'And look at the bar,' said John.

He was right on that front, the audience were buying expensive medicinal spirits.

Miles couldn't go through this every week, he'd have a heart attack. He refused to pay. John said he'd signed a contract.

Miles paid up. He respected contracts if nothing else. He'd been impressed that John had brought one along, he didn't think stand-up comics did that sort of thing.

Business concluded, John left by the back exit. For all his talk of the positive life-changing effect of his performance, he still didn't want to meet anyone who'd actually seen it.

The doorman shook his hand vigorously on the way out.

# 775

As John left the Wellington Arms, Doctor Frankburg Phd, creator of *You Too Can Fly*, was sitting in an uncomfortable chair in a dark and airless room experiencing the tickle from a bead of sweat running down his nose. He watched it drop onto the piece of paper in his hands.

He believed the words he had written to be beautiful on the page but simple and stupid if spoken aloud, especially by him.

## 774

John's phone rang when he was in the taxi.

'John speaki…'

'Where are you?'

'Benny?'

'Why hasn't your phone been on?'

'I've been doing the act. Did you pick up Emma?'

'She wasn't there.'

John had thought it would be funny if Benny was dressed in a way that made him look as if he was in the employ of a South American drug dealer. Chauffeur gear. Big moustache. Mirrored sunglasses. John made a sign saying 'Trophy wife of Señor Heron' for Benny to hold. Perhaps the disguise had been too good.

## 773

Dr Frankburg wiped the sweat from his papers. There was no pleasing rainbow effect, just smudged ink.

'Could we open a window?' he asked.

## 772

Benny hadn't been able to find Emma. He hadn't seen her at the airport. She wasn't at the flat. She wasn't anywhere. She'd got off the plane and vanished.

'Is her luggage there?' said John.

'No.'

## 771

There was only one item left on the carousel but it wasn't Emma's. It was a small brown briefcase which went round and round and round on its own. It stayed so long, it got caught up with baggage from the next flight. When that was all taken, it was left alone again.

It had the name Ronald Henderson on the tag.

## 770

John's taxi sped through the city.

He'd read a fairy tale once. *Long, Broad, and Sharpsight.* A prince had to keep an eye on a princess but each night she was whisked away by a wizard. Sharpsight could see to the ends of the earth and would spot her. Long could stretch tall enough to run them there twenty miles at a step. Broad could drink the sea and fetch her from the ocean bed. They'd always find her. Always bring her home. Neither John nor his friends had any of these attributes.

## 769

'We can't open the windows, we get traffic noise,' said a sound technician.

'Never mind then,' said Dr Frankburg.

'Try not to pop your Ps this time.'

'What?'

'Your Ps are popping.'

'Right. How awful. I'll watch that.'

Dr Frankburg coughed, a light turned from red to green and he continued recording.

'It is very important for you to realise that fear is a learned behaviour. As a newborn baby you were not frightened of spiders or snakes, of lifts or aeroplanes, open or confined spaces. There are many people and places which—'

'Cut, cut. Those Ps, Dr Frankburg, can you ease off on them?'

'I'm sorry, I'm not really very experienced at this.'

'You don't say.'

Dr Frankburg didn't need to be a trained therapist to detect in the resigned tones of the sound engineer hostility and contempt.

## 768

John Heron's taxi driver looked at his passenger and resolved to have a hip flask handy in future, so next time a passenger's wife went missing he could offer refreshment. It would get him better tips.

John asked him if he knew what the Divine Wind was. The taxi driver didn't. He looked at John anxiously in the rear-view mirror and wound down his window. The last thing he needed was a gassy passenger.

## 767

Samuel Thorn watched the darkening landscape flit past. The lights in the train had appeared brighter as the view outside grew gloomier, and Samuel was able to see the reflections of other passengers in the windows.

He liked this effect. It appealed to his theatrical nature. It was how phantoms could get represented on stage. Trick of the light. Pepper's Ghost.

He could watch the passing fields, lit by the setting sun, and as it cross faded with the lights in the train the image of the woman sitting on the opposite side of the carriage superimposed itself on the landscape. Hovering over it as if projected onto the sky.

## 766

Following the success of *You Too Can Fly*, Dr Frankburg felt he could dispense with the voice-over actor and narrate *Conquer Panic* himself. It would be much better if the listener knew that the words spoken were actually the doctor's. It would lend the proceedings an air of authenticity.

If anything took the gloss off the success of *You Too Can Fly*, it was that on the cassette sleeve was the credit 'Read by Samuel Thorn'. Quite small and hard to find as it was buried away amongst 'Additional thanks' and under 'Recorded at Fine Sound Studios', but there all the same. Like a splinter under the nail.

Frankburg had received a letter from an American psychoanalyst saying how his tape had not only helped her through a long haul flight to Australia, but she'd found it rather sexy too, and looked forward to meeting him in person at the Boston conference she'd discovered they were both to attend.

...I can go to conferences now you see, now I have your tape to get me through the flight. Yours in anticipation, Clara Redlake.

## 765

When Clara Redlake had asked for a stamp to the UK, the post office clerk had tried to look down her top. Clara had interpreted this as a result of denied suckling rights as a child.

And lust.

She'd also felt pretty pleased.


## 764

Dr Frankburg had been called many things, but never sexy, not even by his ex-wife. He was too flattered to explain that the voice wasn't his, but instead wrote back immediately saying he blamed his smooth voice on his Welsh roots and he too was looking forward to making her acquaintance.

He spent the weeks preceding the conference practising his impression of Samuel Thorn and praying that she didn't look too carefully at the credits.

His own voice was a pleasant Solihull Birmingham and since Wales was only a hundred miles to the west, Frankburg assumed there must be a similar dialectic root.

Whether there was or not, it didn't help him crack the accent and despite trying to speak this way exclusively, alarming many patients and fellow professionals ('Are you eating a hot potato, Dr Frankburg?') he found if anything he was veering further and further away from the valleys.


## 763

Michael Davies drank Scotch. Near misses always hit him hard. Beth told him forty-five times thirty-seven was 1,665 not 1,480. Michael told her sums were for weak and unoriginal minds.

'Numerophobia,' said Beth.

'Will you fuck off with this?' asked Michael. He thought Beth made these phobias up.


## 762

Frankburg asked the sound engineer for a glass of water. Memories of the Boston conference made his mouth dry and his larynx contract. He had turned up to see his astonishingly beautiful admirer, Clara Redlake, at the conference's opening dinner, hair shining in the evening sunset, backlit by the lights of the Boston harbour, laughing politely at a *bon mot* from an erect delegate, and he had faked tonsillitis to cover his unmastered Welsh.

Hoarsely introducing himself as the man behind *Overcome Your Fear of Flying*, he apologised for his rasping voice but said that it was a pleasure to finally meet.

Clara Redlake, brushing his apologies aside, had been full of admiration that he'd struggled to Boston at all. Dr Frankburg had told her he was sure his lost voice made him a better listener and made a joke that all therapists should lose their voice once in a while. Clara had laughed.

He'd spent a charming evening in the company of a woman who was not only full of sympathy for his condition but said it added an even more exciting level of anticipation for when it was back to its full strength. He'd said, 'Too kind', but thought the condition was probably going to last for at least a couple of days, certainly for the duration of the conference.

'But what about the paper you are to deliver?' she'd said.

Dr Frankburg had forgotten about that.

## 761

At that same conference a woman called Ali Bronski had talked her way past security by claiming to be a case study. That was why she'd misplaced her identity card. She said she was schizophrenic and she'd helped herself to vol-au-vents and cava.

## 760

'Yes, the paper,' Frankburg had choked. 'Will you excuse me?'

He'd grabbed a brandy from the drinks tray and run to the toilets.

Inside a cubicle he ordered his thoughts.

'Five Miles High: Alienation and Isolation Amongst the Jet Set' was the keynote address; it was ready, honed, it was his finest work, his *coup de grâce*. And he had a point to prove. It was a room full of analysts, stuck-up Freudians, many of whom found Frankburg's brand of cognitive behavioural therapy a bit quack and told him so to his face now and then.

A bad throat was going to come across as an attack of nerves dealt with in a very schoolboy fashion.

Then he'd heard a cough from the next cubicle. A female cough.

'Hello?' Dr Frankburg said.

'Hello.'

'Sorry, am I in the ladies?'

'Unless I'm in the gents.'

'How do we find out?'

'We look at the sign on the door.'

## 759

The distinction between the sexes is significant for Lacan. In *The Agency of the Letter in the Unconscious* he has two drawings. One is of the word 'Tree' over a picture of a tree – the signifier (word) over signified (object). Then there is another drawing, of two identical doors (the signifieds). But over each door is a different word: one says 'Ladies' and the other says 'Gentlemen'.

Lacan explains:

'A train arrives at a station. A little boy and a little girl, brother and sister, are seated in a compartment face to face next to the window through which the buildings along the station platform can be seen passing as the train pulls to a stop. "Look," says the brother, "We're at Ladies!" "Idiot!" replies his sister, "Can't you see we're at Gentlemen".'

'For these children, Ladies and Gentlemen will henceforth be two countries toward which each of their souls will strive on divergent wings…'

## 758

'I'm sure it's my error,' Frankburg had said. 'I rushed in here. I'm a bit distracted.'

'Why?'

'Oh, big paper to deliver tomorrow, it's a long story.'

'Are you Dr Frankburg?'

'Yes, as it happens.'

'You don't sound like your tape.'

'I'm aware of that.'

'Are you unhappy with your paper?'

'No, it's damn good, it's just I can't really read it out myself without...'

'Without what?'

'I haven't got the right voice.'

'Sounds all right to me.'

'I need my tape voice, I need the Welshman. As I said, it's a long story.'

'Right.'

There was a pause.

'Perhaps you could get someone else to read your paper for you?'

That would do him. It was practical and practicable.

'What's your name?' he asked.

Ali Bronski flushed the toilet and Frankburg missed it.

'...if you like.'

'Sorry?' said Dr Frankburg.

'I said I could read it out for you if you like.'

Frankburg cried, 'Ha!' popped the lock of his briefcase with sweating hands and slipped the speech under the cubicle wall. As the speech made its journey, it scooped up pubic hairs from twelve different women.

'It's all typed up and double-spaced,' he said. 'Helvetica, very clear font.'

'It's very neat.'

'Thank you. And thank you for doing this.'

'Not at all. The whole conference is looking forward to it, it would be a shame if it wasn't heard.'

Oh, too kind, Frankburg had said and they arranged to meet outside.

He'd heard her cubicle unlock and the toilet doors open and close. He'd heard the brief hum of the conference as she exited.

He'd assessed the pitfalls and could see none. There was the longer term problem of his voice, of course: he couldn't keep up tonsillitis forever. He and Clara Redlake might get married or something. At some point he'd have to come clean. But that was the future.

For now, the paper was secured. And having someone read his work for him might actually do it some good. Give him the air of a maestro who had a glamorous apprentice eager to make sure the great man's word was heard. And she had sounded pretty glamorous.

Unfortunately, she had been nowhere to be seen when he exited the toilets.

## 757

'Shall I have another crack at it?' Dr Frankburg asked the sound engineer in the recording studio.

'I think you'd better.'

'Have you got any tips perhaps? About the popping?'

'We could hire Samuel Thorn.'

'Yes, well, that's not an option, is it?'

'Expensive, is he?'

'It's got nothing to do with money. Let's just do a take, shall we?'

He cleared his throat.

Frankburg tried to follow his own teaching on dealing with pressure moments. He tried to let his lungs fill with air, he tried to relax each muscle one by one, he tried to picture fields of wheat.

'We haven't really got time for this,' said the sound engineer.

## 756

So that had been that. He'd looked around the conference hall but he had no idea what the cubicle woman looked like.

Frankburg bolted Boston.

Note to the conference organiser, sudden illness, swollen glands, probably tonsillitis, sorry to let everyone down, will call in a few days.

Taxi to the airport.

He was home ten hours later. Ironically, he really did have a fearfully sore throat. He put it down to having spent so long faking one for Clara Redlake but it was more a hysterical spasm of the larynx. Plus he'd picked up an infection on the aeroplane. Something to do with the air conditioning.

He'd laid low for three days, didn't answer the phone, didn't read his mail, ate soup.

When he felt better he'd played his answermachine.

One was from Clara Redlake sounding peeved that he'd abandoned her to a 'forward Freudian' but nevertheless expressing a hope that he'd recover soon and that he should call her when his voice had regained its reverberating power.

The second was from the conference organiser expressing polite sympathy but making it clear that he believed Dr Frankburg had pulled a sickie. He went on to say how perhaps it was for the best as Frankburg's absence permitted the inclusion of a last-minute offering from a talented young therapist who brought the house down with a highly original piece about air travel.

Frankburg felt a tide of injustice well up inside him and punched the wall.

Message three was the voice from the toilet cubicle apologising for hijacking his paper but claiming she'd improved it somewhat by giving it the punchier title 'Fear at Thirty-Five Thousand Feet'. She pointed out that they hadn't properly met, and so introduced herself as Ali Bronski. Hi.

Then the phone clicked off.

The robotic answermachine voice asked if the messages should be erased and Frankburg had stabbed the 'yes' button furiously.


## 755

'And so I want you to slowly rise up, fill your diaphragm with air once again. Expel it slowly through your nose. Have you taken your breath? Good. You are now ready to leave the house. Well done. Today will be a wonderful day.'

Frankburg motioned to the sound engineer.

'That it?' said the engineer.

'That's it for the words. You can put the music on now.'

'When do you want the music to start?'

'Start at the point where I talk about the fizzing ball of energy circling the pelvis.'

'Right.'

'Are you giggling?'

'No. Fizzing balls, got it.'

'Good. Send a copy to the office when you've done it.'

Following the Boston fiasco he'd decided to record his own tapes. He'd been pestered by an irritating woman who claimed to be Samuel Thorn's agent, insisting he use Samuel again and maintain some continuity, but his mind was made up. After spending so long trying to imitate the Welsh accent, he didn't think there was much to it and was convinced that Clara Redlake could learn to love the Solihull vowel sounds just as passionately.

He had plans to send his new tape, *Conquer Panic*, to Clara before anyone else. Say he was experimenting with a new voice and ask her, professionally, if it was any better. If that didn't work then sod it. It was hardly worth the grief, no matter how flame-headed she was.

Dr Frankburg walked swiftly from the recording studio to the car park. He had a late session with a client and his popping Ps had made him pretty pushed.

## 754

Benny was tired of being Unfunny John's friend. He binned the stupid disguise and went home. He was secretly glad he hadn't found Emma too. She had a habit of looking at his physique. Not appreciatively, anatomically.

'Tanned skin,' she'd said to him once, 'tough work on the slab.'

## 753

In Worcester, New York State, Clara Redlake listened to the news. It mentioned the bomb found under the car of a pharmaceutical CEO and she groaned inwardly.

Like Frankburg, she had an extensive and varied list of clients. One of whom, Edward Wiltshire, or Edward the Fireman if you will, displayed barely suppressed hostility towards the medical profession as a whole and had regularly expressed his commitment to JUSTICE and POSTIVE ACTION.

Like Frankburg, she too produced self-help tapes. But they were purely experimental and weren't available commercially.

1.  *Managing Anger In Urban Life.*
2.  *Beating Paranoia.*
3.  *Becoming Attractive.*
4.  *Asserting Your Rights.*
5.  *Petty Crime part one – Running Out of Diners.*

6.    Petty Crime part two – Hoax Calling.

7.    Appearing Heroic.

8.    Eliciting Sympathy and Money.

They were designed as distractions. Every time a subject felt on the brink of disruptive or significant antisocial behaviour, they could run through one or more of the tapes and have walk-through experiences of normal life, in all its shades and varieties. Those tapes that were gently transgressive also encouraged a degree of moral reflection. Tape five for example instructed the subject to return to the diner and repay the proprietor twice over to compensate for both the food and his loss of faith in human nature.

Edward the Fireman thought the tapes sucked. He said he didn't need therapy any more as he had found LOVE and A CAUSE and when one had found LOVE and A CAUSE one's thoughts became crystal clear.

Clara asked him if she could pay him to try the tapes as she needed—

'A what?' asked Edward. 'A lab rat?'

She said she wouldn't have put it like that.

He said he didn't mind. He'd been one before.


## 752

In New York City, Edward the Fireman moved onto tape three, *Becoming Attractive*. He left the upmarket department store and went to a bar uptown where he looked everybody in the eye and smiled at them winningly. No one was responding.

Though the tape doesn't mention it, he'd get much further if he took off his headphones and put on some cologne. The tapes were full of little flaws like this. Edward made a note of it on the drinks coaster.


## 751

Clara Redlake kept the radio tuned in to see if anything else developed. She tried to determine whether Edward would feel ashamed or exhilarated by his car bomb operation.

Then she realised she had no proof he'd done the deed so resolved not to bring it up. Unless he did, of course.

## 750

Samuel Thorn was on a train to Birmingham as flight SA841 touched down. His agent had put him on one.

She'd asked him how he was feeling these days and he'd told her he still had off days. She'd said that was understandable. Sam had said nothing, picked some fluff off his jacket and had said no thank you to tea. He drank some now though, sold to him at the buffet coach by a woman who recognised him from a cereal commercial. What a big bull of a man, she thought.

The train slowed. In Sam's hands were his CV and his photo. He hated actor's photos. En masse they were a macabre sight. Glossy ten by eights. Black and white to hide imperfections in the skin. Some looking slightly over their shoulder to give the impression of depth and three dimensions. Peculiar lifeless eyes. Shadows emphasising bone structure. Insufferably knowing. Needy. Vain. His own was just as bad. He'd thought of Descartes' *cogito, ergo sum* as the flashbulb popped so that he would appear profound. It didn't work, he looked like a man trying to remember if he'd left the iron on – or constipated.

Samuel was reading a script for a new drama set in Yorkshire entitled *Graft*, a gritty story about a bunch of people who all had tough lives, tough jobs, and tough skin. The audition was in Phoenix TV's production office in central Birmingham.

Phoenix TV had made, or had tried to make, the ditched sitcom *Tunnel Vision* and their finances were on thin ice. Grit was a seller so grit was being made.

Samuel told his agent the show didn't sound much fun.

His agent had said it was pretty grim. She told him most of the characters died.

Then there'd been a very awkward pause.

His agent had apologised and said she could've put that better.

He'd told her not to worry about it...

## 749

Late, sweating and tearing down the dual carriageway approaching the city, Dr Frankburg was caught by the same speed camera that had captured Michael Davies.

'Damn you!' shouted Frankburg, but pressed on at the same speed nonetheless. He drove through the same underpass and was dimly aware of ferocious tyre skids in the road.

Two roundabouts and a back road later, Frankburg parked up and sprinted to his office.

## 748

...But Sam's agent did worry about it.

Until five months ago, Sam had been her highest earner, her only earner. He was loyal. He'd stuck with her even after the *You Too Can Fly* fiasco for which she'd waived royalties and then seen it shift more copies than *Gielgud Reads Dickens*. She'd even managed to fluff getting him the sequel.

A bigger agency were courting him so she arranged for him to read for *Tunnel Vision*. A new BBC sitcom about the lives of a team of sewer workers in London. They needed an ox with a kind face and he got the job. He sent her roses and she wept with relief.

Then tragedy visited the set.

Halfway through filming, with three episodes completed, one of the actresses, a twenty-seven-year-old Scot called Kirsten, committed suicide in her hotel room.

Samuel took it hard. He'd believed there was a spark between them. Some chemistry. They were both Celts. They'd endured similar life events: late career changes, and the loss of a parent when they were very young; she a mother, he a father, both due to illness. Questionnaires in trashy magazines told them they had things in common.

The production closed down immediately.

There were a few news items on television, not many, Kirsten was an unknown. There had been some newspaper coverage and a small obituary with a family snapshot. Kirsten with Dad.

The programme's director said that the country had lost a very, very talented performer.

Samuel and Kirsten's last conversation had been on the set of *Tunnel Vision*. Samuel had been cleared to go. She had to stay to film an extra bit on her own. A running feature of the show was that each episode would end on a different character stuck down the sewer. It was Kirsten's turn that week.

He threw a prop faeces at her.

His last words to her had been 'Hey, catch'.

This shit was resting on Kirsten's bedside table when she was found. Samuel hoped it didn't undermine whatever dignity Kirsten had sought in her end.

He attended the funeral which was held in a little crematorium. She'd been a nurse before she was an actress. Most of the mourners were hospital staff. He was the only actor there. No one recognised him.

Samuel lost interest in his life. He had no inkling that she was about to do something of that magnitude and he felt terribly ashamed that he didn't see whatever it was he should have seen.

He met with her father and had found a man as devastated and in need of reassurance as himself. They spent an ineffective hour together and got nowhere.

After a while he decided there was nothing else to do except wait until things felt better. He'd met her father twice since that time. On both occasions he'd fancied he'd seen some slight improvement.

## 747

Samuel had once played the voice of Jonah in a series of Bible story cartoons for children. Schools bought the video to jazz up religion classes, and it still got broadcast from time to time. Samuel wished the run would end because he somehow felt that as long as he was out there as Jonah, his presence would bring misfortune upon his companions.

## 746

The train wasn't getting any faster. Phones started going off.

Samuel read *Graft*. It bored him to tears. There was grittiness in bus stations, grittiness in housing estates, grittiness in betting shops and, as his agent had mentioned, some gritty deaths.

Written by Cody Jameson...

## 745

In a café with a dress code. Table service, linen napkins, and free coffee refills. Not very gritty. Not gritty at all in fact. Apart from a hobo on a bench outside, it was about as gritless as you could get. Bloody hypocrite.

## 744

The train came to a complete standstill.

'Wonder what this is?' said a middle-aged woman. She didn't have any interest in the incident but had recognised Samuel from a made-for-TV costume drama where he played a massive blacksmith with a glistening torso.

Samuel cupped his hands round his face and peered into the darkness. He couldn't see anything. He let his breath steam up the window.

'Perhaps it's more leaves on the line. Ha,' said the woman.

Samuel smiled politely and went back to the script.

The woman decided she wasn't very good at flirting and kept quiet.

## 743

*Graft* love scene. Quite tender. Some nudity.

Samuel still had a big slab of a chest but there was give in the stomach when he prodded it. Perhaps he should visit a gym.

The brakes were released with a hiss. The train edged forward and the carriage cheered.

It pulled into Birmingham International at walking pace. It was the station for the National Exhibition Centre and the airport only. A nowhere place. Most places had a station stop, this place was solely a station stop.

But there was activity here.

Sam couldn't get a clear view as there was a waiting area in between the two platforms, but through its windows he could see that a police cordon and some temporary screens had been erected on the adjacent platform. He counted ten police officers. Some talking to members of the public and taking notes, some directing the passengers alighting from Sam's train up the stairs and away from the scene.

There was the muffled crackle of walkie-talkies and the flash of a photograph from within the screens.

The scene was lit by orange station lights. Blue was green, white was orange, red was redder.

## 742

Jonah enters Birmingham, thought Samuel, and someone is smited.

Jonah was a passenger too, but on a boat. Fleeing the presence of the Lord. His fellow mariners asked him to jump ship to calm the boiling sea. And Jonah did it as well, for the general good.

In the Jonah cartoon Sam remembered having to say the lines 'The world will be a safer place without me.' Splosh.

## 741

As the train pulled away, Samuel saw a young police officer turn away from the screens and put a hand up to his face. He stayed motionless like that for a few moments, his eyes closed, shoulders bunched. He then rubbed his face briskly, gathered himself together and turned back.

Samuel kept looking at him until he was out of view.

At New Street Station he saw notices being put up informing passengers that, for the next two hours, return trains would not be stopping at Birmingham International and that a bus service was being organised for those inconvenienced.

The image of the young policeman was still in Sam's mind as he checked into an anonymous city centre hotel. This officer had experienced a terrible yet momentous moment, and it was to Samuel's nagging shame that rather than sympathise with this young man, he was memorising the turn, the covering of the face, the expression, in order to accurately duplicate it should a future acting moment require it.

Many profound moments had been ruined in this way.

The receptionist who gave him his key looked depressed. Samuel didn't ask her why. Didn't want to be told that her test results were positive, or that her house had burned down, or that her marriage was off.

Samuel refused the offer of a porter and ran to his room and switched on the television not wishing to hex anyone else that day.

## 740

Edward the Fireman took his headphones off. He asked the barman if he could put on *The Penny Lock Show*. The barman refused, his clientele didn't dig Penny Lock.

'How can you say that?' said Edward. 'It's an excellent show. Today it's "Love At First Sight".'

'Too slushy,' said the barman.

Edward was outraged. 'Love is deep and committed and REVOLUTION-ARY.'

'Revolutionary?' said the barman.

'GREAT ACTS are performed out of love.'

The barman told Edward to either leave or keep his voice down.

Edward thought about listening to tape four, *Asserting Your Rights*, which would walk him through little confrontations like this, but he didn't think the barman would wait while he rewound it, so he just got up and left. Besides, the joint left a nasty taste in his mouth. Or it could have been the cheap bourbon.

## 739

Samuel Thorn checked to see if his room had a shower or a bath. It had a bath. Kirsten had been found dead in a hotel bath. Drowned. It would give him nightmares if he stayed.

He'd better get the room changed.

## 738

Edward rang *The Penny Lock Show* from a call box and got through to Tamy.

'I fell in love on one of your shows,' he said.

'With Penny?'

'Not Penny, a caller. Who could fall in love with Penny?'

'Some people do.'

'Not me.'

'What show was it?'

'"Fight the Good Fight". Will you put me on?'

Tamy thought about fast-tracking Edward. 'Fight the Good Fight' had been a goodie.

# 737

I didn't think it was a goodie. I thought it was a baddie. I listened to it in my kitchen. It was supposed to be about consumers winning small battles against faceless corporations: 'I bought a washing machine which span out of control and I kicked up such a stink I got a holiday in Yosemite...', but then a woman came on who claimed to be part of a small but dangerous underground outfit which had pledged to commit acts of violence against anyone owning shares in pharmaceutical companies. She called herself Activist 345 and said that major drugs manufacturers were guilty of grotesque market protection. Millions in the third world were consequently suffering needlessly, agonisingly, and since this was being done in order to gratify shareholders, shareholders were going to have to face up to what was being perpetrated for their benefit.

Tamy had sat in her booth and chewed her fingernails and didn't know whether she wanted her CEO father to be listening or not.

Penny Lock asked what the organisation's name was, Activist 345 said it was called TWA. Third World Army. Penny said wouldn't it get confused with Trans World Airlines? Activist 345 said only a corporate whore would say something so flippant.

I gasped and dropped a plate. To my knowledge, no one had ever called Penny a whore before.

Penny got hardline and pushed Activist 345 about the kinds of acts this organisation committed, Activist 345 became emotional and said that she herself hadn't physically attacked anyone, simply filled up shareholders' cars with pig's blood, or sent pictures of disease-wracked Africans to their children with the note 'This is what daddy and mummy are doing'. But the organisation was getting stronger and more dangerous, and it would only be a matter of time before extremists joined the struggle and less targeted violence would occur.

Like?

Bombs, replied Activist 345. Kidnapping. Hijacking.

She said she was suffering an ethical crisis which was why she was calling the station. To urge any shareholders listening to either transfer their shares to fairer-trading companies, or else keep a very, very careful look out. She didn't want anyone's death on her conscience.

Penny said the phone lines were going crazy.

'I denounce Activist 345's insane practices,' said a caller.

'Which companies exactly does Activist 345 take exception to?' asked another.

'Would the TWA blow up the Jimbo Jellybean corporation? Their jellybeans bring me out in a rash,' said another.

I tried to call and defend Penny against the charge of 'whore' but I didn't get through.

Then Edward was put on. The first time anyone from our family gets on air and it was him. I smashed another plate. Deliberately this time.

He said he understood Activist 345's emotional crisis, her dilemma, the need to do something drastic because you felt it was right only to see it careering out of control and cause horrifying damage. He said he was a retired fireman...

'Ha!' I said in my kitchen.

...who'd quit because of the stress. Did the listeners know that only the US President had a more stressful job? He said he'd invested an inheritance in unethical shares without thinking. He said he got scared that the TWA would blow him up leaving his children fatherless...

'Ha!' I said again.

...and for what? So that he could get a few unearned dollars off the suffering of the African poor. He said he wanted out.

Penny let the programme finish with both him and Activist 345 weeping.

I called up Edward afterwards and asked him what he thought all that proved. He said it proved there were still people out there concerned with the pursuit of JUSTICE. He said Activist 345, WHAT A GIRL.

## 736

Edward put in another quarter.

'Penny doesn't want you on today caller, she's got a man who's in love with his monkey, and a couple of stalkers.'

'I won't be slushy,' said Edward.

'If it was up to me I'd put you through but I've been given the thumbs down.'

'I see.'

'I'll take your number if things get slack.'

'Forget it.'

Edward put the phone down. It occurred to him that if Activist 345 was listening to the show she might think him sloppy. And he didn't want to be thought of as sloppy. He wanted to be thought of as steely. Steely and ruthless. He wished his bomb had gone off.

He'd call the show when he had something to brag about.


## 735

Dr Frankburg's nine o'clock appointment, a pilot called Graham Johansson, wasn't coming.

Frankburg cursed. The office was gloomy and depressing in the evenings and Dr Frankburg felt uncomfortable with the responsibility of securing the shared-use premises.

He didn't like sitting there on his own.

It was in this room that his wife had decided he was insufferable and had walked out on him telling him he could have everything, every single thing, she didn't want any of it, not even money. It was also in this room that he had told his daughter that the offspring of separated parents often turned out to be highly motivated and successful people, and although it was all very traumatic now, he was confident she'd feel better very shortly.

She then changed names, disappeared and hadn't contacted him in three years.

Frankburg had been stunned by the abruptness of it. Still was. He told himself he'd botched it. Playing the game of reality with no real cards in his hands.

Frankburg resolved to move offices.


## 734

Samuel picked up the hotel telephone and dialled zero.

'Reception?'

Sam didn't answer. He was staring at the television screen.

It was a local news item. A camera team had made their way to

Birmingham International Station and a reporter was interviewing a senior policeman who wore a bright tie but a grave look.

He confirmed that a man had jumped in front of a train and had been killed. They were still making enquiries but they'd ruled out assault. It seemed the gentleman had jumped onto the track of his own free will.

BANG!

The man was carrying identity on him when he died, but next of kin were to be informed first.

The reporter thanked the police officer.

The police officer thanked the reporter.

'If you need help with using the telephone, there's a card on the table by the side of the bed.'

'Oh sorry, this is Samuel Thorn, could I have a room without a bath, please?'

## 733

Frankburg switched off the heater and gathered his notes together. Eight pages for Pilot Graham Johansson. This constituted four sessions. Johansson's notes were brief. But then they'd only just started.

Session one had remained the easiest session to transcribe because Mr Johansson hadn't said a single word.

He'd chosen to sit in the chair opposite Frankburg rather than lie on the couch to one side. It gave a better view out of the window. From that window you could see the aeroplanes in the distance making their approach to the airport. Around six would descend during a one hour session. Johansson would watch each one.

He was an impressive looking man: six feet three, solid, very well groomed, with fair hair, a faint accent in his voice, well-defined features and good teeth. Capped?

Session two had more content. Some personal details had emerged.

Family: father Danish, mother English. Both alive. Only child.

Graham Johansson: forty-six years old. Single? Pause. Yes. Frankburg had underlined the pause. Something to return to. Born and educated in Copenhagen. Trained as a pilot in England. Full captain for five years. Lived in

Warwickshire. Preferred short hops to Europe and Atlantic flights to the US, didn't like the long haul East.

Session three, at first, seemed to be going the same way as session one. In the lengthy silence Frankburg remembered the psychologist R.D. Laing had recommended that a catatonic client become a life model. Frankburg had chuckled and Johansson had looked up. To cover the chuckle Frankburg had asked Johansson why he felt the need to come. Johansson answered that he'd been thinking a lot about what it was to be a pilot. What it represented and how it related to one's life on the ground. Johansson had asked to hear the doctor's theories about flying and leaving home, flying and nationality, and flying and escape.

Frankburg said he'd rather hear what Johansson himself had to say about these issues. Johansson replied he didn't really know, just that he'd been thinking about them a lot.

Frankburg wondered whether to give Johansson the Laing line about playing the game of reality with no real cards in one's hands but realised he wouldn't know how to answer if Johansson asked him what he meant.

Session four.

'A passenger once asked me about the safety of his novelty religious artefacts. In the hold he had 300 waterproof bibles, 250 edible rosaries, a dozen whistling popes, and a crate of crown of thorns which glowed in the dark.

'I told him not to worry. I said if the plane were to crash in the sea, in the middle of the night, the glow-in-the-dark crown of thorns would mark the way. They would float to the surface of the sea and look like runway lights. Beautiful in a way. And the bibles would be washed up on the Caribbean Coast. They would be hired out by deckchair sellers. And as for the edible rosaries, perhaps the fish could eat them.

'I was disciplined for mentioning a plane crash to a passenger.'

'Do you often think about the plane crashing?'

'Yes.'

'Why?'

At that point Johansson had decided that was enough. He was out of energy. He looked tired. He'd flown to Barcelona and back. Frankburg said it was a very beautiful city. Johansson said he'd only seen the airport.

'There's still a few minutes left if you want them.'

'No, I'm dog tired.' He picked up his coat.

'And next week?' Frankburg had asked.

'Could we do Tuesday nine o'clock? I'm coming back from America.'

## 732

Johansson was still in America. Smoking cigarettes in Manhattan. He was using a brass lighter which was engraved with the words 'Love G.J.'. He flicked the lighter open and sparked the flint which lit the flame. He flicked the lighter shut, sparked the flint again which lit the flame again.

He was booked to fly SA841 to Birmingham but he cancelled when he knew Emma Heron was to be aboard.

He complained of a stomach upset and rescheduled.

## 731

Frankburg locked his filing cabinet and switched out the lights.

His notes didn't add up to much yet but Frankburg wasn't worried about slow progress; he'd had some clients for many years, who refused to do the self-help activities he set them but liked coming back and talking. Some had hung on for over a decade.

Frankburg sensed that Johansson wasn't one of these types however. Despite the Scandinavian introspection.

He left the building wondering what had happened to him.

## 730

Johansson was watching an old episode of *Tales of the Unexpected* where the owner of a remote paradise island offered a visitor a gamble. If the visitor could light the lighter ten consecutive times he would win the island. If he misfired, and only flint sparks flew, he would lose a finger. The owner's wife had taken the bet a number of times and was consequently stumpy. Her wedding ring was barely on.

Johansson wished such an island existed because on current form he'd have won it ten times over.

## 729

Michael Davies told his wife he'd had a near miss.

'Don't tell me that,' said Beth. 'Why do you tell me these things? I'm flying tomorrow and here you are telling me... I need to hear that everything is running like clockwork, I need to hear that the margins of error are... I don't need... I need...'

Michael said he nearly hit a woman in the middle of the road.

'Oh.'

He said he stopped and shouted at her.

'Did she say anything?'

'I thought she was going to.'

'What did she look like?'

'Brown hair, cut short. Big coat, cream colour, which was open and she had a sweatshirt underneath. Light blue, I think, although the lights were making everything look yellow. It had writing on it. And a hood.'

'How tall was she?'

'Not very tall, normal, your height. She had jeans on, I think. And she had a big suitcase. A solid one. It had wheels on one corner and she was pulling it along.'

'What about her face?'

'Didn't really see it.'

'Did she look like me?'

'Why would she look like you?'

'Well did she?'

'What do you mean? Scarred?'

'Scarred, or scared.'

'No. A bit scared, perhaps. She was pale.'

'Sick?'

'No more... I don't know, I can't think of the word.'

'Ill? Nauseous? Panicky?'

'She didn't look like you.'

'Ashen?'

'All right Ashen. She looked ashen.'

'Anything else?'

'I don't remember anything else. Stop asking.'

Beth thought if the woman looked like her, Michael probably tried to run over her deliberately.

'I got distracted by that tape, *You Too Can Fly*,' said Michael.

## 728

Dr Frankburg was struggling with the alarm to his office building. Pig-headed piece of shit. After trying three different four-digit numbers, all of which he was sure had worked in the past, the machine flashed up the curt message that the user had one more opportunity to get the code correct otherwise the system would disable itself.

'Fuck it.' He took the threat seriously and left the building. The place was locked up and secure. No one took any notice of alarms anyway.

## 727

From across the road Cody Jameson watched Frankburg give up and walk away. She watched him limp a little and wondered what he'd done to himself.

## 726

Frankburg's car was parked in a street half a mile away. His earlier sprint to the office had strained some mysterious ligament and he cursed the complicated design of the knee.

He hobbled past the Wellington Arms and noticed in its emerging clientele symptoms of post-traumatic stress disorder. He passed an advertisement for an airline, and then he passed a telephone box and the two things together made him enter it and call up Graham Johansson. It was a legitimate call. Not curiosity, just rescheduling.

The phone was answered by an answermachine which had so many pips denoting other messages that Frankburg put the phone down.

A taxi drove past the telephone box as Frankburg put his diary back in his suitcase.

He walked to his car. It chirped at him brightly. Now why couldn't all alarms be that simple?

## 725

The taxi contained an uneasy John Heron. He too had been listening to the pips on an answerphone confirming that Emma still hadn't arrived home. He looked at his watch. Ten thirty. The plane had landed three and a half hours ago. He took out his phone again and stared at it hoping it might buzz and 'wife' appear on the caller display.

'Take me to the airport,' he told the taxi driver.

## 724

The taxi did a U-turn and cut through the car park of a big city centre hotel. Its passage was noticed by Samuel Thorn who watched it idly from his new hotel room which was smaller but bath free.

It had a worse view but a better mini-fridge.

Night-time taxis prowled the city.

He drank gin.

It had been a while since he'd been in Birmingham. The city had been busy in the meantime. Many new buildings were up, much was unrecognisable from his last trip. And they were still at it. Silent now, the cranes and JCBs massed on a patch of developing ground over the road would crank to life the next morning. Billboards were everywhere anticipating a glittering future.

Samuel liked construction work, it was solid. He enjoyed seeing foundations laid. Seeing how far down they went.

## 723

The reason the receptionist was depressed was because the hotel had been earmarked for demolition. She would have to get a new job in a new town and probably never see the handsome porter again.

## 722

The TV broke Sam's gin spell. Local news had returned to the incident at the train station.

A reporter told him that the police had confirmed that the train jumper's name was Ronald Henderson, a retired doctor from Aberdeen.

Samuel stared bleakly into the screen. He let his eyes unfocus till he could see himself superimposed over the family portrait of Mr Henderson.

Ronald Henderson was the father of Kirsten, the sitcom suicide. The man whose mental strength Sam had confidently thought was improving.

Samuel Thorn hit the streets, cursing curses.

## 721

Ronald Henderson's suitcase was finally picked off the carousel by an airport employee and put into lost property.

## 720

'Hi, I'm not in right now. Leave me a message.'

Bleep.

Sobbing.

'Pick up, you bastard, I know you're there.'

More sobbing.

'I'm coming back. I'm coming back, OK? Stay where you are. Don't fucking move.'

Muffled sound of someone kicking the telephone box.

'Bloody, bloody stupid...'

More sobs.

'Why is this happening? Penny, don't let him leave.'

Pip pip pip pip...

## 719

'A suitcase?' asked the policeman on the phone. 'Not a briefcase.'

'Definitely a suitcase,' Michael Davies said. 'Samsonite, those silver ones, looks like you're transporting nuclear waste.'

'And you don't remember anything else?'

'That's it, except she had a shoe missing.'

'What sort of shoe?'

'I don't know, it was missing, wasn't it? But if it was anything like the other one...'

'I think it's safe to assume it was.'

'Well, you're the detective, but if it was then you're looking for a trainer, white, a black stripe.'

The policeman asked if Michael had a work number.

Michael told him not to call him at work.

The policeman asked why not.

Michael told him he was an air traffic controller.

The policeman said he wouldn't call him at work.

'Hope you find her,' said Michael.

'I hope we do too, sir.'

Not a chance, they both thought.

'Thank you for your call.'


## 718

'This is a call for Miss Emma Heron recently arrived on flight SA841 from New York, could you please contact the information desk. Thank you.'

John Heron wanted to tell the woman who'd made the announcement that it was Mrs Heron, not Miss. If Emma was in the airport and she heard herself referred to as 'Miss' she'd fling her wedding ring in his face saying, Was that what he wanted? Cos that would be absolutely fine by her. She'd done it before.

'Thanks,' he said.

'Pleasure. I'll do another one in five minutes if she hasn't appeared.'

He sat on a luggage trolley.

A minute passed. He wished he wasn't wearing his stupid dinner suit. Security personnel walked by.


## 717

Cody Jameson made a move on Frankburg's building.

Just then an old Nissan pulled up and out came a stocky, long-haired man carrying a small parcel. He left the car door open and the stereo boomed as he trotted up to the door of the office block. Selecting the letter box marked 'Frankburg', the man posted the parcel inside and hopped back into his car.

*Conquer Panic* dubbed and delivered.

The music became a muted series of thumps and the car sped off. Cody decided to have one more cigarette, just to be on the safe side. The gritty scriptwriter assured herself that if she was caught she would say she was doing gritty research. And it wouldn't matter if she was caught because getting caught was pretty gritty too.

## 716

Frankburg himself was driving home. He took a slower pace. No camera would catch him out this time. He took it carefully around the labyrinthine underpasses and one-way systems. A figure stood on a bridge overlooking the road. Frankburg kept his eye on him anxiously. He knew some people with pathological problems often threw things onto car windscreens.

## 715

Samuel Thorn sniffed the night air and smelt exhaust fumes, cooking fat, and failure.

After Kirsten died, Samuel gave Ronald Henderson words of encouragement. Told him Kirsten had been a wonderful woman. Told him time was a great healer. Said he was strong enough to get through it. Said he understood how he felt. Told him God worked in mysterious ways,

Ronald told him he knew these things. Told him to please stop speaking.

Sam thought: the man's getting better.

Then Ronald jumps in front of a train as Samuel enters Birmingham.

Perhaps this curse would infect Samuel himself one day and he'd suddenly shoot himself in the head.

Or jump off this bridge.

He stopped and stared down at the traffic flitting beneath him. Watched it speed under his feet. Listened to the Doppler effect. Hypnotising himself.

He wondered what it would take to clamber over the railings and jump into the path of one of the cars. This big old BMW, for example, being driven by an apprehensive middle-aged man who stared wide-eyed at him before swerving into another lane.

The moment passed. He was low but not low enough. He walked on.

From the other side of the road he heard the smashing of glass. Trouble ahead. He about-turned. He was reassured by this reaction. It seemed that an instinct of self-preservation was still working.

## 714

Attracted by the faint smell of chopped liver, an Alsatian pulling a security guard enthusiastically explored John Heron's small holdall. Minutes later, inevitably, John was in the airport's police holding room, deeply regretting bringing his gun to the terminal.

## 713

Cody Jameson held her breath.

After the glass had smashed, she'd heard footsteps but they'd turned and hurried away. She let her breath go and allowed her heart to slow before proceeding.

She reached into the broken pane and lifted the latch that would open the whole window. She pried the window free of the metal connectors which, had the alarm been set, would have alerted the police station. As it was, the LCD by the door was still gamely prompting the absent Frankburg to have another stab at the code.

Writers are thieves, she told herself.

Cody slipped into the building. She orientated herself. She waited for her eyes to become accustomed to the dark.

Not so long ago, Cody had broken into a house and started rooting around for trophies which would characterise the break-in. Mementoes. Mementoes unblocked the blocks. Started narratives. In this particular house she'd stolen a photograph, but as she'd crept into what she believed to be the study, her torch had picked out a sight of such breathtaking horror that her knees had buckled and she had crumpled quivering to the floor.

The far wall of this room was awash with blood. It seemed to have both old and new smeared and spattered all over it. There were patches which glistened in the light as if it had been spurted there by a victim only hours before. There was a stench which was sweet and rotten by turns and mingled with an unsettling burning smell.

Cody, throat aching with the effort of holding in her screams, had edged away from the wall only to find her hands and feet puncturing bags of gore which had been left on the floor.

What beast's lair was this? What unthinkable acts had taken place in this room?

Horrified to a degree never before or since experienced, Cody had somehow managed to locate the window and scramble back through it.

Stumbling and sobbing to her car, she'd made an anonymous call to the police alerting them to a dangerous psychopathic butcher living in Walton Street and then went on a long holiday.

The Frankburg building was her first break-in since then. It seemed clean. There was no blood on the carpet. At least none that her torch could pick out.

Cody followed a corridor which led to a stairwell. The doors to individual offices were locked. She climbed the stairs and found that all the second-floor offices were locked too, and so were those on the third floor. So was Frankburg's.

She put her eye to the keyhole but saw nothing. She put her nose to the keyhole and sniffed the air from inside the room but could only smell the metal of the lock. She slipped a note under the door.

She went back down to the ground floor and stole the package that she had seen being delivered. It was in a Jiffy bag, addressed to Dr Frankburg, and it felt like a tape.

Good enough, she thought.

## 712

The young policeman stood staring at the mess on the Wellington Arms' back curtain and sobbed. The poor man had twice this evening been confronted with spattered human being. He was beyond the poetically turned concealment of emotion that had so struck Samuel Thorn on the station platform. The world had become a barbarous and hellish place. He could only howl.

'I know,' said Miles. 'Is that funny? Do you think this is what people expect when they come to a comedy night? No is the answer.'

The young policeman ran for the door.

'Don't worry about him,' said his colleague. 'It's been a trying evening.'

'For him and me both,' said Miles.

'I just need you to confirm a couple of things about John Heron, sir.'

## 711

Samuel Thorn returned to the hotel and emptied the mini-fridge.

He looked at himself in the mirror and gave himself the caption 'Jinxed Man Touched by Tragic Events'. He thought now would be a good time to cry but didn't want to watch himself doing it. Too narcissistic.

He watched anyway, then fell into bed.

He didn't set his alarm, he'd let the diggers wake him up. They always started early.

## 710

Cody listened to the tape.

'Hello, I'm Dr Frankburg Ph.D. If you have already heard my tape *You Too Can Fly* you will know that there will be times during this tape when I will be encouraging you to concentrate solely on my voice. This is to draw you into a state of deep relaxation. So I'm asking you now to find an environment which is free from distractions. One where it is safe to close your eyes.'

The voice sounded hesitant and nervous. He sounded much older now. He'd looked much older too.

'We've all felt panic at one time or another, from getting lost in a supermarket as a child, to losing one's house keys. Or perhaps you have faced a more serious threat, illness, physical danger, or emotional damage, the loss of a friend or family member...'

Did she hear his voice crack?

'...Many things give us reason to panic, and for most of us it is causal and we understand why we feel this way. Finding ourselves lost in a strange place is real. Identifying a threat to our life is real. But for some, panic emerges for no apparent reason. There seems to be no cause, and often no escape. This tape will talk about that sort of panic and will give some strategies for dealing with it. I hope it will be of some use.'

Cody didn't think it would be any use at all.

She didn't think anything her father ever said was any use.


## 709

Dr Frankburg left a message with the pilot Johansson.

'Graham, Frankburg here. Just checking that everything's OK. I imagine you got held up somewhere. If you would like to reschedule, please give me a call. Thanks.'

As an afterthought: 'I'm afraid I'll have to charge you for the session as I didn't receive a cancellation call within twenty-four hours. 'Bye.'

Frankburg put the phone down and immediately criticised himself for being petty.

He criticised himself further for ringing at all. Perhaps Johansson lived with a partner who didn't know he was seeing a therapist. He could have caused all sorts of difficulties.

Frankburg wished he'd brought Johansson's notes home to check if he was attached. Sometimes he behaved like a student.

He drank a bottle of wine and went to bed.


## 708

John Heron sat in the interview room at the airport, drumming his fingers.

'OK, you can go,' the policeman said as he re-entered the room.

The police had checked out his story and confirmed the gun was real, but unloaded and only used for theatrical purposes. A prop. The licence was authentic.

John's records indicated a minor traffic offence but nothing to suggest he was anything other than what he claimed: a comedian.

The policeman was interested to note that this sort of misunderstanding had happened before to John Heron, when officers were called to investigate a claim that he was presiding over a diabolical slaughterhouse. But that incident had been cleared up. And as far as he was concerned, so had this one.

'Thank God.'

'Don't bring guns to the airport, sir. It makes us edgy.'

'I appreciate that. I'm sorry.'

## 707

Less than a hundred metres away from John stood his wife, Emma Heron. Near but still missing.

She went straight to the ticket desk and asked to be put on the next available plane bound for New York.

Airline employee Angela found her a seat on the midnight flight. Angela remembered Emma. She'd seen her and an elderly gentleman leave the airport together earlier that evening. Angela had seen how the elderly gentleman supported himself on her arm and noted how considerate Emma appeared to be.

Perhaps they were grandfather and granddaughter.

She'd seen the elderly gentleman take a cassette out of his pocket and put it in the bin liner carried by Rose the cleaner.

She'd seen Rose take the tape out and put it into her personal stereo. Rose had come over to Angela and asked her to listen to a bit of the tape because the voice was dishy. Welsh. Broody. Angela had said no, she was a bit busy.

Emma was looking tired now. Angela thought Emma could do with a bit of lipstick, a touch of rouge. Her face looked dead.

Emma paid with a credit card and checked in her Samsonite.

Angela asked if Emma had packed her suitcase herself.

Emma nodded.

Angela asked if Emma was carrying any electrical devices.

Emma shook her head.

Angela asked if the elderly gentleman she'd seen earlier would be travelling too as Angela would be happy to hold back the seat next to her.

Emma said the elderly gentleman had fallen in front of a train and so probably wouldn't be checking in.

Pause.

'Righto,' said Angela.

## 706

John was escorted from the airport in order to prevent him from pulling some stunt with his prop gun. If he hadn't been flanked by two security officers he might have noticed Emma make her pale and one-shoed way to departures.

## 705

Cody put the tape amongst her other mementoes.

A china dog from a house in King's Heath – the starting point for a story about fairgrounds.

A postcard from the Seychelles taken off a notice board in Stetchford – an article on tropical diseases.

A copy of *Twelve Angry Men* taken from the bag of a city centre shopper – a magazine piece about sweat marks on shirts.

According to an illustrated medical dictionary, the photo she stole from the butcher's house was of an appendix.

Mostly, though, she had mementoes from Frankburg's house. Her portable radio because the world kept turning. Her woollen jumper because the nights were drawing in. Her first 'suicide' note – 'Dad, by the time you read this I will be dead, thanks for everything.' Somehow Frankburg had known it was a fake.

Frankburg waited six months for her to crawl sheepishly back. When she didn't, he'd called the radio and they'd made an announcement: this is an SOS message for Lily Frankburg last seen in Birmingham. Would Lily Frankburg contact the Birmingham Free Hospital where her father Dr Roger Frankburg is dangerously ill.

He hadn't really been ill and he'd hung around the hospital waiting for her to call. Fifteen clients rang in instead, panicking. He was ejected from the premises.

So he'd held a sort of memorial service. Invited everyone he could think of. He figured she'd turn up if only to see who attended.

But she didn't. She wanted to but she didn't want to blow it.

No one at the memorial service believed she was dead either. Frankburg cut a rather tragic figure, speaking at a makeshift pulpit about a daughter who he was pretending was dead whilst scanning the faces of the guests trying to find her. It was an uncomfortable and depressing occasion and many people left halfway through, telling him to pull himself together.

Cody was outraged that he didn't believe her note. Apart from anything else it was hostile literary criticism. She wondered which words were phoney. If she wrote a better note he'd stop looking for her and start grieving properly.

He'd certainly start grieving properly if he saw her dead body, but she didn't want to think about that too much.

## 704

Beep.

'Hi. Graham, or rather Mr Johansson. Sorry, shouldn't've called you Graham. Rather presumptuous. It's not that sort of call... um... I think I'll try this again. This is Frankburg, by the way.'

Click.

## 703

Cody had compiled a top ten writers' last words:

10. 'Now comes the mystery.' Henry Ward Beecher.
9. 'Light more light.' Goethe.
8. 'Severn – I – lift me up – I am dying – I shall die easy – don't be frightened – be firm and thank God it has come.' Keats.
7. 'Nothing but death.' Jane Austen, on being asked what she wanted.
6. 'Don't let the awkward squad fire over my grave.' Robert Burns.
5. 'I believe I'm going to die. I love the rain. I want the feeling of it on my face.' Katherine Mansfield.
4. 'It has all been very interesting.' Lady Montagu.
3. 'Lord, take my soul, but the struggle continues.' Ken Saro-wiwa.
2. 'What is the answer?' (no answer comes) 'In that case, what is the question?' Gertrude Stein.
1. 'Is it not meningitis?' Louisa M. Alcott.

Cody put 'Dad, by the time you read this I will be dead, thanks for everything' in that company and conceded that perhaps it did lack a certain something. The others also had the advantage of witnesses and a tangible corpse. If there was no corpse, the note had to be damn good.

## 702

Beep.

'Mr Johansson. Frankburg here again. Listen, just disregard my last message.

And the one before. Of course I shan't be billing you for the missed session. I don't know why I mentioned it. You can give me a discount flight to Geneva or something instead, ha ha. Give me a call when you're ready. 'Bye.'

Frankburg put down the phone.

## 701

Cody boiled the kettle she'd stolen in February. She drank from the cup she'd stolen in April. She settled on the chair she'd stolen, with difficulty, in May. Then she wondered if she'd been stealing her old life back. Bit by bit.

She listened to *Conquer Panic* through to the end. Her father talked about fizzing balls of energy and some piano started playing. Rather nice.

She felt her eyes filling up a bit.

## 700

In New York City, Edward the Fireman sat in a diner and caught the end of *The Penny Lock Show*. A woman was saying her husband was a plastic surgeon who'd fallen in love with her while she was under his knife.

'What were you having done? If you don't mind my asking,' said Penny Lock.

'Breasts.'

'OK.'

'Great big breasts.'

'Well, that's nice.'

'He did a beautiful job but kept calling me back to check up on them.'

'Uh-huh.'

'He wanted to see me again, you get me?'

'I get you.'

'He offered to do my nose for free.'

'Right.'

'And offered to give me big lips and higher cheeks and a tummy tuck.'

'And has he done those?'

'Yep. I hardly recognise myself.'

'And is that a good thing?'

'Oh yes. It's good to get involved in your partner's career. I think it's the key to a healthy relationship. That's what I wanted to say to your listeners, get interested in your husband's work.'

'Let them slice you up?'

'If appropriate.'

'Well, there you go. Thanks for calling.'

'My pleasure.'

## 699

Beep.

'That was a joke by the way, about the ticket to Geneva, I just meant to say it was fine about the session. OK, speak to you soon.'

## 698

Edward shook his head sadly. The show was losing its way.

He looked around at his fellow diners. A blonde drinking a milkshake, too young for him. A brunette querying the bill, too petty. A redhead cleaning her glasses, too shortsighted.

He ordered meatloaf and fries. The waitress? Too downtrodden. None of them had passion. None had zeal in their eyes. He knew that if SHE was in the diner he'd know her immediately.

Edward moved on to tape five, *Running Out Of Diners*. His food arrived. Halfway through his meal he put down his cutlery as instructed and walked into the toilets. He entered the far cubicle, locked the door, opened the window and slipped through into the yard taking care not to snag his headphones lead. He jumped the wall and ran away. He got a stitch and slowed to a walk. The voice on the tape made no concession to indigestion and asked him to jog another twelve blocks just to be on the safe side. Edward switched off his walkman and was sick in a bin. Self-help tape five got the lowest marks yet.

## 697

I think he should listen to the radio more. Find some music. Might calm him down. Sisterly advice.

## 696

My radio is quiet. It may be blaring out but I can't hear it. I would've thought there'd be something, at least for the fishermen out at sea. I'm flying through time zones but feeling no change. Feeling light.

I put the radio to my lips to feel the vibrations. Ah, there's something.

'Rhapsody in Blue' as covered by Tommy Tempo's Nite Moods Orchestra. The piano part is taken by Tommy himself on the Wurlitzer, dancing on the pedals and pulling out all the stops. His Wurlitzer can do all the instruments but he keeps his orchestra on. Good old Tommy won't let them go. You can't beat the live sound. Who could replace Lips McReady on the oboe? Or Sticks Allen on snare drum?

Tommy will be turning back from time to time and smiling. He's got a dazzling smile.

## 695

…Hmm hmm hmmm hmmm hum. Dancing on kitten heels. Tingling on the skin. This is what Edward should be listening to. If he finds her, he could take his young lady friend, his young activist, to a Tommy Tempo gig. It's hard to think of TARGETS and WIRING when the clarinet hits the high notes…

## 694

…two three two, two three two… hard to be a hot head Wiltshire when you've learned the two step…

## 693

…keep concentrating…

## 692

…

## 691

…

## 690

. . .

## 689

. . . we should have all been taught the two step. All three Wiltshires. I should have set an example perhaps, being the oldest, but I've got two left feet.

## 688

. . . I think mother was exhausted by us. After Edward, her reproductive system packed in and she had to have her womb surgically removed.

I'm thinking now that she went into the hospital and begged or paid them to take it out.

## 687

. . . ba da boom ba da bee . . . keep the beat Tommy . . .

## 686

. . . Edward raged through school, a sprawling epic drama in which he was the central player. He questioned everything. He fought everyone. Young, idealistic men and women lined up wanting to be the Understanding Teacher Who Pulled Edward Round. He left them all scarred and shell-shocked. He was given career advice. He could hardly credit the nerve of this at the time. He was being offered guidance from individuals whose own imaginations hadn't leapt beyond a career in the schools they'd only just left.

'You seem very keen to leave, Edward,' said the teacher during one of these sessions. 'Why's that, do you think?'

'You seem very keen to stay,' he responded. 'Why's that, do you think?' He's always had a smart mouth.

## 685

. . . could talk me into anything.

He talked me into setting fire to the school. He said it would be a fitting and cleansing end. It was old and full of paper and went up like a torch.

## 684

WHOOSH. Bricks snapped, windows melted, wood popped. Edward still smelt the burning wood sometimes. Still felt the heat on his face.

## 683

...our sister got caught in the flames. It seemed she liked to hide in the library and secretly read the books. Sometimes she slept there. She was woken by alarms and had to jump out of a window but she got badly burned and cut.

I think she's forgiven us. She's a very forgiving person.

## 682

Beth liked the story of Monsieur Chabert the Fire King, who had, in 1818, became known for not only eating and breathing fire but also stepping into a 400-degree oven with a raw leg of mutton then emerging at a proper time with the leg in hand perfectly cooked.

Skin of men is characteristically thicker than skin of women in all anatomic locations. It is thickest on the palms and soles and thinnest on the eyelids and postauricular region.

Even so, Beth wishes she knew how Monsieur Chabert had done it because she herself feels eminently flammable.

## 681

Beth is my twin but we don't look much alike. That's my fault though, and Edward's.

## 680

Edward said he didn't feel guilty about the fire. Said war had casualties. I said what war?

He ran away and tried to find one.

I had postcards from him from time to time.

In Europe in the early seventies, he said that every young conscionable citizen of the world was becoming a freedom fighter. So he went to Germany and wrote 'Don't' argue – destroy' on a wall. He was smitten with the chic young Ulrike Meinhoff and was hoping a bit of slogan daubing would get him some notice by 'people who knew people'. Wish you were here, he said.

He went to Italy where a Roman called Francesca took him to the universities of northern Italy where counter right-wing feeling had distilled into organised revolutionary resistance.

Francesca claimed to be one of the founder members of the Red Brigade and showed him how to make a bomb out of soap.

He told Francesca he'd burned down his school, and she took him to bed. He probably didn't mention burning his sister in the process. I guess that would be a turn off.

Edward wrote to me about fascism, the function of universities, the glorious tradition of kidnapping. He spoke about the resistance movement across Europe becoming unified through the desire to end the imperialist feudal system and through a generalised opposition to the Vietnam war. Wish you were here, he wrote.

He told me to join The Angry Brigade. I told him I'd joined an airline company. I told him to come home.

He said I shouldn't feel guilty about the school incident but it was all right to feel sad for the victims. Or, rather, victim. I said I felt both in huge measures.

Edward told me it was excellent that I had become an air stewardess. He said that the Baader-Meinhof and the Palestinians were starting to hijack planes and he felt the movement should have someone on the inside. I said what movement? He said THE movement. He had started to talk in capitals.

## 679

I was a very good stewardess. I told Edward I was POLITE, FRIENDLY and certainly not ON THE INSIDE.

Starting off on short European routes, I soon switched to a carrier heading east and finally settled on a Hong Kong route. It took me far, far away.

During my first months of work, a mixed gang of West German and Palestinian terrorists hijacked an Air France plane on its way to Uganda and demanded the release of jailed terrorists. Israeli troops stormed the plane and killed seven of the hijackers. The news described it as the first major defeat of international terrorism.

BLACK BOX

We were given training. A marine came in and told us what to do if we were faced with a similar situation. Told us how to poke them in the eye. A negotiator came in and told us how to keep them calm. The airline CEO came in and said we probably wouldn't be faced with the situation at all and no one should worry.

I asked Edward if he'd been SUCKED IN. He said he'd hardly admit it in a letter.

He said don't ask questions and I won't be told lies.

He asked me to tell him which flights I worked as he'd hate to burn up another sister.

I asked about Francesca. He said she'd lost heart with direct action and had qualified as a vet. She'd moved to Firenze where she cured the pets of wealthy animal lovers for exorbitant sums of money. He wondered what had happened to commitment.

## 678

Edward asked if I could forward his letters to Beth as she returned all his. I said she returned all mine too.

## 677

I am an ex-stewardess now. A cold one. With no blanket and no nuts.

## 676

I wonder if Beth would like Tommy Tempo? Perhaps I should have sent her a tape. I could've typed on the envelope so she wouldn't know it was from me and thrown it away without opening it.

## 675

The radio's quiet now. Perhaps Tommy is on a break.

## 674

Or my batteries are flat.

# 673

...Have I done that?

# 672

...then.

Edward wiped the sick off his mouth and walked down 14th street. Past a big apartment block. Inside one of them the lights were off but someone was home.

A breeze carrying traffic noise and Edward's footsteps filtered through the apartment's ventilation and did its best to dilute the whisky fumes and cigarette smoke which had settled around the room.

The apartment's occupant, pilot Graham Johansson, was wishing sleep would come more easily.

The phone rang. The answermachine took the call.

'Penny? I hope this is the right number. This is John Heron, Emma's husband. I'm ringing from England and I wanted to know if you knew where Emma was. Did she say anything to you? Could you give me a ring when you get this message? Sorry, I don't even know what time it is there.'

The answermachine pipped an acknowledgement and re-set itself.

'Messages received – two.'

Graham Johansson sat in a chair in the darkened room and watched the red light on the answerphone go on and off and on and off.

Blinking red lights usually denoted a system failure. A critical situation imminent. A pilot would prefer to go through his entire career without seeing flashing red lights. But here one was. It was strange to see it in the still calm of the room.

Mind you, the tone of the messages suggested a system failure had taken place so perhaps it was appropriate.

Johansson did a quick calculation. Emma caught the seven am flight, seven hours to Birmingham, add on the time difference, making touch down about seven o'clock. It would now be one in the morning UK time and she hadn't contacted her husband. Not surprising that the guy's worried.

He stood up, a bit unsteadily, and pressed a button to hear Emma's voice.

Sobbing.

'Pick up you bastard I know you're there.'

More sobbing.

'I'm coming back. I'm coming back, OK? Stay where you are. Don't fucking move.'

Muffled sound of someone kicking the telephone box.

'Bloody bloody stupid...'

More sobs.

'Why is this happening? Penny, don't let him leave.'

Pip pip pip pip...

The message was left at four ten pm US time.

'Erase messages?' asked the machine.

Johansson pressed 'yes'. On the whole he thought it would be better if Penny didn't hear them.


## 671

John didn't know what to do next. Stay by the telephone, or search the streets.

Everyone had been called. Friends. Hospitals. He'd reported it to the police. It had been logged and they said they'd keep an eye out. They took a description.

He rang the morgue. Emma's boss said she wasn't in the staff room, did John want him to check the body drawers? John thought it was a little early for that.

'She's hidden in there before,' said Emma's boss.

John didn't want to know.

Emma's parents were in sheltered accommodation. He rang their house-keeper. She hadn't seen nor heard from Emma. Did he want to speak to Emma's dad? John said no, he didn't want to worry him. The dad didn't like John. Thought the marriage was a shit idea. Didn't like John touching his gun. At their wedding the vicar had asked if anyone had any objections to the marriage taking place and her dad had coughed loudly as if to make an announcement. Everyone laughed nervously. He made a speech at the reception about fathers and daughters. Saying how he'd be there for her if it all went tits up. Fathers and daughters! Fathers and daughters! He'd thumped the table. Knocked his champagne over. Emma had re-filled his glass and told him to sit down. Gently though.

He'd be glad Emma had pissed off.

## 670

Johansson slumped back in the chair and decided not to call his own answermachine in Warwickshire. He knew what his messages would be.

One from the airline concerned about his late cancellation of duty in respect of flight SA841. The same message would confirm his re-booking on SA109 the next day and probably express concern that his mobile phone wasn't switched on.

It might, if the airline representative was sympathetic, hope that Johansson's stomach bug didn't give him too much discomfort. It would certainly remind him of the need to supply a doctor's note confirming health before he flew. Procedure, nothing personal.

Another would be from his mother, who always rang up on a Tuesday.

Perhaps one would also be from his therapist, Dr Frankburg, about his missed appointment.

He really ought to try and continue his cure. After all, you never knew if breakthrough was just round the corner.

He found a therapy section in an old yellow pages.

An advertisement: 'Fear at 35,000 feet. Altitude therapy for those too scared to look down.'

It looked like a mobile number and he dialled it.

## 669

Ali Bronski tried not to cry as her phone lit up.

It sat in the middle of an empty floor and vibrated as it rang, like a beetle caught on its back.

The display read 'call'.

And that's all it is, Ali told herself.

After stealing and delivering Frankburg's paper at the conference in Boston, she'd benefited from a number of referrals which impressed delegates had passed on to her, and a succession of formidably damaged individuals had appeared, punctually, one after the other, looking for some way out of their nightmarish existence. Hope in their eyes that Ali would be the one who would drag them from their mental misery and show them how to live brighter, happier lives. Ali was encouraged to place an ad in the NY telephone directory advertising her services.

But she wasn't properly qualified and many of these poor souls died by their own hand. Ali didn't want to have anything to do with anyone on the edge any more. And yet here was the fucking phone bleeping and buzzing at her.

## 668

Her father, Dan Bronski, would like to tell her that she is young enough for a career change, adverts didn't mean anything, old yellow pages got thrown away, masks could be dropped. He'd like to tell her about the joys of A New Beginning but he doesn't know where she is. Besides, he is one of those people on the edge too.

## 667

'Go away,' Ali shouted at her phone.

She used to think her ineffectiveness was due to the lack of a supervisor and that transference was the problem. The only professional she knew was Frankburg but before she'd had time to ask if bygones could be bygones he'd threatened to call the police and have her charged with intellectual theft. She said she didn't steal his paper, he'd given it to her. He said in that case he'd have her charged with speaking the words of another man in a conference context. She said she didn't think that was a crime. He said well, it should be, and refused to help her.

So Ali stopped seeing people, there were only so many deaths you could have on your conscience.

## 666

Ten more rings, Graham Johansson said to himself.

## 665

Ali drummed her fingers on the floor.

'Call' could also be the fat and sweating man who had approached her in Boston and told her he was a representative of a branch of the intelligence service which was interested in adding to its knowledge of individuals who had, or might be prepared to destroy him or herself for the good of the cause. A leering individual who said that if she were to pass on the details of any client capable of committing acts which entailed their own extinction, suicide bombs and so forth, he and his government would be eternally grateful. With no repercussion upon herself. Purely routine but these were dangerous times. His eyes had flicked to her breasts every half minute. He'd given her his card. He said she should get used to him contacting her now and then, out of the blue.

But he'd stopped calling on the whole. Perhaps he had bigger fish to fry.

## 664

Technically this gentleman *used* to be in the employ of the intelligence service. As it happens he's down on his luck and rather hungry and would give his left leg for a bit of fish to fry, of any size.

## 663

'Call' could be her father, of course. Poor man, probably worried sick. Ali could give him five minutes. Blood was thicker blah blah blah.

Ali picked up the phone.

'Hello?'

The guy at the other end of the phone sounded drunk.

'I wanted to know if you could fit me in for a session this evening?'

Perhaps not drunk, Scandinavian.

'Tonight?'

'Yes. As soon as you can in fact.'

'I don't really do this any more, I...'

'Please, it's very important.'

'What's the matter?'

'I'm a pilot. I have a therapist in the UK, I was due to see him this evening but I cancelled and didn't get on my plane. I fly tomorrow and I could do with talking to someone.'

'Why?'

'You're asking me why?'

'Yes.'

'Well, I'm . . . unhappy.'

'Anything else?'

'Look if you don't want to . . .'

'It's not that . . .'

'Your advert seemed to fit.'

'It's never brought me a pilot before.'

'That surprises me.'

'Me too. I thought you were a depressed bunch.'

'We are. At least, I am.'

'Yes.'

Pause

'So, what do you say? Can I come?'

'I've retired.'

'Oh.'

'Or rather I'm taking time off from extreme cases. Are you an extreme case?'

'I don't know.'

'You see, I couldn't guarantee to pull you back from the brink.'

'Does that mean you won't talk to me?'

'Well, we're talking now so we're already beyond that. We've started whether I like it or not. I'm just telling you that because I've retired this is normal talk, not professional talk.'

'That's all right, I'm feeling better already.'

'Really?'

'You must be very good.'

Pause.

'I won't be held responsible if you take a turn for the worse.'

'OK.'

'I'm not in the best of states myself.'

'I understand.'

'I haven't got a chaise longue.'

'I'm fine on a chair.'

'I haven't got any of those either.'

'I'm sure we'll work something out.'

'You might find that I do all the talking. I've got a lot to get off my chest.'

'We can just play it by ear.'

'OK, then.'

'Shall I come then?'

'If you like.'

'I would like.'

'Drop over at nine thirty, I can do you an hour or two.'

She gave him her address and recommended a subway stop then hung up.

Ali went to see what state her 'consulting room' was in.


## 662

Clara Redlake put a lobster into a pot of boiling water and listened to the hiss and whistle of its expanding air pockets. It sounded like a scream if she let her mind tell her that. She turned the radio up loud to cover any other upsetting noises and drank a glass of white. No further pharmaceutical attacks had taken place during working hours. She wondered if her tapes were having a calming effect.


## 661

The pharmaceutical CEO hired a call girl. He reckoned he deserved it after finding a bomb under his car. He booked into the Hotel Monumental and called a number and an escort arrived thirty minutes later. Pretty quick. Express Tarts, he thought. He let her in the door and offered her a drink. She looked like his daughter Tamy. Same hair, same eyes. He found it disconcerting so he asked if she had a wig, she said no. How about some tinted contacts? She said no. She asked him what he wanted. He told her to take her clothes off and so she did. She said, 'Now what?' She even sounded a bit like Tamy. He asked her to speak in a different accent. European or something. She said, 'Now vat?' He said forget it, it wasn't working for him. He paid up and told her to go.

He thought about ringing for a blonde but decided not to.

Felt that God was telling him not to push his luck.

Instead he called a number and half hoped no one would answer.

'Who is this calling?'

'It's me,' said the CEO.

'About time, you arsehole. Damn you. Why won't you return my calls?'

'I'm returning them now.'

'You better have something damn good on the table.'

'The matter's over, I thought I made that clear.'

'Over? You son of a bitch.'

'I'm calling you, aren't I?'

'Have you ever spent any time in a Turkish prison?'

'Let's not get into this, shall we?'

'Ratty mattresses, puke on the floor?'

'Yes, all right.'

'Dirty protests on the walls?'

'You were well compensated.'

'I haven't been compensated at all, you fucking piece of shit. This is the whole Goddamn point, Jesus.'

'Well, there must be some hold up then. It's a complicated operation, the money needs to go through various procedures, third parties. I've got to cover the company here.'

'I'm practically starving to death.'

'I'm sure it'll work out soon.'

'You piece of shit.'

'Stop calling me that.'

'Piece of shit.'

'Look, I wanted to ask—'

'You piece of shit.'

'Will you listen?'

There was some muttering.

'I need to ask you, did you put a bomb under my car today?'

'What?'

'It's a simple question. There was a bomb under my car, did you put it there?'

There was some laughing and then some coughing.

'So, is that a yes?' said the CEO.

'Did the bomb go off?'

'No, it was a crap bomb.'

'The bomb was made of crap?'

'No, it was crappily made.'

'Shame.'

'Was it you?'

'If it had been me, you arsehole, it would've blown you and your big fucking German car to the fucking moon.'

'OK, well, do you think you could ask around?'

'No, piss off.'

'Just ask a couple of questions.'

'Piss off.'

'Use your contacts.'

'Piece of shit.'

'I'll try and hurry up the money.'

'Arsehole.'

'You ask your Government buddies and I'll hurry up the money, how about it?'

'Arsehole piece of shit.'

'OK then, I'll call you tomorrow.' Click.

The CEO took a taxi home. After a bomb under his car, 'piece of shit' was water off a duck's back.

## 660

The ex-government agent muttered 'piece of shit' again and slammed down the phone. He'd learned that the benzodiazepine he'd taken could cause emotional anaesthesia but at that moment no such side effect had presented itself. Indeed, the ex-government agent was feeling acutely connected to sensations of rage, resentment and malice. He thought whoever had tried to blow up the piece of shit deserved to be shaken firmly by the hand.

He sat in a chair in an airless room. He'd kicked down its door, waved his (expired but convincing ID) at the terrified squatters and had eaten their abandoned food. He still felt dizzy though. Shakedowns always took it out of him.

Eighteen months ago, his legitimate investigation into the illegal marketing of improperly tested pharmaceutical products transformed into very unofficial industrial espionage on behalf of that self-same drug company. Finding himself irresistibly drawn to both the company's CEO and, particularly, the CEO's access to massive payoffs, the government agent gathered evidence against a competitor thought to be knocking off one of the CEO's valuable and patented psychotropic drugs. Caught with his hands on the rival's drug recipes in a building in Istanbul, the government agent was thrown into a Turkish prison. At which point he became the ex-government agent.

After three weeks on a urine stained blanket in solitary confinement, he realised that his faith in the CEO was misplaced and an early release would be entirely dependent on the clemency of the Turkish legal system. He was released a year later, five stones lighter, and with something of a chip on his shoulder.

Back in America, he pestered his old colleagues for the names of insane, wild-haired fanatics who might be persuaded to strap dynamite to their bellies and rush headlong into the pharmaceutical CEO's offices, blowing the building, and everything in it, to smithereens. He wanted to see the CEO's limbs fly through the air, he wanted to stand and watch and, perhaps, catch a hand, or an ear. His colleagues weren't interested. They told him to do it himself if he was so fussed about it. That's if he could get any dynamite around his rapidly expanding gut.

He went to Boston to find himself a sympathetic psychologist. Many told him the people he sought didn't go to therapists. A few told him they'd spill some names if he told them who shot JFK. Most didn't speak to him at all having noticed his ID had expired.

Ali Bronski had told him that in her opinion a couple of sessions on the couch himself wouldn't hurt. He said her couch would suit him just fine, he was more than willing to lie anywhere she told him.

## 659

The past year and a half year had been so desolate that he'd even managed to think back fondly to his agency days, deluding himself that he'd been a pretty flashy investigator. As it was, prosecutors had rejected over ninety per cent of his cases due to weak or insufficient evidence, minimal federal interest, or because there was 'no known suspect'. He had a terrible scorecard and if the Turkish police hadn't locked him up, his own government probably would have done so sooner or later.

But with news of bombs under cars the ex-government agent felt the delicious breeze of justice playing over his hot and angry skin. The waft from the cloak of a masked avenger prepared to pierce the fatty and diabolical heart of one who poisoned the earth and twisted nature and, more importantly, owed him an awful lot of money. It made his eyes close and his mouth smile. It tickled his belly, coaxing a little chuckle, it caressed his groin and made Ali Bronski pop into his head.

He dialled her number to see if she knew who this Carbomb Charlie might be but her phone just rang and rang and then got switched off.

The ex-government agent was no chess player but something about that cool breeze was telling him that he had the CEO's king under pressure. Or he could take a pawn at the very least.


## 658

Johansson scribbled a note and left the apartment.

He had an hour to kill. He tried to make a decision. Left would take him towards the east side, right to the west.

Made no odds. He picked the west and started walking.


## 657

Had he turned east he'd have bumped into Penny Lock who was just rounding the corner. She could reasonably be called a celebrity but no one recognised her unless she opened her mouth. That suited Penny fine though, as most of her 'fans' were oddballs.

She was carrying a bottle of wine, two fat steaks, and a funny story about a plastic surgeon and his implanted wife. She figured Graham's stomach bug had been created by the release of ten-days tension built up during Emma Heron's visit, and meat and gags would go some way to making things up to him.

Emma had rather lost them their *joie de vive*. One night, drunk in a bar, she'd asked them if they knew the poem *'Umi Yukaba'*, or 'Going Out to Sea'. They'd said no.

> *Umi yukaba* (If I go away to sea)
> *Mizutsuku kabane* (I shall return a corpse awash)
> *Yama yukaba* (If duty calls me to the mountain)
> *Kusa musu kabane* (A verdant sward shall be my pall)
> *Ogimi no he ni koso shiname* (Thus for the Emperor's sake)
> *Nodo niwa shinaji* (I will not die peacefully at home)

'Very ... um,' said Penny.

'Mournful?' suggested Graham.

Emma said she had hundreds of them up her sleeve and told them to get her another drink.

It hadn't been a very successful visit on the whole.

Penny chose her own phone-in subjects and, after three days of Emma, she chose 'Guests From Hell'. Emma asked what she was trying to say? Penny said nothing, said the station chose the subjects. Emma said the station should do 'I Think I'm Already Dead'. Penny thought it was a little bleak. Emma suggested 'What's The Fucking Point?' Penny said they couldn't swear on air.

## 656

In her apartment block's lobby she took out a key and opened the mail box marked 'Ms P. Lock'. Some people called her Pad. That was Emma's gag originally. Emma still called her that. She said as an old friend she was allowed.

Penny checked her mail. Nothing.

## 655

In celebrity interviews Penny always said her favourite show was 'Flight Fright'. Graham Johansson had rung in to 'Flight Fright'.

He said he was a pilot. She didn't believe him at first, there had been fake pilots ringing all day, but he had such good stories that she'd let him stay on the air.

He was the last caller. After the show ended she'd kept him on the line.

They met up for coffee. Drinks. Dinner. Night stays.

Soon, as far as any pilot can move in, he moved in. He didn't have much stuff, most of it was in the UK, but he was doing the Atlantic routes and it suited him better than hotels.

He'd asked her if she could say hi to him on the radio when she signed off the show. She said why? It was just a dumb show. He said it made him feel good, it was a simple request.

She said OK.

'That was the *Penny Lock Show*. Love to Graham and love to you all.'

If she forgot, he'd say, 'Is it really so, so difficult?'

If the celebrity interviewer pushed her, Penny said her second favourite show was 'Fight the Good Fight' although in truth she'd found it a bit hairy.

'And you were called a whore,' the celebrity interviewer would say.

## 654

Riding in the elevator, Penny wondered if Emma was having domestic problems. She'd been gloomy to start with and had got worse the nearer she got to flying back. Emma told her not to worry, said it was the morgue-attitude.

Penny wondered if Emma's stand-up comic husband was taking showbiz cocaine and screwing groupies. No. He wasn't the type. Wasn't much of a comic either, as far as Penny remembered. He'd been a better magician.

The last time Penny had seen John's act was his one and only outing as 'Screaming Johan' where he'd bellowed into the microphone for two minutes then suddenly stopped. A technician rushed onto the stage thinking the microphone had broken but it was just that John's voice had packed up. He gamely tried to continue but nothing was coming out so he left the stage. Penny would have been surprised if that sort of performance got him laid much.

Emma said she'd once been out to dinner with her husband and he'd pretended to get paralytic shellfish poisoning. He told her he'd tasted alkaloid neurotoxins in his *moules marinières* and said that if he didn't get to a hospital within thirty minutes diaphragmatic paralysis would set in followed by respiratory failure and death. The restaurant's sweating maître d' had called an ambulance. John had recovered three miles shy of the hospital. He thought Emma would be pleased they'd avoided paying for the meal as they were on an economy drive. Emma wished she'd had a fucking poisoned mussel handy. It had been their wedding anniversary.

Penny had nodded sympathetically, Emma said John thought pretending to die was funny. Well, death wasn't funny, death was a serious business and a day at the slab would teach him that. Penny knew that. Calm down. They were in the Metropolitan Museum and security were getting edgy. Emma apologised and looked at mummies.

Later, in the Farmer's Market in Union Square, cold, blue, smelling of apples, they'd bought cider and picked out food to cook when a young man wearing headphones bumped into Emma, knocking her cider over Penny's trousers. She shouted at him. he looked as if he had done it deliberately.

He apologised to them. He said, slowly and deliberately, 'I am so, so very sorry. I am just the clumsiest dolt around. Could I buy you another one?' He then waited ten or so seconds during which no one spoke. Then he asked, 'How can I make up for this?' and Emma had said, 'Kill me.' He'd looked a bit confused and said, 'My pleasure, have a nice day,' and then he walked away. Emma said he stank of lighter fluid.

## 653

Clara Redlake had watched the whole scene from a bench. She thought she'd better make some changes to the 'Managing Anger in Urban Life' tape. It was the first one though, there were bound to be some tweaks required. She ran after Edward and took the headphones off, saying that was probably enough for the day. He said the tapes didn't allow for encounters with people more fucked up than the people she was trying to cure. She said she didn't like the term 'fucked up'. Edward said he called it as he saw it. He said he'd need more money if he was going to continue as her lab rat. Stop saying that, she said.

## 652

'Penny, gone to clear my head. Back at about eleven. Graham xx.'

## 651

Penny stripped the bed that Emma had slept in.

Emma and Penny first met the day after a Pan Am flight exploded over

Lockerbie. Penny had been in Glasgow and had travelled to the town with a little tape player. She thought some vox popping might get her a job on CNN. Emma had made the journey just to look. They found themselves standing by a crater not understanding why they'd come. Emma told Penny about a man from the flight who'd been discovered in a field still strapped into his chair by the seat belt. Sat alone, like a dignified scarecrow. Emma said they ought to find him so they tramped the fields. They walked for miles and miles. Emma found a fork. Penny found a seat buckle.

Emma told her that when she was a girl she'd found a woman in the woods. Emma didn't remember too much about it but some details came back to her occasionally: the awkwardly placed limbs, the colour of the hair. The find made her a celebrity at school. Friends asked her if she saw ghosts. Teachers smiled at her and told her she was a brave girl. She drew pictures of the body. The teachers said well done, nervously. A school psychologist encouraged her to write a story about it so she did. She wrote a good story about it. The head teacher thought it would be a fine idea if she read it out in assembly. A gentle introduction to the concept of death from one with first-hand experience. He would do an appropriate prayer afterwards.

Emma was excited by the exposure. She changed some things the night before and read out a more extreme version in front of 300 children her age and younger. She made it sensational. The body was blood-soaked. The eyes had popped out. The tongue had been found on a branch. The body had come back from the grave and eaten Emma's mother and father.

Many children cried and had nightmares. The parents complained and the head teacher was disciplined. Emma's parents didn't know how to tell her off so they didn't.

Then she moved school. There was a boy there who'd met a Rolling Stone and Emma was low interest so she stopped playing up.

Penny said she'd never seen a dead body. Emma told her CNN probably wouldn't suit her.

## 650

Penny was stuck with two great lumps of meat and no one to eat them with. She checked her messages. Nothing there either. Where was everyone?

## 649

John Heron sat at home with a gin and said, 'I shall now make my wife disappear.'

He took a sip.

'Ta da!'

## 648

Michael Davies slept. His eyes flickered under his lids, following the radar blips.

## 647

Downstairs, his wife Beth felt hungry. Hungry enough to risk Spongiform Encephalopathy in beef, Campylobacter in chicken, Trichinosis in pork, and Enlerocolitica in lamb. She thought about frying some but knew she'd gag at the smell of burnt meat.

She wondered whether to take her book about the Wright brothers with her to read on the plane. Their first flight had been 272 feet, the left wing was struck in landing and four ribs were cracked at the rear left corner. The second had been 664 feet, the machine acted very queerly in side steering and Orville was compelled to shut off power to avoid running into a fence. Third, 774 feet, Wilbur tried to alter the rudder but it broke in his hand. Fifth, delayed due to hard rain. Sixth, hit a stump. Seventh, landed in a ditch, Wilbur thrown violently out through the top covering, suffering sprained wrist. Eighth, Orville made a complete circle, 884 feet. Six farmers present. Next, a breakthrough 1,041 feet. And so on and so forth.

According to Beth's calculations Orville Wright crashed around 700 times. Wilbur 400, he must have been more cautious.

Perhaps the book wasn't a comfort.

'His winnowing fan is in His hand, and He will thoroughly clean out His threshing floor, and gather the wheat into His barn; but the chaff He will burn with unquenchable fire.' She wouldn't take the Bible either.

She decided to listen to the self-help tape instead.

## 646

Ali Bronski sniffed her armpits and thought she could do with a wash but like the actor Samuel Thorn she got spooked in bathtubs.

# 645

*You Too Can Fly* encouraged Beth to tense and relax each part of her body. Beth did so.

Then it encouraged her to roll her shoulders back and then forwards, then back, then forwards. She did so.

Then a loud siren burst into her ears. Previously softened muscles spasmed, she leapt up and flung off the headphones with a yelp and stared at them as if they were a wounded animal about to bite her.

They lay on the floor emitting tinny sounds of continuing crisis. When she had recovered, Beth adjusted the volume, and put them back on her head.

The siren was still sounding in the background but over the top of it she could hear urgent voices distorted in the besieged microphones.

'500 we just need 500!'

'I'm giving it all I've got.'

'Pull up.' Whoop whoop. 'Pull up.' Whoop whoop.

'Give me… <crackle>… trying to fight it!'

'…more power.'

Whoop whoop.

'Lower the gear!'

'Come on, you can do it.'

'I can't hold her.'

'Come on.'

'We're going down.'

'Jesus. I don't know what to say.'

Huge explosion.

Beth rewound and played it again.

'I can't hold her.'

'Come on.'

'We're going down.'

'Jesus. I don't know what to say.'

Huge explosion.

After the explosion, the Welsh voice cut back in as if nothing had happened.

'…allowing the shoulder muscles to move freely. Good. Let's move on to the neck.'

She switched to side two.

## 644

Manhattan.

Johansson rang the buzzer.

'Yes?'

'It's Graham Johansson, the pilot.'

'You're early.'

'I went for a walk but it's pretty cold so…'

'You could have gone to a bar.'

'I was already trying to sober up.'

'You're drunk?'

'Well, I wouldn't say drunk.'

'What would you say?'

'I don't know.'

'Do you know why you're drunk?'

'Is this how you run your consultations? Over the intercom?'

Ali paused. It wasn't such a bad idea.

'I don't think we'll get much useful work done if you're drunk.'

'I'm not drunk, I needed to clear my head.'

'What's the matter with it?'

'It's been working too hard.'

'Thinking?'

'Yes.'

'What sort of thoughts?'

'Are we really going to talk like this?'

'Why not?'

'Well, it's freezing, for one thing.'

There was no answer.

'Hello?' said Johansson. 'Are you there?'

A blanket fell from a window four floors up. Johansson jumped as it landed at his feet. He stepped back to look up at where it had been thrown from.

The intercom crackled.

'You were saying.'

'Oh, come on.'

'What sort of thoughts?'

Johansson looked at the blanket. It did look pretty warm.

## 643

John snatched up the phone at the first ring.

The airport.

According to a vigilant employee, Angela, an Emma Heron had taken the midnight flight to New York.

'She's just been to New York.'

'Seems she's gone back, sir.'

He put the phone down. He looked at his watch. Two am.

He was half the wiser. He knew where she was, about five miles above the Atlantic Ocean. And she wasn't dead. John felt glad about that and angry about that.

## 642

Side two. Beth found another cut-in section.

'...measured at 500 overcast... one mile visibility in light snow, surface wind northwest fifteen knots...'

'Received.'

'266 you are cleared to 11,000.'

'Received.'

<crackle>

'AF 266, turn left, heading 130 on a southeast course.'

'Received.'

'Cleared to 9,000.'

'Received.'

'...only a few minutes... hold on till then?'

'...upsetting the other passengers.'

'What's the matter with her?'

'Just crying, they think she's crying because something's gone wrong with the plane.'

'OK, see if you can reassure them, we'll try to speed things up.'

'…right…an announcement might help.'

'OK.'

'Control, this is AF 266, we have an unwell stewardess on board, any chance of getting us down quickly?'

'…One moment, 266.'

'She was fine earlier, wasn't she?'

'No, she's been odd all day, just tired perhaps.'

'AF 266 take airway route Victor 132, it'll take a couple of minutes off your journey.'

'Received, thanks.'

'Hope it's nothing too serious.'

'We don't think so, thanks anyway.'

'OK, OK. Cleared to 7,000.'

'Received.'

'You wanna do it?'

'Sure. Ladies and gentlemen this is Co-pilot Johansson speaking. We shall be landing in about twenty minutes time, earlier than scheduled. As I said, the weather in London is slightly overcast but a pleasant twenty degrees. Thank you for flying with us. Cabin crew, prepare for landing.'

'Very reassuring, Mr Johansson.'

'Well, I do my best.'

## 641

It was less catastrophic and much clearer to her, as part of it involved a conversation between a plane crew and a tense air traffic controller who, unless she was deliriously fatigued, was her husband.

Beth stared at the player and wondered why *You Too Can Fly* had sections of blackbox recordings spliced into it.

## 640

'Have you ever wondered what the point of it all was?' asked Johansson through the intercom.

'No.'

'Never?'

'Never.'

'You've never thought, would it really make any difference at all if I just ended it all right here and now?'

'No.'

'Have you ever been on a plane?'

'Yes.'

'Then you must have looked out of the window and seen all the distant lights of a city and thought that each of those lights is lighting up people who are working, driving home, eating dinner, dying, being born, screwing, all that stuff, but you didn't know them and never would. But if the plane were to land in that city rather than your destination, you would meet those people, you'd eat dinner with them, watch some of them die, watch some of them being born, screw some of them...'

'Sounds like a hell of a place.'

'Of all the potential lives you could've had, don't you suspect there's one knocking around somewhere where you matter to more people?'

'Too right, buddy,' barked an old woman's voice.

'What?'

'I tell you I had the chance to move to Connecticut fifty years ago and I swear to God that in Connecticut I'd have never met the kind of low-life husband I've been shackled to all my life...'

'Me too,' piped up another voice. 'I think in Europe the men are more considerate.'

'I nearly took a medicine major, I could have been a doctor...'

'I've always thought that I'd have been much happier in France...'

'What's happening?' asked Johansson.

'You'd better come up,' said Ali. 'The whole block can hear us.'

She buzzed him.

## 639

Penny Lock thinks of tomorrow's show. 'Missing Persons'. She should get a guest in.

## 638

Johansson entered Ali's apartment. She looked at him and he smiled at her. Speaking through the intercom Ali had imagined him in a pilot's uniform. Full braid. Hat. Good teeth. He did have good teeth.

'Sorry about that,' she said. 'Do you want to take a seat?'

Johansson looked around. The place was practically empty. The room into which he'd walked contained a lamp, a book, and a carton of milk.

Ali went into an adjoining room and returned with a small stool.

Johansson walked past her and looked into the room where the stool had come from. Removing the stool had made that room empty. He went into the next room. There was a sleeping bag on the floor but nothing else. She could stay retired as long as she had things to sell.

'Do you live here?' he asked.

'Yes.'

'Where is everything?'

'Here and there. Do you want a glass of milk?'

'Yes, please.'

She went to the kitchen and returned with a small flower vase. She tipped the rest of the milk into it. 'It's quite clean, I often use it.'

'Thank you.'

'Do you want to take off your blanket?'

'I'll keep it on, if that's OK.'

'Sure.'

Johansson supped his milk.

'So,' Ali said, 'you have a better life somewhere else but you missed it. Yes?'

'I don't know what I was trying to say.'

'Come on, you were doing great down there.'

## 637

Beep

'Mr Johansson. This is Frankburg. If you want to change therapists now I fully understand. I've had wine. I apologise.'

Click.

## 636

'I don't think we're supposed to fly. We're jumping ahead evolution wise. I don't think our brains are suited to it, they're too large and their systems fuse and short out. If we are to fly we need smaller ones, like birds. I met an astronaut once. I spoke to him for half an hour and he said he could hardly concentrate any more because he had a complete image of the world in his mind. His perceptions of humanity had changed, he'd stepped back. We're all too tiny. For him it was an issue of scale.'

'Is this how you feel?'

'I don't know. Sometimes.'

Somewhere in the distance a clock chimed ten.

'Have you seen many suicidal people?' asked Johansson.

'Yes.'

'Do I strike you as one?'

'I'd have to see you kill yourself before I made a judgement.'

'Well, it would be obvious then.'

'Pretty obvious.'

There was a pause.

'Would you mind if I slept here tonight?'

'Keep talking. You've still got another hour.'


## 635

The ex-government agent tried Ali again but got no answer. He fiddled with a paper clip and called her a piece of shit. He made his initial out of the wire.

When Theodore Roosevelt asked Attorney General Charles Bonaparte to create a force of Special Agents, Bonaparte suggested that rather than recruit on the evidence of marksmanship, they should have the men shoot at each other and give the jobs to the survivors.

The ex-government agent was glad that recruitment method hadn't been enforced. He'd never been much of a crack shot. He didn't even have a gun any more.

He scratched his crotch and thought that if he got through to Ali he'd call her a sexy piece of shit.

## 634

There are perhaps only three hours when New York and Birmingham are asleep at the same time. That time was now. Even Tommy Tempo had hit the sack. Time was when Tommy could go all night, encore after encore, keep playing till the crowd could dance no more, the men's suits sticking to their bodies and the woman's heels all snapped off. Then Tommy would handpick ten of the finest looking and move on to Barney's and try to drink 'Lips' McReady under the table. 'Sticks' Allen would order champagne then disappear into the toilets with someone. A man, a woman. Sticks didn't care.

That was then. Now Tommy just listened to them playing his records on the radio. Tapping his feet. Totting up the royalties. Thinking Sticks was sometimes a beat too slow. But smiling all the same and dozing off in his chair.

## 633

Johansson didn't use his hour. The blanket, the milk, the empty flat, the low light. After thirty minutes he was asleep.

Ali went into the sleeping-bag room and quietly closed the door. She thought that if Johansson wasn't dead by the morning perhaps she could bring herself out of retirement.

She fell asleep while wondering if she'd be able to fall asleep.

## 632

Ten blocks away Penny Lock was also asleep. Two steaks and a bottle of red consumed solo had put her flat out.

## 631

Air traffic controller Michael Davies dreamt of the blips on his radar screen turning into musical notes. He tried to play the notes on a keyboard in front of him but it sounded terrible.

## 630

Downstairs, Beth had finally fallen asleep. She was on a chair with the headphones on her lap. She flew tomorrow and dreamt of lightning hitting her plane, but the zap made her spine hum and that wasn't such a bad feeling.

**629**

Samuel Thorn dreamt of tying Kirsten to the railway tracks.

**628**

Dr Frankburg had run to the toilet where he was sick. He told himself to stop drinking red wine. Back in bed, he dreamt about diving off the end of Brighton Pier and swimming in the ocean, only to see the pier float out to sea, leaving him treading water in the middle of nowhere.

**627**

His daughter, Cody Jameson, dreamt of blue fizzing balls of energy.

**626**

The taxi driver who picked up Ronald Henderson and Emma Heron from Birmingham airport had been asked to drive around a bit before dropping them off at Birmingham International train station.

He was unaware that taxi drivers had the fifth most stressful job, according to *Aviation World*. Before the fare, he would've been surprised at the fact. After the fare, he though he should go higher. Just behind firefighters.

The old guy spent most of the journey asking the young woman to push him in front of a train.

That's when he wasn't weeping on the phone.

The taxi driver's was asleep too, dreaming of an open-topped taxi cab which catches pullovers that fall from high buildings. His brain confused by the word 'jumpers'.

**625**

Miles, manager of the Wellington Arms, dreamt of being shot.

'Not this one again,' he said in his sleep.

**624**

The ex-government agent's diazepams have taken effect and he was asleep in a chair. The drug has been absorbed in his substantial belly and was being metabolised by his (overworked) liver. His sleep was heavy and dreamless and he didn't wake up as two Spanish-speaking women entered the apartment looking for somewhere to sleep. They saw the ex-government agent slumped, mouth lolling, snoring gently, and decided that he had a friendly face and probably wouldn't try to kill them when he woke up. They lay down next to each other on the opposite side of the room.

## 623

The CEO of the pharmaceutical company was asleep. He, too, had taken a pill so that he won't dream of his limbs being torn from his body by a strange malicious tornado. He's had this dream many times and assumed it would be even worse given the events of the day. He doesn't think of side effects. It's his business not to.

## 622

His daughter Tamy was asleep in a room two doors down the corridor. Her father hadn't kissed her goodnight but had patted her on the head like a puppy. He told her not to open her own mail for a while, especially packages. Tamy wished he was an accountant, or a fireman.

## 621

Retired air crash investigator Dan Bronski was dead drunk. The people who have been enjoying Dan's lavish hospitality all asked where Ali was and he started the evening by saying she was on holiday but finished it by saying she was somewhere in New York and did anyone have any more specific information?

No one did. They put a pillow under his head and a blanket over his body and then called cabs to take them home. The cab company sent three cars over and didn't need to be told the address. Dan's guests always gave them a lot of custom late at night.

## 620

John Heron, exhausted, had the whole bed to himself. He thought he ought to keep the space available for Emma's occupation but couldn't help sleeping diagonally and enjoying the extra room.

## 619

…wake up. Keep concentrating. Don't fall asleep. Who's awake. Who's awake at this point?

## 618

Edward the Fireman was awake. He was supposed to be making fake calls. But pleasant ones. Ones which made the hoaxees pleased they'd been woken up in the middle of the night. Calls which, according to Clara's tape five would make them fall back asleep, reassured that society was essentially decent and considerate.

Edward the Fireman wasn't doing this, however. Instead, he's persuaded the proprietor of a surgical supply store to sell him ten syringes, needles, two scalpels, suture material and lidocaine local anaesthetic, and is lying on his kitchen table trying to look at his liver.

## 617

Clara Redlake was asleep. She's dreamt of lab rats.

## 616

Edward the Fireman was unsure about what he was looking at. He'd injected the anaesthetic in the upper abdomen and cut down to some fibrous material but surgical bleeding was preventing a good view of his anatomy. He swabbed the area and inserted his fingers into the exposed area in an attempt to reveal the organ more clearly. As it happens, Edward had made a very accurate incision and the mystery organ he saw was in fact his liver. Unfortunately he kept passing out every time his fingers touched it.

## 615

Emma. Emma Heron was awake.

She's crossing time zones, wrapped in a blanket, with three seats to herself. She took off one shoe and wondered what happened to the other one before remembering it had split whilst kicking the telephone box in frustration that Graham Johansson didn't pick up.

The captain on her plane spoke to them all. He had rather an automated voice which Emma didn't recognise. She remembered being told that it was possible, these days, to fly a plane solely by computer. The pilot didn't even need to be there. This made Emma think about the voice she has heard. Wondered if there could be such a thing as a kamikaze robot.

She looked around her. On take-off some people had affected a world-weary attitude towards flying. They'd pretended that flying was a bore. They'd pretended to fall asleep. They hadn't looked out of the window on take-off but had busied themselves with important papers. If the plane crashed, however, these people would scream the loudest and pray to God the hardest.

## 614

Edward the Fireman came to and wished he'd thought to place a mirror nearby. He resolved to be more prepared next time. With somewhat shaky hands, he sutured and packed the wound and gave himself another jab of lidocaine for good measure.

Then he fell asleep, or fainted, there's a fine line sometimes.

## 613

...and as for me, I think I am awake. Or in hypnogogia. A waking dream where I am in between awake and asleep, and images are perceived behind closed eyes but are unreal in quality. It is not dreaming, it is not as structured as dreaming, it doesn't form a narrative as dreams do. There is no immersion. There is no rapid eye movement. This is the time before dreaming or just before waking where demons and angels and ghosts visit, but there's paralysis and fear and the body cannot protect itself and the mind is confused.

That's the trouble with hypnogogia, you don't know if you're conscious or unconscious – you don't know anything for sure. You can only feel sure.

But the count is real and I'm down to 613 and everyone else dreams. The stand up, the radio DJ, the burnt phobic, the fake therapist, the real therapist, the attractive red-headed therapist, the writer, the pilot, the air traffic controller, the ex-agent, the CEO, his daughter, the retired air crash investigator, that prick the non-fireman. Conscious in sleep. Eyes twitching under their lids.

There's Kirsten Henderson too. And her father Ronald. But they're both dead now. Their sleep is damn heavy. They'll take some waking.

## 612

...I could wake them anyway, just for a while.

I woke Ronald Henderson in a plane in 1978.

'Would you like a drink, sir?' I asked him.

'A whisky would be fine.'

'Ice and lemon?'

'Lemon? In a whisky?'

'I'm sorry, I was thinking of gin.'

'Why were you thinking of gin?'

'That's none of your business.'

This was our first exchange. Not the best of starts.

## 611

Some people try to be good on aeroplanes. They settle themselves quickly. They always keep their seat belts on. They extinguish their cigarettes. They check the safety card, but only because they are superstitious, not because they have forgotten what to do in an emergency.

They try to ingratiate themselves with the stewardess. They try to impress them with sympathetic smiles, pretending to empathise, pretending to understand.

Sometimes the stewardess will smile back at them, as if finding a soulmate, but secretly they hate these people. They don't know what it's really like to be a stewardess. Why don't they fuck off and keep their smiles to themselves?

## 610

Ronald Henderson was very good-humoured in 1978.

He had a Scottish accent. He told me it was Aberdeen.

He said, 'I have an attitude towards air flight similar to a restaurant. If you make a fuss in a restaurant, God may make the waiter spit in your food. If you make a fuss on a plane, God might send it crashing into the sea. The stakes are higher, of course, but the principle's the same.'

I told him I didn't think that was very scientific. If the plane had crashed every time someone was rude then every single plane I'd been on would've come down. He said he was naturally very egocentric so the rule only applied to him.

## 609

He was a doctor. I liked him. We were flying into Hong Kong. From there he was travelling to Beijing to study medical procedures in one of the city's hospitals. He asked me if I knew anything about Chinese medicines. I said no but I could do with something herbal to help me get over jet lag and varicose veins.

He suggested acupuncture.

When he left the plane, he shook my hand and hoped we'd meet again. I said so did I and, unusually for a passenger, I meant it.

## 608

Emma directed a stream of air on to her face. She remembered John telling her about Houdini's wife and the strain she must have gone through seeing her husband appear to die night after night.

Houdini had an act where he would straitjacket and chain himself into a tight cocoon. The chain was secured with a padlock. The wife's job was to slip him the key during a farewell kiss. It really got the crowd, especially the women, they were very susceptible. Life and death. The simplest deception. Last human warmth before jumping into the icy water. Houdini would have to know his wife though. Know her inside out. Know what she was thinking, how she was feeling. Was she happy? Was there anything on her mind? Because the responsibility was terrifying. His life in her hands. Would she crack? She had such power in this moment. Could he trust her? Did she love him? It was a grave task. A beautiful task. Never was a kiss so important.

Emma said that the wife should've swallowed the key, that would teach him a thing or two about death. John said that would ruin the show.

## 607

Ronald was met at the airport by the senior administrator in the large Beijing hospital, who had taken care of all his travel arrangements for the onward journey and would install him in the house of a family where he was to stay for three weeks.

The house was modest but comfortable and Ronald was made to feel extremely welcome.

It was 1979 and China had recently suffered a terrible earthquake, flattening the city of Tangshan and many buildings in Beijing. The city had only just recovered when Ronald made his first visit. Cracks had been patched up with cement and rubble, hidden by tarpaulin.

## 606

Emma asked the stewardess if she had any scissors. The stewardess said they didn't like passengers to have sharp objects but would nail clippers do? Emma said thank you. She was told that the film that night would be *Enemy of the State* and could be found on channel eleven. Emma said thank you.

## 605

At the hospital itself, Ronald became captivated by a nurse who worked there. She was called Lin and had a very serious face which was transformed by a beatific smile when Ronald greeted her each morning. Ronald had never met such a creature. He had considered himself a lifelong bachelor. Not through a lack of emotional generosity, but because he was waiting for a moment such as this.

## 604

A bolt from the blue.

## 603

Sensitive to the social niceties of his host country, he made the most discreet advances possible. So discreet in fact, that for a while Lin had little idea she was being wooed.

She was twenty years younger than Ronald but was eventually charmed by this soft-spoken Western doctor, so attentive, so respectful of the hospital, its staff, her country, so immersed in her when she spoke to him, so generous, so considerate, so terrible at Cantonese.

A relationship blossomed. Lin still lived with her parents and opportunities to see each other outside work without causing distracting gossip were few and far between. But they managed. A cycle ride, a walk in Beihai Park.

And notes passed to each other. Many, many notes.

## 602

A Chinese love letter is beautiful to look at. Linked strokes, succulent brushes loaded with ink, swiped, porous paper soaking some of it in, leaving the rest balancing on its fibres.

I wrote one to my partner at the time. It said, 'Could you tell me the way to the ticket office?' The only Chinese I knew how to write.

## 601

Ronald was lost. His visit was ending. He wanted something eternal. He wanted to propose to Lin. He wanted her to love his spontaneity.

If Lin wanted to remain in China, so be it, he would stay as her husband. If she wanted to live in the UK, that was fine too, they would find a townhouse in Aberdeen and take up ballroom dancing. Either way, they would be man and wife and, more than likely, breed a number of splendid children.

He appeared at Lin's house with his heart in his mouth. Both Lin's parents were visiting relatives and Lin was alone.

Ronald was unsure of the protocol and so did it the old-fashioned Scottish way. He grabbed her hand, fell down on one knee and ardently proposed.

Then he repeated the words in Chinese.

Lin accepted. Both in Chinese and in English. And French and Italian. She had learned how to say 'yes' in twenty languages.

## 600

'Hai ' is how you say yes in Cantonese. I know how to write it. I'm tracing the strokes on my leg. Up down, up down, across, dot. Yes. Yes. Yes and that was the start of it.

Ronald and Lin drank wine to celebrate, even though it was eight o'clock in the morning. Ronald wanted to get married that very afternoon and wished Beijing was more like Las Vegas.

Lin asked him about Scotland. He told her about the lochs and the glens. The mountains and the towns. He recited some poetry from Burns which he had learned at school but had forgotten he knew. He promised to teach her clay pigeon shooting, even though he'd never done it in his life.

A little conjugation took place. He wanted to strew her bed with flowers but it was raining outside and the petals were soggy.

## 599

I had little conjugations at that time too. Provided by Michael Davies. I described the proposal scene to him but proposal talk made him jumpy and he got us drunk and set off fireworks in the garden to distract me like a child. Then he lurched to one knee, told me that I was everything to him, and sang 'Give Me the Moonlight'. Or 'Moon River'. But didn't propose.

He was a young air traffic controller working out of West Drayton. He was a competitive man by nature so I kept him quiet. He never met my family. The men would've taken him on. They would've hated him and that's always an awkward thing.

## 598

Michael Davies turned over in his sleep and muttered something about guiding a plane through an underpass.

He'd piled up all the pillows around him, sandbagging himself. There was a streetlight outside his bedroom window which was malfunctioning and flashed intermittently. It made his face flicker a sickly yellow. There were hairs on the pillow which were mostly grey. This would depress him in the morning.

## 597

Downstairs, Beth was suffering from sleep paralysis, a conscious sleep experience whereby Beth felt she couldn't move despite the intense effort to do so. Sometimes these dreams were accompanied by strong feelings of dread or fear, but not on this occasion. Beth was talking in her sleep. She was lucid and she believed she was awake. Usually this state could be awakened simply by touch, but Beth was too far away from anyone for this to happen.

'I'm glued to my chair, Michael,' she said.

## 596

Ronald's visit ended and he left Beijing. Under the ignorant gaze of the entire medical staff, Ronald had bowed formally to Lin by way of a goodbye and they had looked at each other, holding the look for a second, and then Lin had turned pale and fainted. Lin was taken home and Ronald drank heavily on the flight.

He looked into the technicalities of emigration. He visited lawyers. He bought a new bed. He visited the gym. He saved money for the return trip and eight weeks passed.

Then he had a letter from Lin saying she would be giving birth to a child in seven months' time.

They'd written regularly since he'd left and Ronald had noticed the tone of her letters had been getting strange. Ambiguous at times. Melancholy even.

He wrote back with a shaky hand saying he was overjoyed at the prospect of a child. It had happened sooner than he'd have wanted but, hell, he was in his late forties, what was the point of hanging around? He'd read somewhere that Mao Zedong had felt that China couldn't have enough children, and flushed by prospective fatherhood, Ronald was in agreement.

Lin took a different view.

She left her parental home and went to stay with a cousin in the quieter south-eastern province of Fujian. To think and to hide her belly.

Her cousin was a stoic farmer who, with his wife, was working too hard under Deng Xiaoping's economic drive to take much notice of her. Lin cooked and kept her head down.

## 595

Ronald decorated his house. He bought cartoon wallpaper and made his study into a nursery. He visited the Chinese Embassy. He wrote a letter a week. Each one asking about the quality of Chinese midwifery and each one asking how big Lin had got. Lin replied bigger, bigger. Don't come for the birth.

## 594

I flew to Hong Kong and back twenty-five times during Lin's pregnancy. Covering 262,700 nautical miles and serving fifty-two pints of gin.

## 593

The baby was born. It was a girl. Lin's cousin got the shock of his life. His wife had clicked and made herself useful with towels.

Ronald wanted descriptions. Lin said she had hands and fingers and arms and legs and a head and eyes and a nose and feet and toes and a mouth...

She said the town was looking at her. She said she sometimes saw eyes peeking through the windows. She thought her cousin was shipping in boat trips of spectators.

Ronald was tearing his hair out.

Let me come because you're sick.

Let me come because you might make the baby sick.

Let me come because I'm sick.

He'd got official permission to fly over but only within a certain time frame. If he let that expire, he'd have to apply again.

Let me come because you have post-natal psychosis.

Let me come because you're more stubborn than your government.

Let me come because if it isn't now, it won't be for years.

Lin relented and Ronald leapt on the flight.

## 592

And so I met him for the second time.

He was pale and sweaty.

He told me the story, I bumped him up to first and gave him free champagne. He left the plane tipsy and optimistic.

I caught sight of him at the airport as he was going through passport control. He looked dazed and nervy. He was clumsy and twitchy. He behaved like a drug-smuggler.

I went over and gave him the number of the hotel where I would be staying for the next twenty-four hours. 'Just in case you need it.'

'Thank you, Stephanie, that's very kind.'

'Don't mention it.'

He rang me while I was asleep. It was two in the morning and he spoke quietly.

'I've got to get the child out.'

'What?'

'I'm going to bring my daughter back to Scotland.'

'What's happened? Is she ill?'

She wasn't ill. Lin was ill. Lin was agitated and emotional. Her thought processes were disturbed, and she spoke nonsensically. She was hallucinating. Eyes in the walls. The stars were looking at her. She hadn't slept properly in weeks and she hadn't smiled at him yet.

I asked Ronald where he was.

He was in Xiamen. He'd taken a bus from Hong Kong and he wanted to get straight back on it. He wanted to take swift action.

He knew how to bring a wife into the UK but Lin wasn't his wife yet. He didn't know how to bring a child in and what did I think? Did I have any ideas? What should he do?

'Ronald,' I said. 'It's a difficult moment, you've been apart for a long time, it's hard to adjust to such an emotional...'

## 591

What's a stewardess to do? This wasn't a case of leg cramp.

## 590

'...Lots of reassurance, you're a doctor, calm everything down. Both of you get some rest. Make decisions in the morning...'

'It's such a mess.'

'It's too much to deal with tonight. Trust me. Sleep on it. See how you feel tomorrow.'

'Will you still be there tomorrow?'

'I'll be right here. Ring me in the morning. OK?'

He didn't answer.

'OK, Ronald?'

'I'm sorry for putting all this on you, I hardly know you...'

The baby started crying and he rang off.

I was sure things wouldn't feel quite so desperate the next day. Sleep would sort them out. Sleep was a good thing...

## 589

John Heron turned over in his sleep. He'd left his bedroom window open and in his dreams he saw mosquitoes fly in and land on his body. They sucked his blood but didn't like the taste and so they left. One of them was sick on his back.

## 588

The ex-government agent woke up with a bursting bladder. He had no idea where he was or where the bathroom could be. Rather than stumble around blindly, he pissed into the apple juice carton by his side. The two women on the other side of the room watched him do this and were glad. The bathroom was right behind them and he'd have probably tripped over them on the way to it.

## 587

The pharmaceutical CEO was lucid dreaming. Aware that he was asleep and aware that he was dreaming. He felt he had power over his dreams. He was suddenly allowed to do what the hell he liked and he liked this control and so he decided to conjure up a blonde. He placed himself back at the Hotel Monumental and made a knock sound at the door and he made the door open and then, rather than a blonde stranger, in walked Tamy. And the CEO lost control of his dream and he was suddenly afraid and he tried to wake himself up before something horrible happened with his daughter.

## 586

Michael Davies dreamt of a time capsule, buried in 1980 and opened in 2000. It contained documents, letters, maps, memories, publications, newsreel, poems, prayers. But as the lid was removed he saw that everything had rotted away because the container leaked. And someone said, 'Oh, what a shame,' and Michael said, 'Thank fuck for that.'

## 585

Emma Heron snipped a lock of her hair and put it in an envelope. She put ten fingernail clippings in there too. Ready to be turned into ashes for use in a commemoration rite. She wondered who to send the envelope to. Not John. He might feel moved by the lock of hair, but the clippings would turn his stomach. She would send it to her boss at the morgue. He would do her a good ceremony. Lots of ritual.

Gene Hackman was on the screen in front of her. Being watched and looking spooked. Taking death very seriously.

## 584

...I woke early and hung around my hotel room until the afternoon in case Ronald rang. But he didn't.

I was due at the airport at four and so checked out at three, thinking I had given good advice. Their reunion must have taken its toll but the human spirit is resilient and sleep was life's great... what did I know? I flew back to England.

I was back in the same hotel two weeks later, different room but a longer stay. I was getting ready to go out with some colleagues when I received a call.

The voice was faint. I told it to speak up.

The voice got louder but I didn't recognise it.

The voice said it was Lin.

I asked where she was. She said she was in Hong Kong. She said she wanted to meet.

I said I was going out for dinner but if she wanted to meet afterwards...?

Yes. *Hai.* Yes. Please.

We fixed up a time and a place.

I was late but Lin was still waiting.

I could see what had attracted Ronald to her. She had a serious but approachable face. Shy but generous. And dark eyes and a dimple in one cheek and long black hair. Tied up with two sticks.

She had taken a seat which had a good view of the door. When she saw me, she half stood and I smiled and so did she and let out a little breath. Relief perhaps.

'Thank you for coming,' she said.

She wore a big overcoat. It was a cold October night but despite the warmth in the room she kept it on. There was an untouched cup of green tea in front of her.

She said that Ronald had said that I'd been very kind. Kind on the phone. Kind with the champagne.

'How did you get here?' I asked.

Immigration had swelled Hong Kong's population to five million but it was still difficult to get across.

'Please don't ask.'

I asked her where Ronald was. Lin struggled to keep her tears back and wished I hadn't asked that either. It meant that I too didn't know.


## 583

The young policeman who watched his colleagues scrape Ronald Henderson from the front of the train had sleep terror. He was experiencing intense dread without any accompanying sensory perceptions or cognitive activity. All those have been used up by the reality of the day. He woke suddenly, drenched in sweat, heart beating rapidly, crying out.


## 582

Lin had been born and raised in Beijing, the only daughter of two teachers. She had been conceived during the final throws of the civil war and born just after the foundation of the People's Republic of China. The year of the tiger. Her mother had taught young schoolchildren. Her father was employed by one of the special universities created to re-educate returning thinkers with suspect backgrounds.

The function of the university was to generate highly self-critical 'autobiogra-phies' before the scholars could graduate and be assimilated into a constructive life at the service of the Republic. Lin's father found the university's project upsetting and distasteful and was soon removed to less contentious teaching posts.

He told Lin she should always be proud of her story, however it unfolded.

Lin lived through the Hundred Flowers project and the Great Leap Forward. She lost two uncles in the famine of the early sixties. She became a nurse during the Cultural Revolution.

She'd had a steady life during an unsteady time and now the reverse was true.

## 581

I told her she was looking well, under the circumstances.

She thanked me politely but knew it wasn't true.

She recollected only vaguely what had happened the night Ronald rang me but she knew that at some point she'd fled the house. Ronald was unable to follow her because the baby was upset. She was unclear about where or in what state she'd passed the night but when she returned to her cousin's house the next morning, both Ronald and the baby had disappeared.

In fact, the house was completely empty. Her cousin would normally return at lunchtime but he didn't appear until six. She asked him what had happened but he wouldn't say. She pestered him all night until he finally admitted that he'd taken Ronald to a friend of his who was able to arrange something.

'Arrange what?' I asked.

'Arrange a way to get back to the UK with the child.'

I was astonished.

'And your cousin did this?'

Lin nodded.

'So what happened?'

That was what Lin was waiting to find out.

## 580

The policeman lay back down in his bed and counted his heart beats. Quick then slower then slow. He didn't want to get scared of sleep. He read in *Law and Order Gazette* that his profession was seventh in the stress league. *Aviation*

*World* thought *Law and Order Gazette* had nicked their research and were pretty pissed off about it. The policeman wondered if surgeons, taxi drivers, undercover agents, CEOs, firemen or the US President were having a worse night than he was.

He told his brain he was done with sleep terror and hoped his brain took some notice.

## 579

Lin had left Xiamen.

'Where are you living?' I asked.

She said she was fine.

'How can Ronald contact you?'

She wasn't sure.

'What are you going to do?'

She didn't know.

I gave her all the money I had, told her I'd find out what I could and left her with her cold green tea.

Two weeks later, I received a message at the airline at Heathrow saying that Ronald had called and there was a number for me to ring as soon as I got the message.

Ronald, as he freely admitted, had lost touch with reality in Xiamen. He was in a strange place with a new child, the mother of which was a danger to herself. His only allies were two anxious and exhausted relatives, breaking under the strain of keeping a child hidden from Lin's parents.

Xiamen was on the coast, about 300km from Taiwan. Lin's cousin had arranged, for a fee, a boat trip to a safe docking point in Taiwan, from where Ronald had made his way to Taipei and got a flight to Dhaka. From there he had flown to Germany and then on to the UK.

## 578

Surprisingly, the most comfortable part of the journey had been the boat trip from Xiamen to Taiwan.

The owner of the vessel had made below deck almost snug. Ronald had been worried about the baby getting seasick but the rocking had had a cradle quality to it and she barely woke.

He sang her every song he knew.

Land was sighted during 'Auld Lang Syne'.

## 577

Ronald asked where Lin was.

I said I'd seen her in Hong Kong.

How was she?

Bad.

What should he do?

I didn't know.

When was I going back to Hong Kong?

Tomorrow.

Would I see Lin?

I didn't know.

How could he get her over?

I didn't know.

I didn't know anything.

## 576

Michael Davies shouted out a name in his sleep. It wasn't Beth's, but Beth heard it from downstairs and it broke her sleep paralysis and she stirred in her chair.

## 575

Graham Johansson started awake and knocked over the small vase of milk by his side. Ali Bronski heard the noise from the next room but didn't wake up as it fitted in with the dream she was having. Shooting bottles off a wall.

## 574

Dan Bronski half woke. One of his guests had left her purse in his house and she'd rung the doorbell so she could retrieve it and pay the impatient taxi driver.

## 573

Penny Lock started in her sleep because in her dream Alexander Graham Bell had come on to her 'Big Breast Implant' phone-in to say this wasn't what he had in mind when he invented the telephone.

## 572

For the second time Lin found me in my Hong Kong hotel.

I told her Ronald and child were well. Well and worried.

Lin said that was good because she had a plan.

That was good too, I said.

She wanted me to help her get into my plane's undercarriage and hide there during the flight to England.

'Oh,' I said.

'It is a tried and tested method,' she said.

'Well...' I said.

'There is a lot of room in there,' Lin assured me. 'You just have to be careful when the wheels are lifted up.'

She made it sound as if she was merely negotiating a tricky bunk bed in a sleeper carriage.

'Um...' I said.

## 571

Edward used to say that he had no respect for authority and it was a liberating feeling.

He said if it felt right and you could deal with the consequences then you did it. But it had to feel right. I asked him if burning down the school had felt right because it hadn't for me. He said it hadn't for him either but he didn't think either of us were old enough to understand our feelings.

He said despite that, it shouldn't stop us from...

From what, I asked him.

From DOING THE RIGHT THING.

I said I did try to do the right thing.

He said that was my trouble, I didn't know the difference between doing the right thing and DOING THE RIGHT THING.

## 570

Beth dreamt of being born out of her mother. Out of our mother, I should say. And Edward's. In her dream she comes out before me, but only by a few seconds. Our father picks us both up and says, 'We'll call this one Beth and we'll call this one Steph.' And our mother says, 'Haven't they got soft skin?' And our father says, 'Yes.' And Beth says, 'Not for long.' And no one seems surprised that she's spoken.

## 569

Edward dreamt he was Prometheus bound to Mount Caucasus where an eagle preyed on his liver. He was being punished for giving fire to the world.

## 568

Lin asked me when I was returning to the UK.

I said the day after tomorrow.

She said that was when she would like to go.

She asked me if I would help her.

I said I would try to 'DO THE RIGHT THING'.

She said was that a yes or a no?

I didn't know.

She said, 'Let's meet tomorrow, you can tell me then.'

She hung up.

I spent the next day at the airport looking at stowaway routes.

I found that the baggage handlers and other cargo workers had various ways of accessing the runway level and one was through a security door which was released by punching in a code and showing identification. From there a system of corridors led to an area where baggage emerged on the moving escalators from the check-in area.

The cargo area itself had many stacked shipping crates providing promising cover en route to the parked planes.

I discovered this by expressing a flattering interest in the baggage process to one of the airport staff who, reassured by my authentic airline identification, showed me the exciting journey of a suitcase from check-in to hold.

I asked him if he was on duty the next day. Which he was. I said I'd see him then. His name was Sunny.

Another security guard checked people going in and out. I didn't manage to get his name.

I met Lin later that evening.

Lin asked if it was a yes or a no?

I told her that getting to the undercarriage involved sneaking through security doors, distracting guards, hiding, running a lot, and hoping for the best.

Lin thought it was an ingenious plan and didn't see how it could fail. Was it a yes or a no?

I told her that I'd fashioned some wings from a couple of umbrellas and Lin could fly herself to England.

Lin told me not to be silly. Yes or no?

I said yes.


## 567

I gave Lin my second stewardess uniform to wear. I only had the one identity badge but the uniform would be useful camouflage at a distance. Lin bought a Chinese-English dictionary and was developing her vocabulary. Lin said the colour of the uniform reminded her of pus.


## 566

That night I slept badly. It was cold and I put an extra blanket over my bed. At three o'clock, I got up and packed the blanket in my suitcase to give to Lin. She was going to need all the padding she could get.

I called Michael and told him what was going to happen. I regretted it almost immediately.

'That's insane, why?'

'She's a friend.'

'What kind of reason's that? What's the matter with you?'

I didn't know.

'Is she paying you?'

I didn't answer.

'Christ,' said Michael as a thought occurred to him. 'When does it get in?'

'About three in the morning.'

'It'll fly over my space, I'll have it on screen. What's the flight?'

'AF 266.'

'God, I hope I don't get it...'

I cut him off.

I may have dozed off again by six but only for an hour or so.

I spent the following day walking the streets of Hong Kong.

## 565

I was on the bus en route to the airport by four o'clock. It was an evening flight. Lin would have night cover.

The other crew members asked me if I was OK, they said I looked pale. I told them I was feeling a bit queasy but would be all right once I'd cleaned up my first dollop of passenger sick. They laughed and didn't mention it again.

I met Lin at five.

I gave her the blanket.

'Do you want a drink before we go?' I asked her.

'No, thank you.'

She was a bit smaller than I was and had altered the uniform to fit her. She'd done a good job. We looked like two sick stewardesses.

She asked if I was ready. I squeezed her arm. She gave me a little smile and we headed towards the security door.

## 564

We walked down staff-only corridors. Our heels clip-clopped loudly. Our jackets shook at each heartbeat.

## 563

At the security door we met another baggage handler coming through.

He asked us what we were doing.

I said I was giving some keys to Sunny.

Lin gave him a beautiful smile. He held the door open for us. Like a gentleman.

## 562

Security checked my identification.

He asked about Lin.

I said she was with me.

Lin gave another smile.

He needed to see her pass all the same.

Lin said she'd have to run all the way back to the staff room.

He said even so.

I said we were looking for Sunny. I said we had a surprise for him. I asked if Sunny had been checked through.

He looked at his papers. He couldn't see the name.

I asked if that was it on the paper behind. And I entered his little booth.

He told me I shouldn't really be in there. I said I liked the smell of his aftershave. He said he wasn't wearing any.

I said I found that very surprising.

His phone rang. I shuffled passed him and knocked something onto the floor. He tried to pick it up and answer the phone at the same time. I said, oops, silly me.

In the confusion Lin dropped below his eyeline and darted through. She was light on her feet. She didn't make a sound.

He turned back. I said Lin had gone to get her badge. I said he should be nice to her when she returned.

He said he would, but it was more than his job was worth blah blah.

I said I understood.

He let me pass.


## 561

I hurried to the gate.

Corridors. Passages. Then out into the cold and the noise and the smell of spent fuel.

The plane was seventy metres away. Hump-backed. Little tiny eyes. Impassive. Others parked beside it, in formation.

I saw metal cargo crates, luggage trolleys. I saw lights and heard bleeps.

There was an expanse of flat empty tarmac from hangar to wheels. No-man's land. The silent sprint.

I couldn't see Lin and I hated our plan. I thought our plan sucked.

An official with a hard hat and earphones asked me what I was doing. I thought I was DOING THE WRONG THING.

I waved my ID around nervously.

I said I was looking for Sunny.

I said I was due to fly soon. I gestured towards the 747 parked behind him. I said wasn't it noisy? Wasn't it cold?

## 560

Movement. A little flicker. Shadows cast by floods flitting between carts and bollards and crates.

A dash. East to west. No shoes. For better grip. Head down. Hair tied tight. Fists clenched.

## 559

I asked the official where the canteen was.

He started telling me.

I asked him to take me there. He said no, why should... I said at least set me on my way.

He said he had work to do on the plane.

I said it was such a labyrinth.

I stared at his eyes. Hoped he couldn't see reflected movement in mine.

He asked me if I was all right.

## 558

He gave me directions.

I pretended to get confused.

He gave me them again.

## 557

Struggling. Slipping. Metal smooth. Lubricated. Nothing to hold on to. No footholds. The plane was a big white whale.

## 556

He asked again if I was all right.

I told him I had fallen out with Sunny. He'd stormed out without his keys and I was upset.

He looked confused. Sunny had a wife and I was not her.

I said not Sunny, Sammy.

He didn't know a Sammy.

He asked again to see my identification.

I showed him.

## 555

Swallowed up. Foot disappearing.

## 554

He said Sammy who?

I said not Sammy, Sumy. Wasn't it loud.

He looked incredulous. I was Sumy's wife?

I said yes.

He said Sumy was over the other side of the airport.

I said I thought I'd got the wrong gate. I said I was feeling sick.

He said he wasn't surprised, being Sumy's wife.

## 553

The whale smiled.

## 552

He asked what I saw in Sumy.

I said I didn't know.

I felt dizzy.

I asked him to help me back to the staff room.

He said my hands were shaking.

He helped me away.

## 551

I went to the observation lounge and watched other planes take off. I watched their undercarriages gather themselves up and saw them make slow tilting turns, lights blinking, puncturing the clouds. Thought the belly was the last place in the world I'd like to be.

I ordered tea from one of the cafés and poured in brandy from a miniature.

'To Lin,' I said.

## 550

I boarded the plane. I set blankets. I stowed foil cartons.

Ludicrously, I went to the middle of the aisles and stamped my foot in a regular pattern, bam ba ba bam bam, hoping to get a bam bam back.

'What are you doing?' asked the co-pilot.

Graham Johansson.

'Pins and needles,' I said.

He was fond of jokes. He would laugh at mine and tell terrible ones himself. He said the Scandinavian humour took some getting used to. He said he'd picked up a goodie from a man in a karaoke bar in the city.

He looked disappointed that I didn't laugh at it.

He asked if I was all right.

I said I thought I'd eaten something.

He left me alone. That was good of him.

## 549

Graham Johansson mopped up the milk with his blanket and fell back to sleep. He dreamt of woods and trees.

## 548

Beth dreamt of Heraclitus, who thought the world was made of fire. She poured water on him. Stupid bastard.

## 547

I had to fend off many concerned enquiries during the flight. Mainly from nervous passengers who read in my discomfort evidence that there was something wrong with the plane.

## 546

The plane taxied and took off.

As it started its climb, the undercarriage was raised and I may have uttered a little prayer. A passenger saw me and was sick.

## 545

Deafening.

Pitch black but for the occasional flashing light. Runway hurtling beneath. Wind swirling through her.

The terrifying pneumatic whine of the hydraulics, pushing, contracting. Vast wheels gathering themselves around her.

Burning hot from friction, penning her in, breathing choking rubber fumes into her lungs.

Scrambling away from the monumental mechanism.

Screams merging with the engine wail. Muffled by the closing undercarriage.

A continuous roar. Darkness.

She may have thought it was better to die than endure this.

## 544

I did my duties mechanically.

When we reached cruising altitude, I asked one of the crew how cold it was outside.

Minus thirty, minus forty.

Lin had worn as many layers as she could whilst still looking like a normal person. She had gloves in her small handbag.

I'd asked about oxygen.

She'd produced a small device which had been given to her by a Japanese diver. A canister. A scuba, perhaps a foot long, with a mouthpiece.

'That's it?' I asked.

She'd read about Sherpas climbing great heights oxygen free and felt the Oriental physiognomy was suited to it.

The flight was ten hours. She said she'd take a puff whenever she was feeling woozy.

We'd talked about landing.

After such an ordeal it was unlikely that Lin would have the strength, wit or will to escape from the plane and into a busy London. She had said that as long as there was enough energy left to get her onto the runway she would collapse there and claim asylum, or claim amnesia, or claim something.

## 543

An hour before landing I started crying. I couldn't help it and I couldn't stop it. Some of the passengers started pinging their stewardess buttons.

I was taken to the area by the cockpit and sat down. After a while the co-pilot made an announcement.

'Ladies and gentlemen, this is Co-pilot Johansson speaking. We shall be landing in about twenty minutes time, earlier than scheduled. As I said, the weather in London is slightly overcast but a pleasant twenty degrees. Thank you for flying with us. Cabin crew prepare for landing.'

He wanted to reassure everyone.

## 542

The plane landed and taxied to the gate.

Someone asked if I needed to be taken home. I said no, I was fine. Graham Johansson asked me if there was anything he could do. I said no, he'd been very kind. I said I'd see him in a few days.

I hung around the airport.

I tried to get back onto the runway to see if Lin emerged but they wouldn't let me through. They were put off by my smudged mascara.

I waited around security hoping to hear some news of Lin being taken into custody but there was nothing.

As the morning came and there was still no sign, I had to assume that she had either been whisked away by the authorities or had survived the flight in better than expected shape and had escaped herself.

Either way there was nothing else to do but go home.

## 541

...

## 540

...

## 539

...I must be awake. I've never done a countdown in a dream before.

## 538

Lin's body was found by a little girl called Emma, in a wood six miles out of Heathrow airport.

Lin had died of hypothermia in the extreme cold, and when the undercarriage was lowered she dropped out of the plane.

Emma was on a walk with her family. She'd run ahead and had found Lin in the grass.

Though Lin had fallen a great way, some of the fall had been broken by trees and her body hadn't suffered as much trauma as you might expect. Emma had talked of a lady sleeping in the woods. When her parents caught up with her, Emma had been putting wild flowers in Lin's hair.

## 537

...what would they have been? Bluebells maybe? To go nicely with her black hair and the yellow uniform?

## 536

...

## 535

... Or daisies.

## 534

... Still here. Still here.

## 533

Emma Heron looked out of the aeroplane window and thought of cherry blossoms that fell from the trees in spring. How falling out of the sky could be beautiful.

## 532

Lin had been wearing my uniform and so I was questioned by the police, suspended from work, dumped by Michael, fired, tried, represented and acquitted. My lawyer pointedly asked me if my uniform had been stolen and had somehow ended up in Lin's possession, because if that was the case then there was only circumstantial evidence that I was involved. I nodded. The jury bought it. As I walked from the courtroom, I said I was only trying to do the right thing and I passed out on the steps.

## 531

Michael said he'd take me back. I told him to piss off. He begged. Said he'd made a mistake. Said he'd framed my Chinese love letter to him. I told him it said, 'Could you tell me the way to the ticket office?' He said that didn't matter. Besides, he could indeed tell me the way to the ticket office.

## 530

I wrote a letter to Ronald. Eventually he replied.

He hadn't made an appearance at the inquest or made his involvement with Lin public. He wanted to shield his daughter from such a lamentable start to her life. He wanted to create a new beginning for her. Reinvent her. Give her a better lie to live to. He had got hold of a new birth certificate and had put the name Lei as the mother.

He called his daughter Kirsten. She was christened in January 1980, the year of the monkey.

Ronald suffered.

He didn't know who to hate more, me for assisting in such a stupid scheme, or himself for a million other reasons and counting.

We'd badly let her down. This wasn't metaphorical in my case.

He wrote to Lin's parents, expressing his heartfelt sympathy without telling them of his involvement with their daughter and received a reply which was so full of dignified thanks that he felt like stabbing himself in the guts.

Lin's cousin in Xiamen had not responded to Ronald's letter. Ronald didn't expect him to.

## 529

Samuel Thorn dreamt of jumping in the sea to calm a tempest. 'The world will be a safer place without me.' Slosh. It made it worse, the sea bubbled up, the wind howled and a passenger ferry sank, drowning all on board.

'Thanks Sam,' all the passengers said, sarcastically.

## 528

Ronald retired. Moved cities, and contacted me for the last time.

'Kirsten is my child's name. I have told you this so that if you ever meet anyone called Kirsten you can walk away in case it's her.' Signed Ronald Henderson, 1980.

Then he disappeared.

## 527

I disappeared too.

I took a train to the airport and flew to New York where I found my younger brother Edward in an apartment in Brooklyn.

I screamed at him for two weeks about the casualties of THE RIGHT THING. Us included.

He said the thing that differentiated an ACT from an act was the ability to see the bigger moral picture. GREAT MEN could see the bigger moral picture, little men tormented themselves with sundry fatalities.

I threw a kettle at him.

Edward was no GREAT MAN. While I had my Lin nightmares, Edward was being haunted by our sister's burns. He'd burned himself a few times, over the gas ring. Then he waited for the burns to heal and used sandpaper to try and remove the scars. He tried other treatments too. Invented some more. He wanted to find a scar cure. His arm was a mess. His head was a bit of a mess too.

He became a lab rat. Offered himself up. Skin treatments at first. Then anything.

He took part in an experiment led by the anaesthesia and pain management department in a hospital to help research into patients who claimed to become 'aware' whilst under general anaesthetic, who said they heard and felt the surgery taking place but were unable to move or to let anyone know.

He was knocked out and his brain waves were monitored. The test was to determine the correct dose of anaesthetic for patients before an operation.

After he was brought round, he became convinced that an operation had been carried out on him while he was unconscious and that a number of his organs had been replaced.

That was ridiculous, said the doctors. He didn't have any incision marks. Edward pointed to one below his rib. The doctors said it was too small and old. He didn't believe them. Thought you could do all sorts of things these days. Keyhole surgery, for example. He looked for punctures in the skin.

The notion became fixed. X-rays didn't help him. Who would recognise their own kidney or liver?

He was referred to Clara Redlake whose first step was to encourage him to think that if indeed his organs had been replaced, it was possible they may have been replaced by those of a heroic or glamorous person.

She asked what day the operation took place. He said May 15th, 1998. She did a search. Well, what do you know, she said to him. That was the day Frank Sinatra died.

Edward didn't buy it. He couldn't sing a note.

He joined the fire service but refused to put out fires in certain institutions.

Some deserved to burn, he said. They kicked him out. He called himself The Moral Fireman, if anyone asked.

People didn't on the whole. People tended to avoid him.

## 526

In his dream, Edward was still Prometheus and the eagle was still pecking away at his liver. Hercules arrived. It was Hercules' job to kill the eagle and snap the chains around Edward's body and free him. Hercules was Beth though and she just sat on the edge of the mountain and ate her sandwiches.

## 525

Michael Davies wrote to me in Brooklyn. He asked if it was because he'd overreacted about the stowaway that I'd gone off him, because if it was then he'd done something about it.

I didn't reply.

He wrote again saying that he was serious about having done something about it. His whole attitude towards stowaways had changed. He now did his bit.

I didn't reply. I pretended I didn't live there.

He wrote again saying he hoped I was reading between the lines and that my silence was a sign of me coming round because when he said he did his bit he really did his bit.

I didn't reply.

He wrote again and told me that if he had to spell things out then he would, but he hoped I knew what he was talking about. He enclosed a tape of him singing 'Moon River'.

I didn't reply. My brother asked me how come I got so many letters.

Michael wrote again calling me a stupid cow and telling me he helped smuggle people into the UK, there, he'd said it, was I happy?

I didn't reply. I started burning the letters.

He wrote again saying he didn't mean to call me a stupid cow and went on to say how he thought repressive regimes were very, very terrible things and he felt he was doing valuable work and it had enriched his life knowing that he was helping people for no reward.

I didn't reply.

He wrote calling me a bitch for not replying when he had put his heart on his sleeve.

I kept that one.

He wrote and apologised for the bitch remark and enclosed a 'testimonial' from a Croatian woman saying how brave and saintly Michael was and how he'd saved her life plus the lives of her two small children.

I moved out and found a new place to live. Edward was pleased, he liked his own space. I told him to return all letters and not give anyone my address.

## 524

I moved into an apartment in Queens.

I walked a lot, ate a lot. I worked illegally.

And I hated my name.

I returned to England with my head down and my sunglasses on and I asked Citizen's Advice to give me a form to change it.

I was pickpocketed by someone there for the same purpose. I grabbed her hand and hit her face…

## 523

Cody breathed in and out and in and out. She was having a dream about Zoro. She carried out a heroic deed and, with a whip of her sword, swiped her initial into the flimsy silk of a confounded nobleman. She judged the distance wrongly and, instead of slicing his silk shirt, she sliced open his chest and he collapsed, his heart flopped onto the floor. Bad show, said the onlookers.

## 522

…She apologised. She bought me coffee.

Her name was Lily Frankburg but not for long. Lily Frankburg wanted to be someone else, a writer. She wanted to kill off Lily Frankburg. I asked her if anyone would miss her. She said they ought to. She said they ought to cry their bloody eyes out.

I said my name was Stephanie Wiltshire but not for long. Stephanie

Wiltshire wanted to be someone else. I wanted to kill off Stephanie Wiltshire. She asked me if anyone would miss her. I said no. I said, well, perhaps one or two.

We drank two pints of coffee and chose new names.

We both liked Cody Jameson so we both took it.

We signed forms and changed our signatures.

Her Cody Jameson wrote. Articles. Travel pieces. Fiction. Screenplays.

My Cody Jameson just went back to Queens and, as before, walked a lot, ate a lot and worked illegally.

Her Cody was quite successful. Mine was no different to Stephanie Wiltshire but it was nice to see my name in print now and then.


## 521

Cody woke for a second then fell back to sleep. Another dream started. She was walking through Frankburg's house. It was bigger and had six levels. She found a thesis discarded on the floor, 'How Difficulties in Recognising One's Own Incompetence Lead to Inflated Self-Assessments'. She picked it up and tried to find Frankburg's bedroom in order to slip it under the door. She got lost though.


## 520

Cody asked me about my life. I gave her some stories from my airline days. She published it as *Tales of a Stewardess*. I didn't mind. She gave me £4,000 for them. I didn't tell her the big tale. Not even with names changed to protect the innocent.


## 519

My teeth aren't chattering any more and I don't know if this is a good thing because I don't really know how my body works despite having been bought a copy of *How Your Body Works* as a child. I remember it featured a man who's inside functioned like a complex community. Governed and maintained by a legion of smaller versions of himself. Red overalled men pushed trolleys of red blood cells round tracks in his body and white overalled men pushed white.

They'd pull together to repair wounds. Put up barricades. Keep out infection. The wound gets scabbed over. After a while it looks like skin again. But it's much weaker.

You can find yourself scratching in the night when your brain is asleep.

In the morning you're bleeding. And worse than before.

## 518

So now the morning has come ... it came to the UK first so people woke up ...

## 517

*Samuel Thorn had been right about the diggers. They started at six thirty.

Forty-five minutes later, he was underwater. He thought Birmingham swimmers had a different intensity to London ones. Something to do with the increased distance from the sea.

The water filled Sam's ears and his huge arms ploughed the lengths. Scouring Kirsten's suicide away. Every time he surfaced he saw Kirsten's face also breaking the water. Coming to at the last minute and gasping for air.

## 516

Michael Davies woke alone in the bed.

'Beth!' he shouted.

Downstairs Beth woke. Stiff-necked from sleeping in a chair.

## 515

Dr Frankburg woke alone. He was used to it now though. The radio told him about the death of a retired Scottish doctor who had thrown himself in front of a goods train. Frankburg wondered if he'd been in therapy and hoped not. Bad for business.

## 514

Samuel had bought a newspaper. It said that witnesses had seen a man at the far end of the platform away from the bulk of waiting passengers and that they'd assumed he was standing there in order to have some privacy while he was on the phone.

He was on the phone?

When the non-stopping goods train had trundled through, the man stepped out in front of it.

'It wasn't going that fast,' said one witness. 'I was shocked at the amount of mess it made.'

Very public. Samuel put this down to guilt, to have his only child...

## 513

Samuel was a good kid when his own father died. He was too young to talk things through with his mother. He was too young to talk at all.

It was important for Sam to stay alive and that was what he'd endeavoured to do. He grew big and solid and strong and clumsy. A smart-arsed teacher had called him 'The Albatross', the sea bird which by its very nature (great size, huge wings), is beautiful only when it is high in the blue sky over the oceans but is ugly and ungainly if it is forced to walk on the earth, 'at bay amid the jeering crowd'. And Sam did get a bit of jeering.

The teacher didn't know Samuel's dad had died, otherwise he might not have called him it. Or made the class read *The Rime of the Ancient Mariner*.

## 512

Jonah. Albatrosses. Blah blah blah. No one would die in the swimming pool, thought Samuel. There were lifeguards everywhere. But he left anyway.

He checked his watch. Audition in two hours.

## 511

Cody Jameson woke.

The radio told her that love was on the rocks, yeah.

She jumped in the bath. Scrubbed at her 'Lily 4 Ever' tattoo.

## 510

Beth Davies would be airborne that day. She puked in the toilet.

Michael Davies pissed in the puke and shouted at Beth for not flushing.

Beth rang Dan Bronski. Air crash investigator. She needed a sympathetic ear.

## 509

John Heron had programmed the theme from *Mr Hulot's Holiday* into his phone. It rang and he jolted awake, knocking a lamp off the bedside table. A Jacques Tati start.

'Emma?' he said.

'No, it's Miles. How are you fixed for next week?'

'Miles?'

'From the Wellington. Sorry to ring so early.'

'What time is it?'

'Eight thirty.'

If Emma had got the midnight flight, she'd have landed by now. He ran to the land line. Miles was still speaking.

'...had a good think about it in the cold light of day, I think you're right, we could be onto something. Those people who watched the show last night are almost certainly going to come back, and bring others. I mean, you don't get to see that kind of thing normally, do you? But I was thinking, it's going to be hard for you to shoot yourself again, have you got anything else which might...'

John switched his phone off and called Penny Lock.

## 508

It was still dark in the US. The sun was only halfway over the Atlantic.

Penny Lock heard the phone in her sleep.

There was a part of her brain which was aware of this but it assured her that the call would be from Graham Johansson ringing to say he'd been held up somewhere and not to worry. Penny's brain then turned 'held up' into 'hijacked' and she watched Graham's plane loop the loop.

Red blood cells were bloated with wine. She was dizzy in her sleep.

## 507

Dan Bronski was lying face down on the couch, awake but also dizzy. The booze buzz gone. Body sick. He focused on an old patch of spilt wine. He recreated the circumstances under which the spill came to be there.

He calculated the volume of wine in the glass. The force with which it was knocked over. The speed with which the clean-up operation was conducted.

He deduced that the glass had broken on impact and visualised the possible spread of fragments. Larger pieces would have been cleared but smaller splinters would have scattered around the area underneath the radiator.

Dan stretched out his hand and felt. A small shard stabbed him painfully in the finger.

He watched the globule of blood expand.

He'd been a good investigator.

## 506

John Heron booked a ticket to New York.

If he found Emma he'd take away her passport and cut it up. Or rather, he'd fly back home with her and then take away her passport and cut it up. And her credit card. He'd cut that up too. And he'd buy her a phone. And go back to magic, and cut her up again. And make her leave the morgue to stop her from cutting people up. Or divorce her.

## 505

Dan Bronski. Hidden victim.

Someone who, in the course of his duties, had suffered secondary traumatic stress reactions brought about by contact with massive death situations.

He had fought the empathetic urge for many years, but constant grisly contact had not anaesthetised him, just worn him down.

He could witness only so many isolated body parts, so many interviews with survivors, so many relatives of dead crew, so many last-minute conversations of distressed pilots before hope, faith and trust drained from his body never to return.

He'd been diagnosed as suffering from symptoms ranging from generalised anxiety to major depression.

He wasn't hung up on the medical description. He'd seen too much of things that people should never see.

They let him retire.

At his monumental retirement party, he'd taken a colleague aside and asked him if he thought there could ever be sufficient support systems in place to stop people like them from going off the rails.

His colleague said he should lean heavily on his family and hope to God they were robust enough to take it.

Dan nodded and thought of his one child. Ali.

She did her best. She'd taken psychology at college and was fond of questionnaires.

## 504

'If you had an important decision to make, is there someone you could go to for advice?'

'Yes,' Dan had said.

'If you made a serious mistake, is there someone in your life you could trust to tell?'

'Yes.'

'Is there someone in your life who gives you comfort?'

'Yes.'

'Is there someone who would stick up for you in a fight?'

'Yes.'

'Have you ever blamed God for an air crash?'

'Yes.'

'Did it alter your religious beliefs?'

'Yes.'

'Are you afraid of dying?'

'Yes.'

Ali had frowned. 'If you hadn't said yes to the last question, I'd've said you were OK. As it is, there's a chance you might crack up.'

'That's nice to know.'

'Do you want to change your answer?'

'Perhaps the question says "flying" not "dying". Are you afraid of flying. Who wrote the questionnaire?'

'I did. It doesn't say "flying" it says "dying".'

He snatched up the paper.

'It says "flying",' he said.

'It does not.'

'It does.'

'That's a "d".'

'Funny looking "d".'

'It's a regulation "d". There's nothing funny about it.'

'It looks like an "f" and an "l" together.'

'It doesn't.'

'Here's another. "Have you ever blamed golf for an air crash".'

'God. It says God. That's what my "d"s look like.'

'I can safely say I've never blamed golf for an air crash.'

## 503

Dan heard the phone ring and said, 'Please be Ali.'

'It's Beth.'

Dan said thank you for it being Beth. 'Please let it be Ali next.'

## 502

Michael Davies left for work.

He tried to give Beth some words of encouragement at the door.

'Just, um, keep breathing... try to... you know, breathe.'

'OK.'

Pause.

'I'll listen out for your plane.'

'Thanks.'

Michael didn't kiss her.

Then he thought he should. But the moment had passed.

Philemaphobia, thought Beth, fear of kissing. Or perhaps venustraphobia: fear of beautiful women. She tried to laugh at herself.

## 501

Cody looked at herself in the mirror.

You're a writer, you're a gritty writer.

She left the house.

## 500

Michael Davies drove quickly to the airport. He got a call about the stowaway shift. He hated those calls. They were from some faceless man who needed to know which blind-eye or stupid ground staff worked which shifts. Michael was able to get this information via an airport personnel chatroom.

Michael said he was anxious that the stowaways might freeze and get tangled in the undercarriage and prevent the wheels from lowering and perhaps they should provide gaffer tape.

Before he got an answer. Michael stopped the car by the side of the road and vomited at his repugnant thought. He really didn't have the stomach for this sort of work.

## 499

Dan Bronski rang Beth's doorbell. He was as nervous as a kitten.

## 498

John packed for a manhunt.

He threw a camera into his case.

He ought to take a photograph.

He leafed through snapshots.

Cornwall.

Beach walks.

Wales.

Greece.

Italy.

First day at the morgue.

New house.

New Year's Eve.

A picture of Emma in hospital. Her appendicitis operation. He'd taken a picture of the removed appendix too but it was missing. She'd got peritonitis and had stayed in for over a week. Emma flushed and feverish. She'd hallucinated during the illness. Called him Dad twice. Or bad.

He wouldn't take that picture. He'd take another.

A blurred picture of Emma caught unawares, trying to fly a kite in strong winds. Suddenly worried that it was going to pull her off the ground, she'd let it go and it had disappeared into the distance. She'd shrieked and put her gloved hands up to her mouth, then had laughed and turned to John who snapped her as she looked at him.

John put the picture in a stiff envelope. It was the only one he could find in which she was smiling.

## 497

Emma Heron sat on the floor leaning against the grated shutters of Foot Boutique at Kennedy Airport. When it opened in five hours' time it might sell her some shoes. If she was going to go down in a blaze of glory she might as well do it wearing the strappy number in the window.

## 496

'What is this you're playing me?' asked Dan Bronski.

Beth stopped the tape.

'This is *You Too Can Fly*, a relaxation tape for nervous passengers. You can play it before going on a plane and it stops you from freaking out.'

'Won't the plane crash section unnerve people?'

'I don't know why it's on here, I just wanted you to tell me what was happening.'

'Give me it again.'

## 495

She looked at his face as he listened.

He had more frown lines than laughter lines but that wasn't surprising. Centrally placed, he was equidistant from any airline disaster that might befall the country. When planes missed the UK, he travelled to Asia, or Africa. Crash site to crash site. Hypothesising cause. Examining charred wreckage. Deducing failure. Apportioning blame. The life would wrinkle anyone.

On his birthday, he'd scooped up the remains of a crash in Indonesia. Too many children. He'd found a kiddy shoe. It had a wing drawn on it. He kept it to remind him of Icarus.

Afterwards he'd thrown a party. He invited Beth because she was a survivor and he wanted to have survivors around him.

Michael Davies turned up. He'd quit West Drayton and had joined Birmingham Approach. He'd heard about the party on the air traffic control grapevine.

Michael got drunk and put his hand through a window. He didn't feel the pain so he smeared himself with blood and stumbled into the kitchen and told everyone he was the Aircrash-o-gram. He started singing a ghoulish Happy Birthday. Dan went for him. No one felt like dragging him off.

Beth stepped in and took Michael home.

Michael told her she was beautiful. Told her her hair was the colour of ripe wheat. Said she reminded him of the beautiful Stephanie Wiltshire.

Beth said Stephanie Wiltshire was her twin.

## 494

Lucky old Beth.

## 493

Michael had wept. He bought her things. He said, 'Let me look at you.' He asked how she got the scars on her face. She said Stephanie did it. Michael said he wasn't surprised. Stephanie ruined lives. Beth agreed. Michael said Stephanie let people down. Beth asked if they could stop talking about Stephanie. He said of course. He asked Beth to marry him. She said yes and asked him to set a date.

Dan Bronski wished he'd killed Michael.

## 492

'Chicago, 1987,' pronounced Dan. 'A classic. Pilot had faulty aerilons, something had severed mid-flight. Don't remember the details but he'd lost almost all means of steering the plane. Engine problem too, I think, and they couldn't get the wheels out. They were trying to make an emergency landing and they'd cleared all runways. Nasty impact.'

'Did anyone make it?'

'Oh God, no. Terrible crash.'

The voices sounded different to her now she knew they were dead. Last recorded words.

Shouted, urgent. Comprehensively alive.

…Whoop whoop.

'Lower the gear!'

'Come on. You can do it.'

'I can't hold her.'

'Come on.'

'We're going down.'

And then: 'Jesus. I don't know what to say.'


## 491

Beth asked Michael every year or so whether they were actually going to marry or not. In the end, Michael brought round a ship's captain who'd married them there and then in their kitchen. Their nextdoor neighbours witnessed it and smelt drink on the captain's breath. And Michael's. When it was over, everyone just stood awkwardly in the kitchen. 'Champagne!' shouted Michael, but he didn't have any so they drank a carton of revolting 'Posh Sherry' that he'd once brought back from Nigeria. Someone asked the ship's captain where he sailed his ships. The captain said he captained oil tankers. Oh, said everyone. Nice. He said he'd gone down once in the Pacific and his load had polluted some islands off the coast of Indonesia and almost wiped out a species of bird. Michael ushered him out of the house.

It wasn't the wedding Beth had had in mind but at least it had happened.

Technically he wasn't a real ship's captain any more and Michael reckoned the marriage would never hold up in a court of law.


## 490

They listened again: 'Jesus. I don't know what to say.'

It was spoken by a woman. Dan said he couldn't remember her name but she must have had a battle. Not only with the wild plane but to get to where she was in the first place. On the flight deck. It was a masculine profession. She'd deserved the last words. If anyone had earned them then she had.

Even if she hadn't known what to say.

'Was this all you wanted to know?' asked Dan.

'There's another bit,' said Beth.

## 489

Frankburg took a taxi into work.

'It'll cost you double if you're sick in the back.'

'I won't be,' said Frankburg.

'I'm just saying. To cover the cleaning and inconvenience.'

'I'm fine.'

'Just so's you know.'

'Thank you for telling me. Please take the corners slowly.'

## 488

Cody arrived at Phoenix TV and found the *Graft* team discussing *Tunnel Vision*. The producer had 'a friend of a friend' on the shoot who believed Kirsten had been diagnosed with some fatal disease and didn't want to put herself through a debilitating decline. The casting woman had heard that she was addicted to sleeping pills and that it was an accident. The work placement girl had an elaborate conspiracy involving spurned lovers, pregnancies and political scandal.

'Did she leave a note?' asked Cody.

No one knew.

They all shushed as Samuel entered the room for his audition.

## 487

Frankburg paid the taxi driver double and apologised again.

## 486

Beth pressed play.

'...measured at 500 overcast... one mile visibility in light snow, surface wind northwest fifteen knots...'

Air traffic control was calm, efficient.

'That's Michael's voice, isn't it?' said Dan.

Beth nodded.

'Received.' The pilot.

The pilot had a slight accent.

'266, you are cleared to 11,000.'

'Received.'

The tape crackled for a few moments.

'AF 266, turn left, heading 130 on a southeast course.'

'Received.'

'Cleared to 9,000.'

'Received.'

There was talk between captain and someone who'd come into the cockpit. Hard to decipher.

'...only a few minutes...hold on till then?'

'...upsetting the other passengers.' A female voice.

'What's the matter with her?' The co-pilot, much clearer.

'Just crying, they think she's crying because something's gone wrong with the plane.'

'OK, see if you can reassure them, we'll try to speed things up.'

'...right...an announcement too might help.'

'OK.'

'Control, this is AF 266, we have an unwell stewardess on board, any chance of getting us down quickly?'

'...One moment, 266.' A catch in Michael's voice.

There was a small pause in the cockpit.

Co-pilot: 'She was fine earlier, wasn't she?'

Pilot: 'No, she's been odd all day, just tired perhaps.'

'AF 266, take airway route Victor 132, it'll take a couple of minutes off your journey.'

'Received, thanks.'

'Hope it's nothing too serious,' Michael again.

'We don't think so, thanks anyway.'

'OK, OK. Cleared to 7,000.'

'Received.'

'You wanna do it?'

'Sure. Ladies and gentlemen, this is Co-pilot Johansson speaking. We shall be landing in about twenty minutes' time, earlier than scheduled. As I said, the weather in London is slightly overcast but a pleasant twenty degrees. Thank you for flying with us. Cabin crew, prepare for landing.'

'Very reassuring, Mr Johansson.'

'Well, I do my best.'

Beth switched off the tape.

'How did these recordings get on here?' Dan asked.

Beth didn't know. Michael had sounded like a little boy. Speaking from a time that Beth didn't know and in a way that she had never heard.

## 485

'Hello, Samuel, delighted you could make it. I'm the head of casting for *Graft*. This is the producer. This is Cody Jameson, she's the writer.'

'Glad to meet you. Can I say I really enjoyed the script?'

'Yes,' Cody replied.

The head of casting wrote 'good voice' on her paper.

## 484

There was only one telephone number on *You Too Can Fly*. Beth dialled it.

'Fine Sounds Studios.'

'Dr Frankburg?'

She was put on hold.

While she waited, she was aware of Dan looking at her. She didn't mind, though. Dan had spent his professional life looking at burnt bodies. He'd cried for most of them. He loved it when they lived. He loved the walking wounded.

'We get a lot of this,' said a voice eventually.

'Sorry, I didn't mean to put you out.'

Fine Sounds Studios read out a number. 'That's his work number, we used to have his home one but he told us off for giving it out to people.'

'That's fine, thanks very much.'

'I think the tapes are shit myself…'

'Pardon?'

Click.

## 483

Phoenix TV.

'How are things at the moment, Samuel?' asked the producer.

Television people were very superstitious. They didn't need another *Tunnel Vision*. Couldn't afford another tragedy.

Hiring 'The Albatross' was high risk, thought Samuel.

'Fine, thank you.'

The producer nodded encouragingly. 'Good, good.'

There was a small pause.

'Let's get cracking then. We're going to have a look at scene twelve, page twenty, which is the scene where Bryn first meets Cathy in the bus station. You've just got off the bus and are deciding what to do next. Cody here is going to read Cathy's part.'

'Fine.'

'OK with the video?'

'Yes.'

'Anything anyone wants to add?'

Cody wanted to ask Sam if Kirsten had left a suicide note.

'No.'

'Right. When you're ready then, Samuel.'

## 482

'Dr Frankburg?'

'Yes.'

'My name's Beth Davies and I've just been listening to your tape *You Too Can Fly…*'

'It's not my voice, I'm saying that now because I want to make that quite clear. The man's name is Samuel Thorn, he's an actor, and I don't have his number or know if he's married. I am not Welsh.'

'Er...'

'What you hear is what you get, OK?'

'OK.'

'Because I don't want to get off on the wrong foot. People's expectations are very powerful conditioners and it isn't helpful to get too hung up on a perceived personality behind a voice. I, myself, find Welsh a bit cloying, but that's me.'

'Um.'

'So long as we're clear on that.'

'I think so.'

'Good, how can I help you?'

'I've been listening to a copy of your tape—'

'Do you mean copy as in bought copy, or copy as in taped off a friend?'

'I don't know.'

'Because if it's a bootlegged copy then I can't vouch for its quality.'

'I think it's legitimate.'

'I've lost a fortune somewhere because of people taping tapes.'

'It's a problem, I know.'

'It's also criminal, though it's very hard to make the police take it seriously.'

'I'm sure.'

'I could've probably bought a car with the lost revenue.'

'Indeed.'

Pause.

'So anyway, Dr Frankburg. In the middle of side one and again at the end of side two there are little snippets of recordings from blackbox flight recorders.'

'Are you serious?'

'I was just checking that this wasn't part of the treatment.'

'No, it is not.'

## 481

It was very early in New York but Graham Johansson was already awake. He left Ali's apartment and walked twenty blocks to the Hudson River. A gull was bobbing up and down on the water. It had its beak buried in its wing and it was drifting with the current. Graham Johansson thought it must be nice to sleep on the water, and found pleasure in the thought.

Then the gull tipped over onto its side.

The gull was a bit of old wood. Graham frowned in disappointment and threw his phone at it, but missed.


## 480

Edward the Fireman was awake but post operatively woozy. He checked his wound and found himself quite impressed at the anatomical precision of his initial incision and noted that with diluted doses of lidocaine the pain eased sufficiently to enable rudimentary mobility. Even so he composed some last words using famous ones from history as inspiration. Just in case the day went badly. He liked Louis XIV's: Why weep you! Did you think I should live for ever?

He decided to leave breakfast. There was blood in his Cornflakes.


## 479

Frankburg wanted to hear the tape.

Beth said she had a flight to take and was pushed for time.

Frankburg expressed impatience.

Beth said she was nervous about flying. She suffered from aerophobia and perhaps Frankburg could give her some words of encouragement before she went.

Frankburg said he didn't do freebies and told her his rates.

Beth said he was bloody expensive.

Frankburg said she should listen to the tape if she wanted an affordable alternative. That was its point.

Beth said the tape was fucked.

Frankburg, again, wanted to hear it.

Beth said there was a screaming pilot on his fucking tape.

Frankburg said that wasn't his fault.

Beth said even her prick of a husband was on his fucking tape.

Frankburg said he couldn't be held responsible.

Beth said she didn't know why she fucking bothered.

Frankburg told her to take it easy.

Beth said his fucking tape had made her worse.

Frankburg told her to take a deep breath and picture fields of wheat.

Beth puked up again and gave the phone to Dan.

Dan asked Frankburg what kind of fucking therapist he thought he was.

Frankburg said 'fucking' seemed to be very much in Dan and Beth's minds.

Dan told him to mind his own flipping business.

Frankburg apologised and said he was hungover. He apologised about the contaminated tape and again asked to hear it.

Dan said Frankburg should check his master tape.

Frankburg said he would but asked Dan to bring the tape over to his office, if it wasn't too much trouble.

Dan said it wasn't but he should work on his phone manner.

Frankburg said he would and told him he'd give Beth a free session as compensation.

Beth shouted she didn't want one.

Frankburg asked if Dan wanted one instead.

Dan said he was beyond help but he'd bring the tape over anyway.

Dan hung up and helped Beth into a chair. She smiled at him.

Dan pictured a field of wheat but he was lying back in it with Beth tickling his face with her hair.


## 478

Beth asked Dan what he knew about skin. Dan said it covered the external surface of the human body and was the principal interface between it and the surrounding world.

Beth said that was very nicely put.

Dan said it protected against ultraviolet radiation, temperature extremes and bacteria. It was good for sensory perception and stopped fluid loss.

Not tears though, said Beth.

No, said Dan.

Beth smiled at him again and said that her skin grafting had been done very well, and hadn't masked facial expression.

Dan said she had a lovely smile.

Beth said she didn't think she could manage the flight alone and asked Dan to fly with her for company.

Dan agreed, of course he agreed. Besides, his daughter lived in New York somewhere and he ought to visit more. Beth said visiting family was probably important.

Beth kissed him on the cheek.

Dan said she still smelt of puke.

He put Beth into a cab. He told it to go to the airport. He told the cabby to sing *Don't Fence Me In* by Bing Crosby and the Andrews Sisters if his passenger got agitated. The cabby said he didn't know all the words. Dan told him to hum it.


## 477

Dan drove home to fetch his passport.

He had a filing cabinet in the corner of his bedroom. Inside were hundreds of tapes. Pirate copies of every blackbox voice recording he had worked on. Each tape humming with the energy of the passions inside. His little cemetery. Kept with the diligence of a groundsman but overgrown of late. Dusty now.

He used to think it was his duty to make last words known to those they loved and would sometimes play recordings to them.

An aeroplane had come down in North Carolina and initial findings had pointed to human error. The eighty-year-old mother of the pilot had been informed and could barely speak to Dan out of grief. Grief made worse because of the possibility that her son had made a monumental mistake. A lengthy and painful investigation eventually revealed a million to one chain of events starting from a small mechanical fault leading to an electrical failure which gave the pilot misleading readings. Earlier in the flight, before the problem manifested, the pilot had spoken to the co-pilot about how he loved flying over his home state of Ohio and wondered whether, if he painted the roof of his mother's house bright red, he would be able to spot it on a clear day. He played that part to her over the phone.

He also had a tape where a passenger had burst into the cockpit of a plane that had lost its engines. She was called Melanie and had screamed out her lover's name in the final seconds before impact. Dan had tracked down her lover and called him:

'Mr Arnold?' Dan said. 'Do you know a girl called Melanie Beaumont?'

'Um, yes.'

'You sound unsure. About twenty-three, liked action films. High-pitched voice, easily panicked, fond of gin and tonic, ring any bells?'

'Who is this calling?'

'I'm surprised you don't recognise her because she knew you. I have a recording of her last seconds on this earth and she mentioned your name. She was in a state and quite incoherent but your name definitely comes up. She was surrounded by strangers and terribly afraid and she wanted to die with the right person by her side. And in those final moments she realised it was you. "Jack! Oh, Jack!" That's you, isn't it Mr Arnold? A fling was it? Or something more serious.'

'Look, we were just…'

'Well, perhaps not serious for you but obviously for Melanie.'

'Oh.'

'Something to think about, isn't it? Perhaps you were thinking of calling it off anyway, Mr Arnold, perhaps your wife was asking awkward questions. This crash has rather cleared up the problem, hasn't it?'

'What do you want?'

'I don't want anything, Jack. I'm just ringing to ask if you'd like the tape? As a little memento. It's about fifteen seconds long.'

'I don't think…'

'You don't want Melanie, then? Brushing her off again, Mr Arnold? You really ought to treat these last-minute dedications with a little more reverence.'

Then Dan had put the phone down.

He realised he should let the living bury their dead in their own way and he locked the tapes away and stopped listening to them.

## 476

Now the lock was broken and his cabinet was almost empty.

No Mortonlake 222, ditched in the desert; no Peru 45, shot down; no Kentucky 13, pilot joked about it having bad luck – 'unlucky Kentucky'; no Panama 342, hijacked, terrorist used a phrase book to issue his demands; no

Airfare 432, crashed in the open sea, no Chicago '87 . . .

It was a grave robbing. Almost all gone. Only a few bones.

Dan shook his house down but nothing turned up. He found his hands shaking a little. He put his passport and some clothes into a case and left the house. Even with a distracted mind he could still pack well in minutes. He was used to quick exits.

He drove to Frankburg's and tried to think who, aside from his daughter Ali, had been in his house recently.

## 475

*Graft*, scene twenty, Bryn and Cathy meet.

Cathy – Are you going to just stand there while you get your pants nicked or is this your butler taking them away for washing?

Bryn – Hey, fuck off out of there.

*Stage direction* – Bryn tries to slap away a young thief who's got his hand inside his bag. The thief runs off.

Bryn – Cheeky bastard.

Cathy – I don't think they'll fit him.

Bryn – No.

Cathy – Perhaps he'll sell 'em on.

Bryn – There's a big black market for Welsh pants in Leeds, is there?

Cathy – laughs.

'OK, let's leave it there, I think we get the gist,' the casting woman cut in.

'Oh, right.'

'That was great, thanks, Samuel.'

'Yes, thanks, Samuel,' said the producer.

'Sure.'

'We're casting all today so you probably won't hear till tomorrow at the earliest.'

'OK, fine.'

'Lovely to meet you.'

'Yes.'

'Safe trip back. And thanks again.'

'Thanks.'

He got up and gathered his things together. He'd been in the room approximately four minutes.

## 474

He pushed the button for the lift. Cody ran up to him.

'We've got a lunch break at one. Could I meet you?'

Cody picked a restaurant and told him how to get there. 'On me,' she said.

'Very kind.'

As he entered the lift, he asked, 'How did I do?'

'Bit nervy,' said Cody. 'Watch the lift. It breaks a lot.'

Samuel let the lift doors close and he descended. The smell of Phoenix TV was different. He thought perhaps that after *Tunnel Vision* they'd changed their air fresheners. A voice in the lift told him that he had reached the ground floor. With a start, Samuel realised it was his own voice. An old job of work for the Elite Elevator Company. He wasn't surprised the lift trapped people inside.

He exited the building in a daze and was almost knocked down by a bus. Must learn to concentrate, thought Samuel.

## 473

'Record outgoing message?'

'This is John Heron. I've gone to the US. Emma, if you ring, leave a message, I can pick it up remotely. Anyone else ringing, you leave a message too. Unless it's Miles.'

He caught a bus to the airport. The bus nearly knocked over Samuel Thorn. The bus driver swore furiously at him. John Heron told the bus driver to calm down. The bus driver told John to sit back down in his damn seat.

Samuel waved an apology to the bus with his newspaper. John recognised Samuel from a toilet bleach commercial.

## 472

The taxi driver was on the chorus: 'Let me mmm mmm mmm mm, hum hum hum...'

Beth told him he had a very nice voice.

## 471

John Heron arrived at the airport and picked up his air ticket. He stared at the assistant's name badge, 'Angela.'

## 470

Angela hated name badges.

The company thought it was a good opportunity for customers to talk to their employees on a first-name basis.

Angela thought it was a good opportunity for male travellers to look at her breasts.

## 469

Angela asked if John had packed his bag himself.

John said yes.

Angela asked if John was carrying any electrical goods.

John said no.

Angela recognised the name Heron and asked if John was meeting his wife in New York.

John said he hoped so. John asked Angela to sit him next to someone who might cheer him up.

Angela said there was a clown going to a conference.

John said not clowns. He didn't like clowns.

Angela offered a casino croupier, female.

'Is she sexy?' asked John.

'She has nice hands,' said Angela.

'How about a magician?' asked John.

Angela said there weren't any magicians on the flight, as far as she knew.

John said he used to be one. Said he used to cut Emma in half.

Angela put him next to a dentist and didn't blame Emma for running off.

## 468

Angela saw the whole range of relationship behaviour at the airport. She'd seen couples greet each other at arrivals, hit each other at arrivals, separate at the check-in. She'd seen people sneak away from marriages, reconcile, change plans and fly to Vegas to remarry. Fly to different cities to marry somebody else. She'd seen assignations, impregnations, and molestations. She'd seen people lose children, steal children, give birth.

She looked for rings on people's fingers and different names on their credit cards.

Angela used to be a table tennis player but she quit because she could never get into the England squad. Fucking ping pong.

## 467

'Tell me about Kirsten Henderson,' Cody asked Samuel.

They were eating egg in Mr Egg where you could 'Eat Like A King For A Pound'. The King of where? Sam wondered.

'Do you buy the suicide line?'

'What do you mean? Course I buy it.'

'You were expecting her to do it then.'

'Well, no.'

'You were surprised?'

'Everyone was.'

'Any idea why she did it?'

'I really don't know. Why does anyone do it?'

'Because they're unhappy.'

'There's your answer then.'

'Did she seem unhappy?'

'Well...'

'Did she tell you she was unhappy?'

'No, not in so many words.'

'Did she hint then?'

'No. Not really.'

'Do her family know why she did it?'

## 466

The later edition of the paper made the connection between Kirsten Henderson and Ronald Henderson.

## 465

Cody read the story. She read grief stricken daddy.

'What a sorry tale. Shakespearean.'

'I wouldn't say that.'

'He was on the phone just before he jumped. I wonder who he was speaking to?'

'I don't know.'

'Did you see this one coming?'

'No.'

'Perhaps there was nothing to spot.'

'What?'

'I wonder if he left a note?'

'Look...'

'Did Kirsten leave a note?'

Pause.

'I don't know.'

'Don't know or won't tell me?'

'Don't know.'

'Did the coroner mention one?'

'I didn't go to the inquest.'

'Why not?'

'Can't remember.'

## 464

He was at home. His mother had looked after him. She thought he was always going to take something like this hard. She let him go for walks and read books and hammer on about the Thorn curse. After three weeks she had gently prodded the gloomy sod out of the house.

## 463

'I want to see the note. How do I see the note?'

'I don't know.'

'I'll put you in *Graft*.'

'I don't…'

'I'll cast a foxy co-star for you to roll around with and fall in love with and who won't kill herself out of the blue.'

'Find the note yourself,' said Samuel.

Cody left him with his egg.


## 462

Beth Davies arrived at check-in.

To Angela's eyes, Beth was scarred, married and dry-mouthed. She had a first-class ticket. Angela asked if Beth had packed her bag herself.

Beth said yes.

Angela asked if Beth was carrying any electrical goods.

Beth said no. She said she was meeting someone, Dan Bronski, and wanted to sit next to him on the plane.

Angela said she'd try to arrange it.

Angela wanted to ask if Beth was nervous because she'd been in an aeroplane crash – she looked like she had. Angela wanted to suggest St John's Wort, or Valium, but thought that would be overstepping her duties.


## 461

Frankburg's office.

A note had been slipped under his door.

'Dad. The last note was a cry for help. Now I'm really doing it. I love the rain. I want the feeling of it on my face.'

He ripped it up and chucked it away. He recognised Katherine Mansfield. Lily was such a plagiarist.

A muffled shout came from the floor above.

'Yes, that was me,' replied Frankburg.

Muffled query.

'No, I think the alarm must have disabled itself.'

Muffled insult.

'Of course I remember the code, it's the Battle of Hastings.'

Muffled answer.

'Well, if it's the signing of the Magna Carta, why didn't anyone tell me?'

Muffled response.

'I'm sure the insurance will cover it. Look, is anyone going to Coffee Paradise?'

Muffled response.

'If I treated you to a double latte, would you go to Coffee Paradise?'

Muffled response.

'Allergic to dairy? How awful. All right an espresso.'

Muffled response.

'Well, what would be worth your while?'

Muffled response.

'All right, I'll pay for the fucking window, stop being so petty.'

He closed the door. 'Wanker.' What had happened to camaraderie in the building? Furthermore, his *Conquer Panic* demo tape had not arrived in the post and it seemed *You Too Can Fly* was corrupted.

He rang Fine Sound Studios and expressed outrage and made accusations. The studio replied with ignorance and mystification, assuring him the *You Too Can Fly* master was uncontaminated. They offered to send another *Conquer Panic* over with a sound assistant called FX.

Frankburg told them the self-help market was a licence to print, and there were other studios in the Midlands. They told him to keep his hair on. Frankburg slammed the phone down. It was all very low-brow.

## 460

FX was a name given him at Fine Sound Studios. He loved it. He'd always been called Norris at school. He drove towards Birmingham with a new *Conquer Panic* and the instruction to treat Frankburg like a valued client, despite being a pillock.

## 459

Dan Bronski drove towards the city. If Ali wanted his tapes, she could have just asked him for them. What was he? A monster?

If someone else took them then he didn't know where to start.

It was said that if a fifty-year-old person went to Victoria Station and stayed there for another fifty years, everyone they'd ever met in the first fifty would pass by them in the second. You could say the same thing about Dan's house. He got about as much traffic.

He told himself he would cross that bridge etcetera etcetera. In the meantime, it was important to go to New York and cross Ali off the list.

He hoped he'd find her. Hoped she wanted to be found.

## 458

FX and Dan Bronski converged on Frankburg's office.

Dan introduced himself to FX in the lift.

FX said he was pleased to meet him.

Both of them thought the other was a client.

FX apologised for crashing Dan's session. Dan said he was about to say the same thing. FX explained he wasn't a nut, he was only delivering a tape, *Conquer Panic*. Dan said he was delivering the other one, *You Too Can Fly*. Dan asked what was wrong with the one FX had. FX said nothing he hoped. FX asked Dan if he knew what a fizzing ball of energy was.

## 457

'Take a seat,' said Frankburg. 'Got to be quick, got another one coming in an hour.'

'Another tape?' asked Dan.

'No, another client. I hope to God they don't bring a tape.'

## 456

'...to loosen the tension in the shoulders...'

Damn the Welshman. Frankburg still clenched his jaw, even now. He was about to ask his guests whether they thought the accent was too guttural when:

'266, you are cleared to 11,000.'

'Received.'

<crackle>

'AF 266, turn left, heading 130 on a southeast course.'

'Received.'

'Cleared to 9,000.'

'Received.'

'...only a few minutes...hold on till then?'

'...upsetting the other passengers.'

'What's the matter with her?'

'Just crying, they think she's crying because something's gone wrong with the plane.'

'OK, see if you can reassure them, we'll try to speed things up.'

'...right...an announcement too might help.'

'OK.'

'Control, this is AF 266, we have an unwell stewardess on board, any chance of getting us down quickly?'

'...One moment 266.'

'She was fine earlier, wasn't she?'

'No, she's been odd all day, just tired perhaps.'

'AF 266, take airway route Victor 132, it'll take a couple of minutes off your journey.'

'Received, thanks.'

'Hope it's nothing too serious.'

'We don't think so, thanks anyway.'

'OK, OK. Cleared to 7,000.'

'Received.'

'You wanna do it?'

'Sure. Ladies and gentlemen, this is Co-pilot Johansson speaking. We shall be landing in about twenty minutes' time, earlier than scheduled. As I said, the weather in London is slightly overcast but a pleasant twenty degrees. Thank you for flying with us. Cabin crew, prepare for landing.'

'Very reassuring, Mr Johansson.'

'Well, I do my best.'

## 455

Frankburg recognised the voice of his missing client Graham Johansson.

'Where did you get this?' Frankburg asked Dan.

'It's from a blackbox.'

'Is it recent?'

'No.'

'Did the plane crash?'

'No.'

Frankburg wondered why there was a blackbox recording at all. If there'd been no mechanical or other irregularities, they just wiped the disk clear for the next trip, didn't they?

Dan Bronski said there had been an incident. It involved a stowaway who had died.

Frankburg grabbed Johansson's notes but there was no mention of a dead stowaway. Frankburg wondered when that was going to come up.

'Why is this on my tape?' asked Frankburg.

'I don't know,' said Dan. 'There's another bit too.'

## 454

Beth Davies went into a toilet cubicle at the airport. She locked the door and put a picture of the sea on the wall and an air freshener on the floor. Desert Dawn. She listened to music on her headphones and took a pill.

Her worst flight had been aboard a Lufthansa to Hamburg. Michael had been with her. They'd tried to take their minds of the flight the night before so they'd gone round to see Dan Bronski, who'd not only taken their minds off it, he'd taken their minds off the planet altogether with a drink which he had invented and brewed himself from 'fruits of the wood'. Consequently, Beth had been fighting nausea, paranoia, the fear of death and a hangover as she boarded the plane.

Dan had told them of a recent case where a plane had crashed in the Burmese jungle, not far from the border with Laos, carrying thirty-seven passengers and a small crew. Though the undergrowth was dense and the plane had a fairly supported landing, the passengers had all perished. Dan presumed that the plane had had a massive system failure, and despite the brave efforts of the pilot, the plane's controls were rendered ineffective. It had been a difficult case to investigate because of the inhospitable jungle environment. He'd been confused, however, by the injuries sustained by the passengers. They were still mostly in their seats, buckled up, but had suffered in a way that was not entirely consistent with the impact of an air crash. After many months of investigation, he'd deduced that the passengers did after all survive the initial impact, but whilst injured and helpless in their seats they'd been set upon by tribesmen who'd tortured and abused them. Needless to say, none of this information appeared on the blackbox flight recorder, which had stopped recording once the plane had crashed. Just as well. Dan was glad to be spared that.

As Beth had sat in the Lufthansa seat she'd suffered a rising tide of terror in her breast which the Lufthansa seat belt could not contain and as the plane taxied to the runway the interior of the cabin had started to resemble the catastrophic Laos flight. The German-accented steward running through the safety procedures transformed into a charred and abused passenger. The smell of the airline food became burnt flesh to Beth's nostrils. A boy in the seat opposite sucked his thumb, as if tasting how savoury it was.

Beth had flipped. She'd unbuckled her seat belt and run down the aisle. The other passengers had murmured and one shouted out in surprise. Beth had only heard a loud rushing in her ears and a warm bright light spreading over her eyes and she'd passed out by the exit.

When she came to she was being carried down some steps from the plane to a waiting vehicle which looked like a golf cart. She'd felt clammy and sick but her muscles were very relaxed and she'd let her eyes slip shut again. For the next few minutes she'd just listened to the sounds around her and the play of changing atmospheres on her skin. She'd been brought inside and taken to a room where first aid was administered.

She'd heard Michael's voice from time to time answering questions about her state of health and whether she had any allergies. She'd heard someone else ask if the scars on her face were from a previous aircraft disaster. Michael had said no. Said that was from a different time.

Their bags had been removed from the hold and the plane had taken off, an hour late, without them.

## 453

Beth stared at her picture of the sea and sniffed at her air freshener and let the tranquilliser do its work.

If she turned the music up loud and hummed along, she could almost kid herself that she was in her toilet at home. Although on the whole that was where she felt her worst.

## 452

'Jesus. I don't know what to say.'

Frankburg rewound.

'Jesus. I don't know what to say.'

'FX rewound.

'Jesus. I don't know what to say.'

'Wow,' said FX.

'Tell you what, FX, why don't you run down to Coffee Paradise and get us all a frappacino?'

Frankburg chivvied him into the lift before FX had time to ask what Coffee Paradise or a Frappaccino was.

## 451

Frankburg asked Dan if he thought a self-help tape which was solely the compilation of last moments of other people's lives would be a life affirming one. One which strengthened the resolve in the listener to ensure that each second was lived to the very full.

Dan thought it was possible.

Frankburg asked him if those final screams were really saying, 'There are so many things left undone.'

Dan thought they might be.

Frankburg thought there could be an accompanying book full of suicide notes.

'Dad, by the time you read this I will be dead. Thanks for everything.'

No, he wouldn't use that one.

'Have you got a daughter?' asked Frankburg.

'Yes,' said Dan.

'Do you know where she is?'

'No.'

'No. I don't know where mine is either.'

There was a pause.

'Mine writes me suicide notes,' said Frankburg.

'Really?'

'What does yours do?'

'I don't know.'

There was another pause.

'What's her name?' asked Dan.

'Lily,' said Frankburg.

'That's nice,' said Dan.

'Thank you. Yours?' asked Frankburg.

'Ali.'

Frankburg was ready to say that's nice too but the name Ali Bronski clicked and he flew off the handle. He told Dan that Ali Bronski was a thief and a saboteur.

Dan leapt to her defence as any father should and told Frankburg to watch his tongue.

There was a generalised discussion about whose daughter was the worst and who was the worst dad.

They shouted at each other aggressively for ten minutes during which Dan smashed up Frankburg's chaise longue and Frankburg kicked in his own filing cabinet. Frankburg screamed that Dan had bred an embezzling, fork-tongued, intellectual larcenist as he upturned his table. Dan thundered that Frankburg's next self-help tape should be How to Be So Fucking Irritating You Made Your Family Want To Kill Themselves and put his foot through Frankburg's computer monitor.

They ended up panting and sweating and bleeding in the middle of the room and agreed that they were both sub-standard dads who'd let their daughters down.

## 450

Outside the door, Frankburg's one o'clock appointment decided he wasn't feeling so bad after all and went away.

## 449

Dan and Frankburg sat in the wreck of the room. Dan lit a cigarette, smoked half of it then handed it to Frankburg who smoked the rest. Frankburg showed Dan some of Lily's notes. Goethe, Burns, Austen, Keats. Frankburg apologised for calling Ali Bronski a pirate, Lily was just as bad.

Dan stood, shook Frankburg's hand and drove to the airport.

## 448

Lily/Cody told Phoenix TV they could audition the women fine without her.

She went home and hit the phones to find Kirsten's note. Keats was a ham. Kirsten's note was a proven goodie.

## 447

Beth felt the tranquilliser make her blood sluggish and her heart slow. She exited the toilet cubicle but left the picture and the freshener inside. It might comfort the next person.

The next person happened to be Rose the cleaner. She took the picture but binned the freshener. It smelt off.

## 446

Michael Davies turned pale. Ashen in fact.

'That's you, isn't it?' Dan said.

'Well, I don't know. It's pretty old.'

'It's off a blackbox.'

Michael was on a break. Dan Bronski played him the tape on a walkman.

'This was on the tape I picked up yesterday?' asked Michael.

'Yes. Where did you get it from?'

'A cleaner.'

'Where did she get it from?'

'I don't know, I'll have to ask her.'

'Might be worth it, mightn't it?'

They looked at each other.

'What's the case?' asked Michael.

'Don't you know?'

'No.'

Michael had read about what your face did when you lied. Eyes flicked, nose got itchy, neck pulsed. In an effort not to display these symptoms, he displayed them all.

'Did Beth give you this?' Michael asked.

'Yes.'

'She's heard it then.'

'Yes.'

'Why did she call you?'

'She thought you sounded distressed.'

There was another pause.

## 445

Michael had been distressed.

Two decades younger, sitting sweat-drenched and nauseous, AF 266 entering his airspace, his voice catching, sweat popping.

'...we have an unwell stewardess...'

Trying to ask what the matter was, wanting information, other planes crowding his radar, demanding his attention. AF 266 crawling across his screen like a luminous bug, brighter than the others, heavier, finding it a short cut.

Knocking off. Driving home, shouting stupid stupid stupid.

Waiting in the house for me to come back. Changing the locks so that I couldn't get in, in case I brought the stowaway with me. Standing back from the bedroom window, lights turned off to hide him. Watching me walk up the drive, unsteady, shaky.

Seeing me try to get my key to work and look around as if I've got the wrong house. Watching me try another key and then shout out his name.

'Michael! Michael!'

Hearing me bang on the door and ring the bell and shout through the letter box.

'Michael!'

Seeing me go round to the back door and bang on that. Throwing gravel onto the windows, crumpling up on the drive. Crying, great sobs. Pleading.

'Please, Michael.'

Watching me on the ground for an hour.

'Open the door.'

Seeing me get up and walk away from the house. Seeing me turn at the gate and look up into the bedroom to catch him watching the whole pitiful spectacle.

Getting caught by the look. Spotted. Me seeing him seeing me.

Darting behind a curtain. Peeking out.

And smashing up the place in self-disgust.


## 444

Dan watched a vein in Michael's temple throb like a little heartbeat.

'What are you going to do now?' asked Michael.

'I'm going to do some investigating.'

'Is that necessary?'


## 443

Dan booked himself first class on the one thirty to New York. He got free travel. An unlikely perk of being an (ex) air crash investigator.

Angela at check-in thought Dan Bronski was good-looking in a craggy way, although she thought he'd probably slept in his clothes. She wondered how an air crash investigator would help the scarred lady through the flight. Perhaps he was good at massage. Perhaps he knew the sound of a ditching plane so well he could assure her, every minute, that he hadn't heard those sounds and everything was so far so good.

She found him a seat next to Beth just as John Heron was again being dragged into airport security.


## 442

He was on a 'people to watch out for' noticeboard by virtue of the gun incident the night before. A call to the police officer from that shift confirmed that in his opinion John posed no threat to national security unless he was again carrying fake guns. John wasn't, so he was let go.

John felt like the Cooler King.

## 441

Dan found Beth playing racing-car games. He joined her. They zoomed around a dirt track in Arizona. Taking corners impossibly fast, surviving preposterous crashes. Beth won by four seconds.

'All set?'

'No.'

'How far are we from "yes"?'

'A million miles.'

'New York is nearer.'

'Doesn't feel it.'

'You want a drink?'

'Yes.'

'Nothing like a loosener.'

'Thanks for coming.'

'Don't mention it.'

'Why are you coming?'

'I think my daughter may have stolen all my blackbox tapes.' Plus I love you. He didn't say that bit though.


## 440

Frankburg sat in his office. Bruised, exhausted and surrounded by client notes from his smashed-up filing cabinet. A decade of confession described in Frankburg's spindly handwriting. Hundreds of lives on half a tree. He wondered if any of them felt any better.

He made a paper plane out of a stress case, a man who became so tense his eyeballs filled with blood and couldn't see. Frankburg launched the plane towards the window but it fell short.

Frankburg picked a kleptomaniac and changed the design, he made more folds. It flew two metres and hit his water cooler.

Through his door came a confused and miserable FX carrying two leaking Frappaccinos.

Frankburg asked him if he knew how to make paper planes and handed him a client who had a phobia about buses. The client saw a person die of a heart attack on a bus, then years later the client's father died of a heart attack, now the client fainted on buses.

FX folded lengthwise, a sleek fighter plane. He weighted it with a paper clip.

FX asked why the client didn't just drive everywhere?

The plane soared out the window and halfway across Birmingham.

## 439

John Heron sat in a pub at the airport, drank, and fiddled with his five-year-old wedding ring.

He asked the barman if he knew how to do the Indian rope trick.

The barman shook his head.

John said the top of the rope was hoisted upwards towards the branches of a tree by way of a thin wire on a pulley system while the magician plays a stupid tune on a flute type instrument. Then the magician sends an assistant up the rope who amusingly refuses to come down. The magician pretends to be furious at the assistant's disobedience and threatens to kill her. Then the magician shins up the rope after her. When at the top he throws down bits of butchered lamb, legs, organs, while the assistant screams horribly. The horrified audience thinks that the assistant is being gruesomely murdered, at which point the magician descends the rope with the assistant, now in a skimpy glitzy costume, draped decoratively around him, to rapturous applause.

'Sounds horrible,' said the barman.

'It follows strict historical precedents,' said John. 'I did it myself in a town square in Greece. It was where I met my wife. In a bar. I asked her to be the glamorous assistant. I needed someone who would look good in a glitzy costume and wasn't squeamish.'

'Did she do it?'

'She climbed the rope all right,' said John, 'but then she hid in the trees for a joke and refused to come down. "Bloody come down," I said. "Piss off," she said. "Will you bloody come down?" I said. "No", she said.'

'What happened?' asked the barman.

'I had to descend empty-handed. I was consequently set upon by the enraged crowd whose distressed children still believed Emma had been butchered. "Sick act!" they cried, in Greek, and chased me out of the square. I was arrested and cautioned. I'm often arrested and cautioned.'

The barman shook his head. 'Got to know your assistants,' he said.

'You're right there,' said John.

## 438

Dan Bronski bought Beth a drink from the same airport pub.

They took a seat next to John Heron.

Dan thought that it would be good for Beth to see someone looking more miserable about flying than herself.

## 437

John Heron introduced himself.

Beth Davies asked him if he was drinking because he was worried about the plane crashing.

John looked at Beth's face and started to ask if...

Beth said, 'When people see me anxious in an airport they think I've been in an air crash. If I'm anxious on a train they think I've been in a train crash. If I'm anxious in a taxi, the driver asks if I've had a road accident.'

'What if you're anxious in a supermarket?' asked John.

'I don't know what they think then.'

Baked bean accident, thought John, but didn't say it. Dan looked like a guy who might punch his lights out.

## 436

John said he used to be a magician.

'Have you ever heard of Monsieur Chabert, the Incombustible Phenomenon?' asked Beth.

'Yes,' said John.

'No,' said Dan.

'M. Chabert,' said John, 'would enter a hot oven with a tray of raw meat, When it was cooked he would hand it to the chef-d'oeuvre, then take in another and stay there, singing, "Le Valiant Troubadour", until the second lot was also well done; then he'd come out of the oven and sit down to eat the dinner with his friends, who'd watched the whole performance from start to finish.'

'No burns?' asked Dan.

'Nothing,' said Beth.

'There was also The Incombustible Spaniard, Senor Lionetto. He bathed for five minutes in boiling oil. Then he got out and rubbed the soles of his feet and his hands with a bar of hot iron heated to a white heat. And he put it in his mouth.'

'How did he do that?' asked Dan.

'That's what I'd like to know,' asked Beth.

'Trade secret,' said John, though he didn't know either.


## 435

'Passengers Dan Bronski, Beth Davies, and John Heron flying to New York flight BA 342 please board at gate thirty-three, this is your last call.'

John and Beth didn't move.

'We ought to go,' said Dan, sliding off his bar stool.

'I don't know why I'm going now,' said John.

'To find your wife.'

'I don't know New York, I've never been.'

'It's not so big.'

'I should have brought my gun.'

'You'll feel better on the plane.'

'Anyone know what the "Divine Wind" is?'

'Let's not talk about that,' said Dan, who did.


## 434

John bleeped through the body x-ray.

'I knew a guy,' said Dan, 'an Australian businessman, who once made a joke whilst going through the body x-ray. "My plastic leg is hollow and holds a powerful gun," he said, "I'm going to hijack the plane, ha ha!" The security guards didn't laugh. I think they'd heard jokes like that before.'

'Well, it's not very funny in the circumstances,' said Beth.

'He got taken to the airport security cells where he underwent a full body search. To security's surprise, he really did have a plastic leg. Security let him off, saying he shouldn't make jokes about hijacking planes as it's a very serious issue. He said he probably shouldn't make jokes about having a plastic leg but it was the only way of coping with it.'

'What's your point?' said Beth.

Dan didn't know. He was just making conversation.

John got the all-clear. It was his collapsible wand causing the problem. He always carried it. Old habits died hard.


## 433

Frankburg flew a compulsive hand-washer into the corridor. He flew a cat killer into a lamp shade. He made a self-amputee loop the loop and crash into the wastebasket. FX whooped and said he had the paper plane know-how. FX grabbed 'Dad, by the time you read this I will be dead.'

'Not that,' said Frankburg. He wanted to keep the notes. He liked seeing Lily's handwriting even if he flinched at what she wrote.

He gave FX a transsexual instead.


## 432

Cody/Lily hit the phones.

'*Birmingham Standard?*'

'Bruce McClean, please.'

'One moment.'

Hold music. 'Moonlight Sonata.'

'Bruce McClean.'

'My name's Cody Jameson, I'm ringing about your reporting of the Ronald Henderson suicide at Birmingham International.'

'Yes?'

'You had some background about his daughter, Kirsten. I wondered where you found it.'

'What's your interest?'

'I'm ... I was a friend of Kirsten.'

'Did I get my facts wrong?'

'Some of them.'

'My source was the *Edinburgh Argus*, they reported the...'

'Thanks.'

'If...'

Click.

## 431

Bruce would never make the nationals.

## 430

Dial.

'Directory enquiries, which name please?'

'*Edinburgh Argus*,' said Cody.

'Hold please.'

A recorded voice gave her the number.

'News desk.'

'My name's Cody Jameson. I'm ringing from the *Birmingham Standard*. I'm sure you know that Ronald Henderson died on the front of a Birmingham train yesterday.'

'Yes, we'd got that.'

'I'm doing some background and I remembered your coverage of his daughter's death, Kirsten. Very good.'

'Thank you.'

'Your work?'

'Some of it, yes.'

'What did you make of Ronald? Pleasant man?'

'It was hard to tell under the circumstances, he was very upset.'

'Of course.'

'Why do you ask?'

'I'm just filling in some blanks.'

'Right.'

'Remind me of Kirsten's coroner would you? Mr...'

'Dr Chorley? What have you got?'

'Nothing. As I said, local interest. Thanks for your time.'

Click.

## 429

The *Edinburgh Argus* would never scoop a Watergate but they did damn good celebrity profiles.

## 428

'Directory enquiries, which name please?'

'Coroner's office, Edinburgh.'

'One moment please ... thank you.'

'Cody dialled.

'Dr Chorley please.'

'Who?'

'Dr Chorley? I believe he's the coroner?'

'The coroner here's a Mr Turner.'

'Oh. Has Dr Chorley ever worked in that office?'

'Not as far as I know.'

'Right.'

'I could put you through to Mr Turner's secretary, if you'd like?'

'No, that's OK. I'm trying to track down the coroner's report for a friend of mine.'

'Did your friend die in Edinburgh?'

'London.'

'The report will be with an office there then. London has half a dozen, though. You'll have to check their jurisdictions.'

'Will do, thanks very much.'

'Click.

Dial.

'Samuel, in which hotel did Kirsten die?'

'The Shropshire Regis.'

'Where's that?'

'Islington borders— Hello?'

Click.

## 427

Samuel had been lodged in the Highland. Bigger star. Better area. If he'd died, a different coroner would've picked him up.

## 426

Dial.

'Directory Enquiries, what name please?'

'I keep getting you, don't I? I want the Coroner's Court London, please.'

'One moment please...'

'Probably sounds a bit morbid this...'

Cody rang the offered number.

'City Coroner's.'

'Could you tell me which coroners would deal with a death in the Islington area?'

'Inner North London, St Pancras Coroner's Court.'

She scribbled down the number. She rang it.

'Coroner's St Pancras?'

'I'd like to see the coroner's notes on the inquest of Kirsten Henderson, is that possible?'

'Do you have the deceased d.o.d?'

'Not precisely, within the last seven months.'

'Are you related to the deceased, or do you have a proper interest?'

'Related by marriage.'

Writers are liars as well as thieves, Cody told herself.

'One moment, please.'

Hold music, Bach. She hummed along.

'There is a tape recording of the inquest but you'd have to apply to the coroner to listen to it. The same goes for the transcripts and notes. If you want a copy, there's a fee payable but again you'll have to make an application to receive them.'

'Did you say a tape? A video tape?'

'Audio. But you'd have to come down to our offices to listen to it, we couldn't let you take it away.'

'Could you give me your address?'

## 425

The coroner's assistant got the Kirsten Henderson tape ready. She was very organised. She wore smart clothes and had never lost a file or a tape in her life. The dead were well looked after.

## 424

Dial.

'Hel—'

'Samuel, we can listen to Kirsten's inquest on tape.'

'I don't want to.'

'Wanting to and needing to are two different things.'

'I don't need to either.'

'I'll come and get you.'

'I...'

'Where are you?'

'I'm...'

'You're not in Mr Egg are you?'

'Um, yes.'

'Eat Like a King. I'll call you when I've got a car.'

Click.

## 423

Sam shifted in his seat. His trousers slightly stuck to the plastic.

He fantasised about absolution in Kirsten's suicide note.

'Don't mourn me.'

Or, 'Don't torture yourself, I have just this second decided to do this. Totally out of the blue.'

Or, 'Sorry, Sam, you were the best friend I ever had, if anyone could have stopped me, you could, love Kirsten. Don't forget me.'

Or even better, 'See you in Heaven.'

## 422

Around and around goes the wind, and from its circuits returns again.

## 421

The wind is deflected west. Its path appears shifted because of the rotation of the Earth. This is the Coriolis effect. The force which causes moving objects near the Earth's surface to be turned westward. So everything's heading my way.

Including the sun, which made its way across the Atlantic and brought morning to the US. It was today.

## 420

Penny Lock woke and was sick.

She got some toilet paper from the bathroom and cleared it up. She had polished wood floors so it came up easily.

Balance back, Penny poked the answermachine to see what her gloomy pilot had to say for himself.

Beep.

'Penny, it's John again. Emma's on her way back to the US. I don't know why, and I don't know where you are either. Give me a call as soon as you get these messages.'

Beep.

Penny was sick again.

## 419

Ali Bronski woke.

She sat crossed legged on her sleeping bag and put the final touches to a questionnaire for suicidal pilots.

'Is it important to be smart at all times?'

Gentle start, lead him in.

'Wash regularly for a clear complexion? Brush your teeth? Use floss?'

Cut to the chase.

'Would you want your loved ones around you at times like this?'

Like a chess player she ran over his probable responses.

'Times like what?'

'Just as the plane crashes.'

'Which plane?'

'Your plane.'

'Is my plane crashing?'

'If it was, would you want your loved ones around you.'

'No, but…'

'Would you make sure you said a tender goodbye to them before you went on this flight?'

'Which flight?'

'The flight which is crashing.'

'Why is my flight crashing?'

'It doesn't have to.'

'Why is it, then?'

'You tell me.'

'I don't know.'

'Do you want it to crash?'

'Why should I want that?'

'You tell me.'

And he'd be off. And his cure would start. Ali thought if she could drag Graham Johansson out of the mire she'd feel much, much better about herself.

## 418

Clara Redlake woke. Her alarm was tuned in to the radio and this morning's phone-in was 'Animal Experimentation.'

Clara picked up the phone and dialled the station. She pointed out to the host that at any one time there were thousands of human lab rats in the US testing new drugs or taking part in medical experiments. She said these people were pioneers for science.

The host said humans weren't animals.

Clara said *au contraire*.

## 417

The pharmaceutical CEO woke and wondered if he would be blown up today. In the shower, his mind let him believe the shower head could have been sabotaged and a chemical would react with the water and cover his body with sulphuric acid. He took it apart. It was fine but he couldn't put it back together again. He had a bath instead.

## 416

His daughter, Tamy, woke. She received a parcel in the post. Her father advised her not to open it. Said it should be x-rayed or sniffed by sniffer dogs. He wrote himself a memo to buy a fluoroscope. He said after the bomb under his car yesterday no one should open anything. Tamy said it was a birthday gift. He said he didn't realise it was her birthday. She said she was thirty. He said oh. She opened the parcel to find it was from her father. His secretary had selected the gift, posted it, and signed the card on his behalf.

He said thank God for that. He said happy birthday and kissed her on the cheek. Tamy said yeah thanks.

## 415

Tommy Tempo didn't wake up. He died peacefully in his sleep. There'd be no obituaries in the *New York Times*. Most people had forgotten about old Tommy.

## 414

The ex-government agent woke to hear his phone ringing. He jumped out of his chair alert, defensive, and ready to receive a cold bucket of water in the face or a kick in the balls. An old prison reaction. When he remembered where he was, he sat down again and let the cramp in his calf command his attention.

'Hello?' he grunted.

'What's the matter with you?' said the pharmaceutical CEO.

'Nothing, who's this?'

'It's me. The piece of shit, if you will.'

'Have you got any money for me?'

'Give me a chance, the day hasn't started yet.'

'It has for me, buddy boy. I've got cramp in my leg and in my belly. I need breakfast and I can't pay for it.'

'Have you spoken to anyone about the bomb under my car?'

'No.'

'Are you going to?'

'I don't owe you any favours, sunshine.'

'Just get on the phone and give me a name.'

'Get some money, you piece of shit.'

'I need a name. My daughter's getting parcels.'

'Give me some money.'

'Give me a name.'

'You piece of shit.'

'You're a piece of shit.'

'Give me a name and I'll give you ten thousand.'

'Not enough.'

'For starters.'

'Not nearly enough.'

'A down payment.'

The ex-government agent paused. Then he called the CEO a piece of shit again, but not very forcefully.

'I'll call you in an hour,' said the CEO.

The ex-government agent put the phone down.

Then he noticed there were two nervous looking women huddled on a mattress opposite him and he nearly jumped out of his skin.


## 413

Edward the Fireman changed the dressing on his wound and slowly and carefully got dressed. He chose dark clothes in case he seeped. He bundled up his kitchen tablecloth and threw it in the rubbish.

He was bad today. He needed distractions. From the pain as much as anything else. And he couldn't take pills for it. That would be hypocritical. What would SHE think. Where was SHE anyway?

He thought about another bomb to bring her to him, but thought he might ooze too much of his blood at the scene.

Divert myself, he thought. He picked up tape seven. 'Appearing Heroic'. He headed towards Grand Central Station.

## 412

Graham Johansson walked by the river but didn't smile back at the joggers. He confirmed his flight with the airline. He'd pilot SA 109 to Birmingham later that day. They asked him what had happened to his mobile phone. He told them it was broken. It was actually at the bottom of the Hudson but he didn't mind that at all. On the whole, he'd had more bad calls on that phone than good ones.

## 411

The ex-government agent waved his expired agency identification at the two women who jumped up and ran into the kitchen. He didn't give chase because his legs were still cramped so instead he shouted at them to leave immediately or they'd find themselves in a federal institution. Nothing happened so he shouted again. Then he hobbled into the kitchen to find the two women cooking eggs in a pan. They looked at him nervously and added some herbs and tomatoes. The ex-government agent didn't know what misunderstanding had created this state of affairs but he decided to shout about federal institutions after breakfast. The eggs smelt damn good. Though the apple juice tasted a bit off.

## 410

I woke.

## 409

I looked out of the window on a blue day. It was the 10th of September. The day Guernica was returned to Spain, the day the British Navy lost the Battle of Lake Erie, the last guillotine was used for the last time.

The day I woke up in the Hotel Monumental.

## 408

Cody, dogged. Lying through her teeth.

PC Queely, tired from nightmares.

'The case is still under investigation, Miss Jameson. I can't give you that information. You can attend the coroner's inquest if you wish to.'

'Ronald Henderson was on the phone when the train hit him. I think he was trying to ring me. I was expecting him to call and I was in the bath and then the phone rang and I rushed to it but just missed it.'

'Could have been anyone.'

'I tried to call him back but all I got was the phone's voicemail. Please, I need to know, I need to know if I was the last person he tried to ring, it means so much to me...'

'What was your relationship with Mr Henderson?'

'We were... we'd started seeing each other, he was coming to visit me from Scotland.'

'According to our information he'd just got off the plane from New York.'

'Yes, um, that's right, he was...'

'Coming to Birmingham from Edinburgh via New York?'

She put the phone down. Smart-arsed copper.,

## 407

Ronald Henderson in New York. He'd buzzed my buzzer.

I'd picked up the receiver and said 'Yes?' and a voice had said 'Stephanie?' and it had been Ronald.

Out of the blue.

I dropped the handset as if it had bitten me and I listened to the tinny sounds of his voice telling me that Kirsten was dead. He kept buzzing. He asked me why 'Cody Jameson' was written on the buzzer. He said he'd read *Tales of a Stewardess* by a Cody Jameson and it was shite. He said he knew I was in there.

'Stephanie!'

He told me he'd be dead soon and that that would be that.

'Stephanie!'

He kept shouting until someone else in the block told him to shut up. When he didn't someone must have gone outside and moved him away.

I peeked out of the window and watched him leave. An old, old man. Broken. He turned unexpectedly and looked up and caught me looking and I ducked away.

Then I ran away.

I locked up my apartment. I left it as I had lived in it. Didn't make the bed.

Left the dishes unwashed. There were perishables in the fridge and consumer items in the living room. I took my little radio with me. I could listen to the Penny Lock show for comfort. I checked into a hotel where I woke today.

## 406

The Hotel Monumental. Room fourteen. There were no room thirteens. The Hotel Monumental found that people always wanted to change if they were put into room thirteen so they're now numbered from twelve to fourteen on each floor. The good thing about the Hotel Monumental is that if you put your shoes outside the door they clean them for the morning. If you get in late at night, the shoes are all lined up in the corridor and you have your pick.

## 405

PC Queely put the phone down on Cody and looked at the list of telephone calls that Ronald Henderson had made on the evening he jumped in front of the train.

There was nothing until seven forty which was when Ronald was clear of the airport. At seven forty Ronald made a call. Three minutes later he made another. Three minutes later another. And another. Fifteen calls, all three minutes long and all to the same number, right until he was hit by the eight o'clock freight when the calls understandably stopped.

The number was Ronald's own home number in Edinburgh.

## 404

From her bedroom Ali shouted, 'Mr Johansson!'

No reply.

'Are you decent?'

No reply.

'Are you asleep?'

No reply.

Oh no.

She left her bedroom. Graham was gone. Ali saw a note on the floor. She rushed into the bathroom expecting to see Graham bleeding in the bath.

Empty. She rushed into the kitchen expecting to see Graham hanging from a beam. Nothing. No dead person in her apartment.

She read the note.

'Ali, thank you for seeing me last night. I realise I owe you some money for the session. Please call round to my apartment to pick it up. I'll leave it with my partner. Yours G Johansson.'

He wrote an address at the bottom.

Ali collapsed on the floor weeping with relief.

## 403

Grand Central Station. Edward the Fireman had found a small child looking lost, he picked her up despite the excruciating pain in his abdomen and returned her to her mother. He told the mother that he'd found the child about to fall in front of a train. The mother was full of gratitude but found Edward a bit alarming. Edward the Fireman smiled and took his due. 'Appearing heroic' wasn't so bad.

He was feeling sicker by the hour but he didn't want to go home in case he found me there, furious with him for telling the old man Ronald Henderson where to find me.

He switched tapes and left the station.

## 402

The ex-government agent rang one of his ex-colleagues.

'Don't ever ring this number,' came the reply.

'Hey, come on, we go way back.'

'No, we don't.'

'Sure we do, don't be like that. You and me, the Hungry Ears.'

'What are you talking about?'

'The Surreptitious Entry Team, the times we had.'

'I don't know what you're talking about.'

'Surveillance Steve?'

'My name isn't Steve.'

'Isn't it?'

'You always called me Steve, but it isn't my name.'

'Oh. What is your name.'

'I'm not going to tell you that.'

'Dave?'

'No.'

'Bill?'

'Go away, I can't talk to you.'

'I wanted to ask you a favour.'

'No.'

'Come on, just a bit of information.'

'I'm putting down the phone.'

'Bomb under a car yesterday, just a name.'

'Don't ever call me again.'

'Come on.'

Click.

'Hello?'

Nothing.

'Damn.' He put the phone down.

'More eggs,' he shouted. *'Muchos huevos'*

He rang Ali Bronski.


## 401

Ali answered her phone without thinking.

'Got you!' shouted the ex-government agent in triumph. 'Give me the name of some mad terrorist... hello?'

Ali switched the phone off.

'Damn,' said the ex-government agent. Again.


## 400

Cody looked for some transport.

FX's car was parked near Frankburg's building.

A piece of packing tape slipped behind the window flipped the lock and Cody was inside going through the glove compartment.

Tapes, chewing gum, a magazine about mixing desks.

Cody rang. Samuel.

'I've made an appointment to go and listen to the coroner's inquest tapes.'

'When?'

'This afternoon, five o'clock.'

'I don't want to go,' said Samuel.

'Why not?'

'I want to stay here.'

'Why?'

'You go. Tell me what the note says.'

Cody hotwired the car. She was a very resourceful woman.

## 399

The ex-government agent put on his jacket and stormed out the apartment. Then he stormed back in again and waved his ID at the two women. One of them gave him a bread roll with the rest of his eggs in. He took it. They smiled at him. He half-heartedly waved his ID again then left. He'd boot them out later. Perhaps after dinner.

## 398

Beth, Dan and John boarded the plane.

'Your husband's an air traffic controller?' asked John.

'Yes,' said Beth.

'Would you feel better if he was guiding us in?'

Pause.

'I would feel far, far worse.'

## 397

Michael Davies smoked and wondered if he was in trouble. He rang his contacts abroad and asked them if anyone had been making any enquiries about him. They all said no. He asked if anyone had picked up on his idea to supply stowaways with gaffer tape so they didn't get tangled up in the undercarriage. They asked what the hell was gaffer tape. He said it was like duck tape. They asked what the hell was duck tape. He said it was what Americans called gaffer tape. The guy said did he mean duct tape. Michael said oh, yes, that was what he meant. Then the guy started laughing. Michael told him to shut up. He wondered why he did this anyway.

He told himself he did it to win back Stephanie Wiltshire because, no matter how hard he tried, Beth Wiltshire was not the same thing at all. It had been a stupid idea marrying her.

## 396

A mess of wires around the ignition.

'Lost my keys,' Cody explained. 'Are you sure you don't want to go?'

Sam said he wanted to stay in Birmingham. He said as he was here he might go back to Phoenix TV and have a look at the *Tunnel Vision* footage. He'd never seen it.

Cody said if it was the car then they could go in the train.

Sam told her it wasn't the car.

## 395

John was getting horror stories from a dentist next to him.

Dan asked the stewardess if John could be upgraded to join him and Beth in first class.

The stewardess wasn't sure.

Dan told her about a brave stewardess called Bernadette who, despite fracturing a foot, still had time to comfort a small child as the plane went down:

'It's OK, it's OK, little one. Don't cry. I know it's a bit bumpy but it's nothing to be worried about. It's like being at the funfair. Have you ever been to the funfair? Did you go at night when the stars were out? But it was still warm because it was summer and you were allowed to stay up late. Did you play on the helter skelter? Did you go right to the top and slide all the way to the bottom, round and round, faster and faster? Did you have some candyfloss? It's so sweet, isn't it? It's my favourite too. Ooh, that was a big bump, wasn't it? Just like when you got to the bottom of the slide. Or being bumped by a dodgem car. Did you go on the dodgem cars? It's just like that. Don't cry, don't be afraid, people scream at the funfair too, don't they? It doesn't mean they're really scared. Oh, that was a really big bump, wasn't it? I fell over too. It's funny when I fall over, isn't it? Like a clown at the circus. Shall I fall over again to make you laugh? Don't cry, little one, it'll be over soon. Would you like a boiled sweet? Let's all have one. I bet your mummy would like one, wouldn't she? Would you like to unwrap it for her? Here we go, little one. Down it comes. Just like the helter skelter. All the way down. Hold on to me! Hold on to me tight! Just like the fair! Just like the funfair!'

The stewardess asked him if all that was on the blackbox? Dan said yes, if you listened very carefully. She thanked Dan for telling her that and upgraded John Heron with tears in her eyes.

## 394

Michael Davies sat in the tower and looked out over the runway systems. He gave the plane standing at the head of runway 4 clearance for take off. Someone asked him if he'd slept OK. Michael said he'd slept like a baby. Someone else said babies always woke up. Michael said he was fine. Someone said it was just that he looked a bit tired. Michael told everyone to shut up for Christ's sake.

## 393

The engines whined, the brakes were released and Beth, Dan and John shot down the runway feeling the vibrations under them disappear as the plane left the tarmac.

Beth was sick. She didn't mind that, though, it was a good distraction.

## 392

Michael watched the plane drift away through binoculars. He thought about guiding an approaching jumbo into its path, killing interfering, investigating passenger Dan Bronski. It would get his wife Beth, too, unfortunately.

Mind you...

There was an enormous jumbo coming in from Thailand. He could ram the two together. A great big fiery embrace in the sky.

At the first warning bell, Michael's supervisor led him away from the radar and into a restroom and told him to calm down. Michael asked him if he said the words 'duck' or 'gaffer' tape would his supervisor know what he was talking about? Michael was told to go home.

## 391

'Anything?' asked the pharmaceutical CEO.

'I'm still working on it...' said the ex-government agent.

'Come on, you jackass.'

'Just give me a minute, will you?'

'One name. Ten thousand dollars. Get moving on it.'

Click. The CEO put the phone down. The ex-agent didn't even get the chance to call him a piece of shit.

## 390

Upstate New York. The door of Clara Redlake's Worcester garage opened electronically. She waited till she could see enough daylight before pulling out of the garage, closing the door with a remote as she emerged. A kid delivering the papers watched her go and fell in love with her. Clara admitted that it was a pretty swish manoeuvre.

## 389

I was on the move too.

I checked out of the Hotel Monumental and left a ten dollar tip on the pillow. I had with me a tiny little bag. In it was a phone and a radio and a passport and all the money I could draw out of my bank.

The receptionist told me that it was their pleasure to have me staying with them. I thanked her and said my nights would never be as comfortable again. She smiled but thought that I was probably overdoing it.

I walked to the subway and boarded a train.

It moved quickly through its network of veins and arteries. I imagined I was an antibody. Or a bubble of compressed air about to give the city the bends. Or a gallstone being painfully passed.

## 388

Cody hit the motorway.

She rang Samuel from the fast lane. Asked him if he'd ever played 'Six Degrees of Kevin Bacon' in which actors are connected with other actors by their movie appearances.

Samuel said he'd never been in a film. He'd really only done commercials and voice overs.

Cody asked him to stay on the line anyway. For company.

## 387

Beth held the sick bag in her hand and tapped her feet and rocked forward and back. Skin at her irregular hairline prickled and her breath came in short shallow bursts making her dizzy. Making her sick again.

At times like this, she tried to think of individuals who would be more disturbed than she was, who would need her comfort if they were sat beside her. Beth tried to view the climbing plane through the eyes of Wilbur and Orville Wright. Would they be overwhelmed at the progress of air travel? Probably not. She recently discovered that there were two other Wright brothers, Reuchlin and Lorin, as well as a sister, Katherine. No one mentioned them much. Forgotten siblings. They didn't get flight. If they were beside her now, they would be absolutely terrified.

'There, there,' said Beth, 'there, there.'

## 386

Michael Davies drove around and around. This was the first time he'd been told to leave work. He thought his tenth place in the most stressful occupation league was a disgrace. He didn't reckon firemen had it worse, or CEOs, or fucking football players. He thought even the President of the United States had an easier ride. He certainly got more perks.

Michael called in to a bar and ordered a bloody Mary. It was the messiest drink he could think of.

## 385

Clara Redlake liked driving on America's roads. In the city she walked to marshal her thoughts but it was such a distracting place, it was hard to keep an idea in her head for long. Driving was different. A slowly transforming landscape. Road vibration keeping the mind humming.

Clara drove along Highway 88 towards New York, tuned in to the city's excellent talk shows.

## 384

Tamy asked her father where he was taking her for her birthday breakfast.

'What?'

'Never mind.'

'I said I'd take you for breakfast?'

'Never mind.'

'I've got to go to work.'

'It doesn't matter.'

The pharmaceutical CEO felt terrible. He got his housekeeper to fry up some bacon and a flask of coffee. Then he told Tamy to go and wait in the car.

'Check underneath!' he shouted after her.

## 383

I got out of the train in Brooklyn. Behind a warehouse building I met a man who smiled at me and shook my hand.

I sold him my passport for five hundred dollars and a passage to the next stage.

I was told not to mention my name to anyone. I said I wouldn't.

He asked was I warm enough. I said yes. He said why didn't I travel first class like most Manhattanites? I said I was paying a penance. He said a what? I said I was doing the right thing. He said fair enough. He couldn't care less.

He gave me an address and I got on the subway again.

## 382

Clara tuned the radio. She found another show discussing human experimenta- tion. It must be human experimentation day, she thought. A woman with a hoarse voice was saying how she had a tube up her nose that was fed down into one of her lungs, there was a one in two hundred chance of her suffering a major haemorrhage but she was paid two hundred dollars so she let them do it. A dollar per chance.

An ethical guy said researchers weren't allowed to pressure or induce subjects to take part in trials by offering them large amounts of money.

Clara didn't think two hundred dollars was all that large for a haemorrhage.


## 381

The pharmaceutical CEO drove chaotically through the traffic eating bacon out of a Tupperware box and handing Tamy bits of muffin.

'Is this it?' asked Tamy. 'This is my birthday breakfast?'

'Isn't this bacon good?' said her father and offered her a greasy streak. 'Mmm mm.'

'Drop me off.'

'What?'

'I'll walk to work.'

'What about our breakfast?' He hit a bump and spilt hot coffee over his trousers. He screamed.

'Here is fine,' said Tamy.

Her father stopped the car and kissed her on the cheek, trying not to wince in pain.

'There's some bacon in your beard,' she said.

'Happy birthday, Tamy,' he said. He started rifling in his wallet for some money.

'Don't do that,' said Tamy.

She got out and walked to the radio studio.


## 380

Cody found a Nirvana tape in the car. She rang Samuel again and asked him if he knew what Kurt Cobain had written in his suicide note. Samuel didn't know.

'I'm too much of a neurotic moody person and I don't have the passion any more, so remember, it's better to burn out than fade away. Peace, love, empathy.'

Samuel told her to concentrate on the road, and hung up.

## 379

Clara heard a research guy on the radio ask for volunteers to test an anti-ulcer drug. They'd have to give two blood samples and collect their urine for twenty-four hours in a four-litre bottle. They'd get twenty-five dollars for it. Other volunteers were required to allow blisters to be raised on their arms which would then be syringed and emptied over a twenty-four hour period. He didn't give a price for that and didn't recommend people signed up for both.

## 378

I found the bar I was supposed to wait in and I waited in it. I ordered tea but didn't drink it. I looked at everyone as they came in. Looking for someone to acknowledge me.

A man came in looking for someone. He saw me looking like someone who was looking for someone looking for someone, and he came over. He asked what I was drinking and I said tea. He ordered some too and asked if I was British. I said I was. He seemed surprised but made no comment. He said any friend of Michael Davies was a friend of his. I smiled weakly. He asked me if I knew what gaffer tape was. I told him it was thick adhesive tape that electricians used to stick down cables. He nodded. Then he drove me away in a green sedan.

## 377

The ex-government agent listed his priorities.

1.  Get Ali to give him the name of some, any, disturbed nutcase who might go around planting bombs under people's cars.
2.  Ring back the pharmaceutical CEO, give him the name of said nutcase and collect ten thousand dollars.
3.  Ask Ali if she knew any other lunatics who might be persuaded to blow up the pharmaceutical CEO, for cash, if necessary, once his guard was down.
4.  Ask her out.
5.  Get some more breakfast.

The ex-government agent felt the sun on his back and it felt good. He moved

'Ask Her Out' up to number two. Then to number five. Then he crossed it off his list altogether; what a dumb idea. He moved breakfast to number one instead and headed towards a diner.

## 376

Graham Johansson was sitting still. He smoked a cigarette and thought that, though he was stationary, he was sitting on a globe that was spinning pretty damn fast. Spinning around its axis at 1,040 miles per hour at its equator, slower at Johansson's present latitude. Johansson felt like spinning faster so he told himself that the earth was spinning round the sun at a speed of 18.5 miles per second. Johansson was aware that the solar system took roughly 250 million years to orbit the Milky Way once and in this orbit he was travelling at a velocity of 155 miles per second. He was aware of more to come but his mind wasn't up to the maths.

## 375

Even though commercial aircraft fly up to 35,000 feet, the cabin is usually maintained at pressures equivalent to an altitude of 6,000 to 7,000 feet. This is like travelling to some of the lower mountains near Denver. Furthermore, trapped air will expand, dissolved gas may leave solution, and definitive medical care is not readily available. High above the Atlantic, one is in a state of transient isolation. Coupled with a lower oxygen concentration, this often leads the brain to take, at the very least, a reflective course.

## 374

'Do you think that during the last moments of your life you are more yourself than at any other time?' asked Dan.

'No,' replied John.

'Do you think those last moments sum up your whole life?'

'No.'

'Would you think back over your life in those last moments?'

'Yes.'

'Would you think you'd fulfilled your potential?'

'No.'

'Have you got some regrets?'

'Some.'

'Are there times when you've let opportunities slip by?'

'Yes.'

'Are there times when you wished you'd grasped the nettle?'

'Yes.'

'Are there times when you wished you'd been braver?'

'Yes.'

'Have there been times when you wish you'd been a bit headstrong from time to time?'

'Yes.'

'Do you wish that now and again you'd said "Damn the consequences"?'

'Yes.'

'In the last moments of your life, would things which seemed like big worries at the time suddenly feel not so big any more?'

'Probably.'

'Would you feel silly for worrying about little things?'

'Yes.'

'Have you wished you hadn't worried about making a fool of yourself?'

'Yes.'

'Do you wish you'd danced on more tables?'

'Yes.'

'Do you wish you'd seen more places?'

'Yes.'

'Kissed more people?'

'Yes.'

'Drunk more champagne?'

'Yes.'

'Run faster.'

'Yes.'

'Shouted louder.'

'Yes.'

'Danced harder?'

'Yes.'

'Have there been times in your life which were so exciting you could have said, "I could die happy now"?'

'No.'

'Would you think that if you survived the crash you'd do some of those things?'

'I probably would think that.'

'Do you wish you'd been kinder?'

'Yes.'

'Have you ever wished you had children?'

'Yes.'

'Would you wish you'd had children as the plane was crashing?'

'No.'

'You'd be glad you didn't have to put them through this?'

'Yes.'

'Is it possible to be kind as a plane is crashing?'

'Yes.'

'Have you been in love?'

'Yes.'

'Do you wish you'd been more passionate?'

'Yes.'

'Do you wish you'd written more love letters?'

'Yes.'

'Do you wish you'd made love more times?'

'Yes.'

'Is it possible to fall in love while a plane is crashing?'

'I don't know.'

'I don't know either.'

## 373

I don't know. I headed south in the green sedan. The driver stopped by a hardware store and told me to give him ten dollars. He disappeared into the shop and came out with a roll of what he called duck tape. Then he started laughing. I asked what was so funny and he said he was just following instructions. I asked if there was any change from the ten dollars but he said no.

## 372

'Now that you've answered those questions. What do you think your last words will be?'

'I don't think I'm any further on,' said John.

'Has it not helped?'

'Not really.'

Dan looked at him.

'No. No, it probably hasn't.'

Dan drank some more booze.

'Do we have to talk about this?' asked John.

'It's one of my daughter's questionnaires. Thought it might be useful.'

## 371

Beth sat in the plane's toilet and hummed 'Don't Fence Me In'.

She breathed deeply. Dan knocked on the toilet door and asked if she was OK. Beth looked at her hands. They shook. She asked Dan if an air crash investigator had ever died in a plane crash. Dan didn't think so. Beth said in that case she was glad Dan was aboard. Dan said he was glad too.

He asked her if she thought it was possible to fall in love while the plane was crashing.

Beth thought anything was possible but it would seem a terrible waste if it happened at that moment.

## 370

John asked if there were such things as blackbox recorders for passengers.

Dan said there weren't.

John thought that was a shame. There should be one installed in each seat, just where they had TVs. That way, precious last sentiments could be recorded. Much better than pen and paper where the writing would get rather shaky.

Dan thought it would be bad for consumer confidence.

John thought the opposite. He thought individual blackboxes would be good for solo passengers, just in case they found themselves next to a stranger who meant nothing to them. They could record a message to a loved one, or to humanity. It would be a valuable contribution to the understanding of the human condition.

Dan said it was hard to know what would pop into your head in those moments. Could be anything.

## 369

The green sedan parked up in a side street. I was told to wait in the car.

The driver went into a building. Ten minutes later he returned with another man. This new man asked for more money. I said I'd paid already. And I'd bought duck tape. There was a big argument about money generally so I paid up another five hundred dollars. That wiped me out but I guess it didn't really matter any more.

We all got back in the car and hit the road again.

'Got any music?' I asked.

They played something Cuban.

## 368

'Once,' said Dan, 'in a crash site in Australia, I found a receipt from a supermarket. I was surprised that this tiny piece of paper was legible when there were some full-grown solid people who'd been burnt to a crisp. But somehow this scrap of paper had survived. It showed details of purchases made the day before. A magazine. Chewing gum. Water. Baby wipes. Boiled sweets. Miniature toothpaste. Deodorant. And painkillers. I remember thinking that this was obviously an experienced passenger preparing for a flight. On the bottom of the receipt were the words, "You were served today by Nemone Cooper, if you have any comments about today's shopping trip, please let me know." Nemone. This was the first time I'd heard the name. I wondered what Nemone looked like. Or if she remembered the passenger when she opened up her newspaper and read about the crash. I wondered if Nemone and this passenger had chatted at the cash till. Maybe they discussed Melbourne, or Australia in general. Maybe Nemone asked if the passenger was going with someone special. Perhaps it was Nemone who suggested buying the painkillers. After all, you can pick up all sorts of infections on aeroplanes. Something to do with the air conditioning. There were earplugs on the receipt too. They might have joked about getting stuck beside a crying baby or an insurance salesman and had a laugh together about this. Perhaps this little exchange kept Nemone smiling even after the passenger left the shop. Perhaps the passenger smiled too. Perhaps the passenger smiled again as she looked in her bag of sweets during the in-flight film and remembered her conversation with Nemone. I wonder if Nemone was the last person this passenger thought of before she died. And if the memory of Nemone's smile was, in that moment, stronger than any other memory.'

## 367

The ex-government agent arrived at a diner and ordered French toast and coffee and pancakes and said, 'Leave the menu.' The waitress looked at him and wondered whether he was another runner. They'd had a few of those recently. He made a show of flashing his ID and she seemed happy.

When his food arrived he rang Ali.

Her phone was still switched off so he left a message.

'It's me Miss Bronski. Sorry for shouting "Got you" before. Bit brutal, didn't mean to startle you. I need you to give me a name. Anyone really. Someone on the edge, though, someone who might do something stupid which harms other people. Nothing will happen to them. Well, they might get arrested, but they'll be released and you never know, it might actually do them some good. Make them rethink... I don't know, you're the expert. Anyway, give me a call. Quick as you can 'cos there's this piece of shit... you don't need to know this. OK then... um... yep... so... OK, so do you want to go to a movie? Nothing heavy. Actually, forget it. Just give me the name. Unless you do want to go to a movie. No, fuck this. Call me.'

He switched off his phone and wolfed down his pancakes blushing furiously.

## 366

'You'd utter Emma's name if the plane started crashing?'

'Almost certainly.'

'Say something tender?'

'Absolutely.'

'When did you last see her?'

John thought back. He had refused to give her a lift to the airport and she was grumpy about it.

'Week and a half ago.'

'Did you say goodbye to her?'

'Yes.'

'Did you leave things badly?' asked Dan.

'Not badly exactly.'

'Blandly?'

'Well...'

'Could've been better?'

'Yes.'

'Have you got a photograph of her?'

'In my luggage in the hold.'

'No good to you if we start ditching.'

'No.'

'Would you try to conjure up her face in your mind?'

'Yes.'

'How does she look?'

The kite photo.

'She's laughing.'

'Would you try to transmit a thought to her?'

'Yes.'

'Would you wonder if she knew what danger you were currently in?'

'Yes.'

'Perhaps she would have a terrible premonition?'

'I think she would feel something, yes.'

'Do you imagine her suddenly stopping what she was doing, looking pale because of the premonition, and being asked by friends if anything was the matter?'

'Yes.'

'Do you imagine her saying, "No, everything's fine, I just felt strange for a moment"?'

'Yes.'

'Perhaps she'd be given a chair and a glass of water.'

'Perhaps.'

'Do you imagine her receiving the news and having her worst fears realised?'

'Yes.'

'Have you seen her cry before?'

'Yes.'

'Was it over a silly little thing?'

'Yes.'

'Would it seem like such a small thing in comparison to now?'

'Yes.'

'Did she feel better quite quickly after that time?'

'Yes.'

'But she wouldn't this time?'

'No.'

'She'll be devastated?'

'I hope so.'

'Will you cry for her because she's so upset?'

'Yes.'

'It will be a terrible shock, how will she cope?'

'I don't know.'

'Will she wander around the empty house?'

'Yes.'

'Will she touch all your old things?'

'Yes.'

'Smell your clothes?'

Tears started running down John's face.

'Time heals, though, doesn't it, John?'

'I think so.'

'Do you think over time she'll get better eventually?'

'Yes.'

'Do you want her to get better eventually?'

'I don't know.'

'Do you want her to get over it?'

'Um.'

'Do you want her to recover and pick herself up?'

'I don't know.'

'Do you want her to laugh and meet someone new in the future?'

'No.'

'Do you hope that if she met someone new she'd call him by your name by mistake?'

'Yes.'

'Do you hope that you'd never be forgotten?'

'Yes.'

'Do you think that you would be forgotten?'

'Yes.'

'Do you hate her for forgetting you?'

'The ungrateful cow!' wailed John.

## 365

The ex-government agent was feeling sick what with the pancakes and the cinnamon toast and the croissants which the waitress had persuaded him to try. His trousers gripped his waist and he felt the need to go up a shirt size. He took a pill which was supposed to control his blood pressure but reckoned the coffee would dilute any of its helpful effects. Reverse it probably. Piece of shit pharmaceutical companies.

His phone cheeped. He lunged for it, knocking his coffee over his trousers.

'Ow, shit! Hello? Ali?'

A waitress came over and started to dab the table and then his crotch with a cloth.

'Give me a name,' said the pharmaceutical CEO.

'I'm fucking working on it you piece of shit.'

The waitress stopped mopping and smiled at the ex-government agent. She'd wanted to call her boss a piece of shit when he scolded her about customers who ran out without paying.

'I'll have you a name within the hour, now piss off and get the money ready.'

He switched the phone off and prayed for Ali to ring. He wished he hadn't asked her to go to the movies. What was he? Twelve years old? And what was this waitress grinning at?

## 364

'I didn't mean to say that,' said John.

Dan said if he wanted a personal blackbox he could always borrow his Dictaphone.

John said he thought he'd leave it.

Dan said that if John had shouted 'The ungrateful cow' as his last words, it would have gone in at number one in his top ten plane crash last words.

John asked him what his top ten was.

Dan said:

10. Up. Up.
9. Hang on! (said as an instruction).
8. Hang on ... (said quizzically).
7. I don't think I've seen that before.
6. If you could do that quickly, it would help.
5. What a shitty ... why is this doing this?
4. Yes. I'll try. It's a good idea.
3. Well well well well.
2. We're OK. OK now.
1. Jesus. I don't know what to say.

## 363

'More toast?' asked the waitress.

'God, no,' said the ex-government agent.

He started spending his ten thousand dollars in his head. He'd buy a car so that he could stop using the subways. He could drive over to Ali's place, wherever the hell that was, and take her out into the country. He'd wear a snazzy linen suit and sunglasses and impress her with tales from the Agency. She could wear a summery dress which was all short and showed off her thighs and perhaps a bit of cleavage. Her hair could waft around 'cos he'd bought an open-topped car. She'd have put lipstick on and perfume. She might lean over and put her fingers inside his shirt and nibble his ear.

The ex-government agent got up awkwardly from the table and asked where the restroom was.

## 362

Graham Johansson also had a top ten, or bottom ten flights.

10. Turbulence approaching Dallas, biting his tongue, getting blood on his shirt.
9. Food poisoning above the Pacific.
8. Stacking over Heathrow, running out of fuel, thinking air traffic control had forgotten about him.
7. Someone he was at school with recognising his voice and being shown into the cockpit. This person used to flick his ears in maths class and demand money off him.
6. A fighter pilot who'd seen action in the Gulf War calling him a flabby, shit-eating dumbo jumbo flyer.
5. Pissing his pants above France.
4. A near miss and the cold sweat.
3. A struck-off doctor trying to perform a heroic in-flight tracheotomy using only a coat hanger and brandy: he was hoping it would restore his reputation and bring him back to the profession. Botching it.
2. Dropping a stowaway out over woods.

His number one was the same as Dan Bronski's. The runaway winner. Chicago '87. 'Jesus. I don't know what to say.' A plane he hadn't even been on.

## 361

Dr Frankburg's office was full of paper planes. A foot deep. He started making the Birmingham Unhappy into paper hats and boats.

## 360

Michael Davies, now quite drunk, sick and guilty with stowaway complicity, drove into town and parked his car outside a record shop. He ran in, grabbed a Frank Sinatra tape and ran out without paying. He drove powerfully away.

'Jesus. I don't know what to say.'

A calm voice almost. Clear.

It was his Mrs Johansson. Sally Johansson.

Her plane hit the runway at two hundred and fifty miles an hour. Johansson saw it all from the observation lounge. The 737 twisting and weaving. It was like a cheap remote-controlled plane being badly steered by an inexperienced child. Except when it hit. Then it was a very grown-up ball of flames. No one was going to walk away from that.

He'd bought some flowers. She had been urging him to put some effort in. They didn't see each other enough. He didn't try as hard as she did. She told him she wondered why she bothered sometimes. Graham told himself he'd better pull his finger out or else she'd leave.

He'd bought some perfume as well as the flowers. He'd got the shop to wrap it up for him. The perfume was called *Forever* and he was going to joke that it'd gone off. Try and make her laugh.

He watched the fire engines and ambulances tear after the bouncing wreckage. They covered it in foam when it came to rest.

Flight 283 coming back from Barbados. She had always wanted to go to Barbados. She'd told him that she might even get a bit of a tan, despite her pale skin. Her lovely pale skin.

'Jesus. I don't know what to say.'

He wasn't himself after that. Who would be?

His mother had kept a diary. January 2nd, Graham withdrawn. Jan 3rd, Graham quiet. Jan 4th, Graham off his food. February, Graham ashen. Graham tearful. March, Graham angry. Graham abusive. April, Graham drunk. May, Graham missing. June, Graham letting himself go. July, Graham cruel. August, Graham apologetic. September, Graham tired. October, Graham eats. November, Graham smiles at a joke. Perhaps he's turned the corner.

He hadn't though. Not really.

'Jesus. I don't know what to say.'

It was just a voice and he listened over and over again and he wanted to read something into those last words and there was nothing.

Sally Johansson didn't shout out his name. She didn't cry for the two of them. She didn't wail for their lost life together. Shout for God. Shout for him. She didn't know what to say.

He wanted something more.

Goodbye, Graham.

I love you, Graham.

But it wasn't there. He didn't hear that.

## 358

But she might have been thinking it. He just had to hope she was thinking it.

## 357

Frankburg made a paper swan. Then he unfolded it and read it.

The client was a nurse who felt uncomfortable with medicine and didn't understand drugs so went off to be a fake nurse on a television programme. She did a convincing injection, she looked good crying, she could hit a mark. So she'd decided to quit nursing to be a TV star.

In Frankburg's scrawling writing: nice legs, what's the problem here?

The nurse had a patient with appendicitis who then developed peritonitis and was kept in. She had tubes up her nose and a yo-yo temperature. She would get feverish and dream intensely. She'd shout and disturb the ward. One night the nurse woke her and calmed her down. But just as she left the dream, still confused, she looked at the nurse and touched her face and very gently stroked her hair. She sang her a lullaby. She told her that the nurse looked just like the woman she'd found in the woods. Dead as a doornail. Same hair, same face. The spitting image.

Frankburg wrote: what do you want me to do with this?

The client said she wanted to find her mother.

Frankburg said there were agencies which...

The client asked Frankburg if he had any children. Frankburg said he had a daughter. What did his daughter do? Frankburg didn't know. He said he hadn't spoken to her for a while. Frankburg hadn't been sure whether mentioning it was a good idea, sometimes clients lost faith in their therapists if they had a disastrous personal life. She asked if Frankburg loved his daughter. He said yes, of course. She asked him if he had ever lied to his daughter. He said probably. She advised him not to lie to his daughter. He said he thought it was his job to offer advice. She said you got it where you could.

Frankburg's notes finished at that point.

He wondered if there were any more notes, amongst the ditched planes.

He didn't think so. Sounded like a one-session wonder.

## 356

The green sedan pulled up outside a house. I was taken into a small lounge and told to take a seat. It was comfortably furnished but a little cold and there were pictures of the Madonna and child on the walls. Two Spanish children were inside watching TV. They said *hola* to me. I said *hola* back. I asked what they were watching. They said they were watching TV. My Spanish packed up so I just smiled. They offered me an animal cracker. They seemed very well brought up children. The sedan driver turned to leave.

'What shall I do?' I asked.

'Just wait,' I was told.

'How long?' I asked.

'Till someone comes to collect you.'

'How long will that be?'

'Soon.'

'How soon?'

'Just soon.'

## 355

I watched a cartoon with the Spanish kids. It was about a brain which flew into different heads with farcical results.

There was a brain chapter in *How Your Body Works*. I remember a guy in charge of its operations. A Blofeld in a big chair. He told the heart to keep pumping and told the liver to look sharp. He was in charge of memory too. A filing cabinet room. Manned by renegades. When files were lost, he sent them on missions around the body. They visited the nose to pick up the perfume of an ex-lover. Visited the guts to spasm at a bad mussel. They went outside the body of amputees, occupying the space where the arm or leg had been, sending phantom memories back to the brain. Spooking it. They burnt some files and threw the ashes away. If someone asked about it, they denied all knowledge. They burnt associated files too, just to be on the safe side. It was a rogue department and the guy in charge tore his hair out about it.

I may not be remembering this quite right.

## 354

Beth listened to *You Too Can Fly* in the plane's toilets. She rewound and listened and rewound and listened.

## 353

I fell asleep on the couch. The kids still watched TV. I asked them where their parents were.

'*Donde esta sus madre? Et padre?*'

They shrugged at me and turned back to the TV. Very philosophically, I thought. I dreamed.

## 352

...and here I am... as Beth rewound and listened.

Michael: 'AF 266, turn left, heading 130 on a southeast course.'

Johansson: 'Received.'

Michael: 'Cleared to 9,000'

Johansson: 'Received.'

Co-pilot: '... only a few minutes... hold on till then?'

Voice: '... upsetting the other passengers.'

Co-pilot: 'What's the matter with her?'

Voice: 'Just crying, they think she's crying because something's gone wrong with the plane.'

Beth rewound, tried to confirm.

Voice: '... ph upsetting the other passengers.'

Co-pilot: 'What's the matter with her?'

Voice: 'Just crying, they think she's crying because something's gone wrong with the plane.'

Rewind.

Voice: '...eph's upsetting the other passengers.'

Co-pilot: 'What's the matter with her?'

Voice: 'Just crying, they think she's crying because something's gone wrong with the plane.'

Rewind.

Listen for the word.

Voice: 'Steph's upsetting the other passengers.'

Co-pilot: 'What's the matter with her?'

Rewind.

Voice: 'Steph's upsetting the other passengers.'

Rewind.

'Steph's upsetting the other passengers.'

Rewind.

'Steph.'

Rewind.

'Steph.'

## 351

What do I want Beth to be thinking now?

I want her to be thinking fondly of me. Trying to remember some better times. Thinking about mucking around in the quarry near our house. Thinking about climbing trees.

I want her to be coming over to New York to talk to me. Perhaps she is. Perhaps she wants to patch things up. Perhaps she's got some old photos in her bag she wants to show me.

I won't be at home of course, but it would be nice to think this is what she might be doing.

## 350

Beth shouted to Dan from the toilets. He rushed up to the door.

'Are you all right?'

'Is this the stowaway tape?' she asked Dan.

'Yes,' said Dan, surprised. 'How did you know?'

'My sister was on the flight. You can hear them say Steph if you listen closely enough.'

'Do you need anything?'

'What a question.'

## 349

I dreamt about the Wright family. Lorin, Reuchlin and Katherine skulking and scowling as Orville and Wilbur get into the papers, as Orville and Wilbur are given awards, prizes, keys to the city.

I dreamt of an advertisement being placed in the *Evening Item* announcing another record attempt by the Wright Brothers. An enormous crowd gathers in anticipation. At three thirty in the afternoon two figures emerge, in spectacular, if overblown flying regalia, and are met by thunderous applause. Uncharacteristically, a large bucket is passed around by Katherine Wright, which is quickly filled with dollar bills and notes of an even high denomination.

Katherine looks uncomfortable and embarrassed by the skimpy costume she has been made to wear. The brothers, who have yet to take off their obscuring flying helmets and scarves look oddly ill at ease. One of them is swaying slightly and the crowd don't remember the other one being quite so short.

At the appointed time, the plane is wheeled to the edge of the run. The two brothers appear unfamiliar with its workings and the crowd soon become restless by what is evidently pointless fiddling and prevarication. At last, after a brief and angry exchange between them, the taller brother makes an announcement. He stands awkwardly and unsteadily on a wooden crate, pulls off his scarf and with his voice slurring from too much booze proudly announces the inaugural flight of Reuchlin Wright, and his sophisticated brother Lorin Wright, the older, less successful but infinitely more talented brothers of the OH SO FUCKING FAMOUS ORVILLE AND WILBUR, WHO COULD DAMN WELL GO AND FUCKING FUCK THEMSELVES! Though this would no doubt come as some disappointment to everybody, Reuchlin assures them that, assisted by the glamorous Katherine, he and Lorin would effortlessly outstrip the previous distance record currently held by their upstart idea-stealing brothers, and would more than likely fly into Canada.

With that, Reuchlin stumbles off the crate and attempts to crank up the propeller. Lorin is ordered to get off his fat arse and help, allowing the nearest bystanders a clear view of the streak of urine on his trousers. Shouting obscenities at the crowd and offering Katherine's body to the first man to get the damned plane started, the propeller suddenly spins into life, taking off two of Reuchlin's fingers and hurling Lorin into the rudder. With the engine spinning powerfully due to Orville's expert maintenance, the plane lurches along the runway, dragging Lorin and a screaming Reuchlin towards the fields beyond. In a few minutes they are all but lost from sight, a trail of crushed crops and broken fences marking their painful and wayward journey.

Beth has this dream too, sometimes. Twins are lucky like this.

## 348

'Can I do anything for you, Beth?' asked Dan, still standing faithfully at the door.

'I hope so,' said Beth.

I hope so too.

Beth isn't bringing photos to show me. She has in her bag hundreds of letters written by her husband Michael to me in New York and returned to sender. Each one painfully expressing Michael's preference for a different Wiltshire sister.

She looked at herself in the mirror and thinks about a different haircut, different clothes. She tried to remember what she looked like when she was fourteen.

Smooth.

'Are you still there, Dan?' she asked.

'Still here.'

'OK.'

'OK.'

## 347

John shouted to Dan from his seat. 'Last night I shot myself on stage. The audience were appalled. I've never heard a hush like it.'

'I'm sure,' said Dan.

'Now I'm thinking about a plane crash site being faked. Setting it up early in the morning in a public park. The police and firemen and investigators and rescue workers all standing round a charred and smouldering calamity, trying to deal with the horror of it. Crowds gathering. Suddenly the blackened bodies all stand up, picking bits of fake flesh from their bodies and taking a bow. Is there any merit at all in this image?'

Dan thought.

'No,' he said.

No, thought all the other passengers.

'There was once a well-known bullet catcher,' said John, 'who had an act in which he caught a bullet in his teeth from a gun fired by a member of the audience. So that the gunpowder didn't fire a real bullet, a catch was slipped surreptitiously by the performer before handing the gun to the volunteer. On this occasion the audience member knew how the trick was done and, in order to expose the bullet catcher, he refused to let him touch the gun before he was due to fire it. Astonishingly the bullet catcher allowed the act to continue knowing that the gun was primed and fully loaded. Why did he do this? Was he terrified that his secret would be exposed? Could he not stand the shame? Who knows. The volunteer hesitated and looked confused. He had expected the bullet catcher to call it off. 'Take a good aim and fire at me, sir,' cried the bullet catcher. The crowd, too, by this time was barracking this volunteer whose hand was shaking and sickly sweat could be seen breaking out over his face. 'Shoot,' they all shouted: 'Shoot the man.' Terrified and appalled that what had started out as a clever unmasking of the bullet catcher had turned into this horrifying spectacle, and with the crowd ringing in his ears, the volunteer shot the bullet catcher through the head, killing him instantly. Blood, screams, you can picture the scene.'

'Yes,' said Dan.

'Emma told me that story.'

'I'm not surprised.'

## 346

The ex-government agent sat in the toilet of the diner and tried to fantasise about Ali Bronski in a summery dress. The second he achieved a degree of tumescence someone rapped on the cubicle door.

'Give me a minute, will you?' said the ex-government agent.

'Goddammit, what are you doing in there?'

The ex-government agent's blood flow gave out and he decided to have a shit instead. Much more straightforward.

## 345

Ali Bronski read the address on Graham Johansson's note, got in a cab and told it to drive east.

The taxi driver told her that Manhattan adult residents hailed cabs an average of one hundred times per year. He himself was one of New York City's 11,787 medallion taxicabs. That was a cab for every six hundred odd people. He would average around thirty fares per shift. Nine out of ten drivers were immigrants speaking a total of sixty different languages, most commonly Urdu, Punjabi, Arabic, Bengali, Russian, German, Japanese, Twi, Ibibio and Estonian.

Ali asked him to say something in Twi. But he couldn't.

'What's your line of work?' the taxi driver asked Ali Bronski.

Ali said she was a pilot.

'No, really,' said the taxi driver.

Ali said she was a surgeon.

'Come on,' said the taxi driver.

Ali said she was a call girl.

The taxi driver still didn't believe her but wanted to this time. Ali told him to drive a bit faster.

## 344

At KKRC the receptionist had bought Tamy a cake. A production assistant had bought Tamy some bubbly. A sound engineer had bought Tamy some fancy knickers. Tamy took them into her producer's booth and thought they were all better gifts than her father's.

## 343

Ali Bronski arrived outside Penny Lock's apartment. She paid the taxi driver and switched on her phone. It beeped at her. She listened to the ex-government agent's message twice because he seemed to have his mouth full.

Ali Bronski buzzed 'P. Lock' and asked if she was the partner of Graham Johansson. Penny said yes. Ali said she'd had a message from Graham to call round. He might have some money for her.

Penny Lock let her in.

Ali asked her if she was the talk show host Penny Lock. Penny said yes and she ought to be getting to work.

'I love your show,' said Ali.

'Thank you.'

'"What Would It Take To Kill?" was profound.'

'Well, that's very kind.'

'I rang in myself once.'

'Did you really?'

'"Fight the good fight", I was the freedom fighter.'

'Oh God, really?'

## 342

Edward the Fireman stood outside a big glass-fronted building with a smashed vase at his feet. He was telling anyone who'd listen that it was an anniversary present for his GREAT LOVE. Passers-by gave him a look of sympathy. One or two gave him a couple of dollars. The smashed vase and the winning demeanour were supposed to be what was eliciting sympathy and money (tape eight) but what was mostly doing it was the blood from his wound, which was dripping onto the pavement.

## 341

'Fight the good Fight' had won Penny a small Talk Show Award. It was a statuette of a microphone, silver, and it took pride of place on Penny's dining table. Penny wondered if she was near enough to grab it in case she had to bludgeon Activist 345 in self-defence.

## 340

The ex-government agent had listened to 'Fight the Good Fight' with his heart pumping powerfully in his chest. His past employers had contacted him asking if this was his idea. He'd said no he didn't know anything about it. He didn't know who the woman was. They'd said they damn well hoped not as he could find himself in a lot of hot water.

The ex-government agent had given Ali one thousand dollars to do it and had spent the next week in the vicinity of the pharmaceutical CEO's house waiting for someone to blow it up. Or set fire to it.

## 339

Ali needed the money, and when the fireman rang in it seemed it wasn't such a depraved project after all. Ali's tears were genuine.

The ex-government agent wasn't quite as moved. He didn't like hearing grown men cry. Made him stick his fingers in his ears and go la la la la.

## 338

'So, Activist 345, how are you?' asked Penny with a nervous smile.

'I'm fine, you can call me Ali, though. I don't go by Activist 345 usually.'

'I understand.'

'It was a fake call. I didn't really do any of those things. It was phantom terrorism. Introducing concern in people without actually doing anything.'

'Right. I see.'

'I did it for money.'

'OK.'

'Mind you, there are a lot of small shareholders around who are normal, respectable people who wouldn't ever consider themselves a target of terrorism. Perhaps they might worry about getting caught up in a generalised attack, but would never think that they were being targeted individually. I think it's very unsettling to think that you might be, don't you?'

'Yes.' Penny scrolled through her own portfolio. Oil companies. Probably best not mention them.

'And that fireman guy sold his shares, didn't he?'

'No, he was a fake caller too, it turned out.'

'Really?'

'He didn't have any shares. He wasn't a real fireman either. He said he was in love. He asked for your address after the show. We said terrorists didn't give out their address. He said, "Of course, stupid of me".'

'Oh.'

'He was good though, wasn't he?'

They stood for a while thinking. Both of them feeling they'd been kind of duped.

'Do you want some coffee?' offered Penny.

## 337

Edward passed out on the pavement. He came to five minutes later to find his takings from his smashed vase trick gone. Lying on the ground he removed Clara's self-help tape from his Walkman and threw it into the road. Then he took the others out of his pocket and threw them into the road too.

A kid passed by and said, 'Don't you want these any more?'

'No,' said Edward.

The kid ducked between cars and picked them all up and took them away. Edward wanted to tell him they'd do more harm than good, but he didn't have the strength.

He tuned in the radio and listened to that. Just till he was strong enough to stand.

## 336

The ex-government agent returned from the diner's toilet to his table. The waitress asked him if he needed anything else, the lunch menu would start fairly soon. He said no.

On his phone was the message: calls missed – one. He stabbed its buttons.

'This is Ali. I think this better be the last time we speak. For what it's worth, I've just seen a man called Graham Johansson, a pilot who might fly his plane into the Atlantic Ocean. I wouldn't arrest him. Look what that did to you. And no, I wouldn't like to go to the movies but thank you for asking.'

## 335

'Graham came to see me last night,' said Ali Bronski.

'Really?' said Penny Lock.

'He asked me if I'd ever seen a suicide before.'

'And have you?'

'Yes. Graham asked me if he reminded me of the suicide I'd seen before.'

'And did he?'


## 334

Gentle thrashing. Bubbles. Struggling but so sluggish it looked like flapping or swimming.

Trying to be helpful. Trying to do the right thing.


## 333

'Not really, no.'

'That's good.'

'He finds it hard to fly since his wife crashed on the runway in Chicago. I think he's...'

Ali stopped talking. It was evident from Penny's face that she was unaware that Graham had been married.


## 332

Beth ripped up her return ticket. She didn't want to get on a plane again. She didn't want to go home again. She didn't want to see Michael again.

She ripped up his letters into tiny little pieces and flushed them down the aircraft's toilet.

Dan told her about a postman who kept every fourth letter he was supposed to deliver. Every fourth; he was very strict about it. There'd been love letters, bills, junk mail and postcards, job offers and dear Johns, rejections, good news and bad news, jokes, wedding invitations, notices of eviction, court orders and pay cheques, good luck cards and sorry to hear cards, letters to Santa. He'd amassed over sixty thousand pieces of mail. They'd been in the cargo hold of a doomed aircraft. The postman had been flying because he liked his destination's stamps. He'd wanted to read each letter on a beach in the sun, and construct a map of everyone's life. When the plane crashed, all the letters burst free of the hold and billowed into the sky. The breeze had taken them, and spread them, and they drifted to the earth in a cloud.

As Beth watched the plane's toilet flush suction suck the pieces away, she liked to think of them falling over the Atlantic and a fisherman in a little boat looking up and saying, 'It's snowing.'

## 331

Michael Davies was wandering around departures. He wanted to get hold of Rose the cleaner and tell her that instead of giving him *You Too Can Fly* she should have left it in her bin like she was damn well paid to do.

## 330

'Yes? Well?' said the pharmaceutical CEO.

'Graham Johansson,' said the ex-government agent.

'What?'

'I said Graham Johansson.'

'That's it?'

'That's it, that's your name.'

'He put a bomb under my car?'

'Almost certainly.'

'Almost certainly?'

'It's a pretty good shot.'

'How good? Give me percentages.'

'I'm ninety, maybe ninety-five per cent certain.'

'And that's the word from your Government pals?'

'That's it verbatim. From the horse's mouth. Now, the cash—'

'What is he? Some fucking Greenpeace kid?'

'No.'

'Drug addict?'

'I don't think so.'

'What is he then? Why does he hate me?'

'I don't know.'

'Is he animal liberation?'

'I believe he's a pilot.'

'A what?'

'An airline pilot.'

'You're kidding me.'

'No. Now, this money, I want it in unmarked—'

'You're telling me an airline pilot tried to blow me up?'

'Yes, so the bills should be no greater than—'

'What airline?'

'I don't know.'

'You don't know what airline he works for?'

'No.'

'Perhaps it's fucking Concorde.'

'I don't think it's Concorde.'

'Jesus.'

'So anyway—'

'He sounds Swedish, is he Swedish?'

'Um, yes.'

'You don't know.'

'I do know, he definitely Swedish.'

'He could be Danish. Or Finnish.'

'He could be but I don't think he is, I mean I know he isn't.'

'You're making it up.'

'I'm not making it up.'

'Who gave you this information?'

'I'm not at liberty to say.'

'This is shit.'

'It's a reliable source. That's the word, the word is Graham Johansson, a Swedish pilot, take it or leave it.'

'I'll leave it.'

'What?'

'A fucking airline pilot for Christ's sake.'

'Hang on—'

'What kind of information's that?'

'It's damn good information.'

'It's crap.'

'What about my money?'

'Sing for it.'

'You piece of shit!'

'Oh here we go.'

'You fucking piece of pissing shitty piss!'

'A Scandinavian airline pilot. Those well-known fanatics. Mother of God, what am I, an idiot?'

Click.

'Don't hang up on me you fucking piece of piss!'

Nothing.

The ex-government agent let out a howl.


## 329

The tyres screeched as Beth Davies, John Heron and Dan Bronski landed in the USA. They didn't hear the screech. Just felt the bump.


## 328

'Ali, give me another name. Please. Anything. Someone nuts. No fucking pilots. Oh, Jesus.'


## 327

I was woken by the door opening. The Spanish kids were still watching TV but the cartoons were over and it was a talk show. 'God Is Coming Between Us'. A fat man was weeping because his devout girlfriend wanted to 'wait'. The audience were of the opinion that God didn't come into it, and the girlfriend just didn't want his belly all over her.

The green sedan driver came into the house and gave the children some peanut confection. Perhaps he was their father. He gestured for me to follow. I walked outside. It was hot and humid. Choking. I was taken to another car.

'Has it got air conditioning?'

'This isn't business class, lady.'

He didn't need to take that tone. I'd paid about the same as business class. I was driven away.

## 326

Beth Davies, John Heron, and Dan Bronski queued at immigration control. Beth filled out her visa waiver and thought the USA sounded phobic. It feared visitors bringing communicable diseases. It had mysophobia: fear of contamination.

## 325

Someone brushed past John wearing Emma's preferred perfume. He watched her for a while. She looked nice. A part of John wondered what his life would have been like if he'd married her instead. Woke up with her. Went out to dinner with her. Got her to do the Indian rope trick. He'd have to get her to change her perfume though. She didn't look like she worked in a morgue either.

She sneezed and didn't cover her nose.

John went off her.

## 324

I was driven along a highway. I didn't look outside. I looked at an ashtray feature in the door. There was a butt inside. I wondered who had smoked it. Wondered whether it had been their last cigarette. It was smoked down to the filter and a bit beyond. I asked the driver for a cigarette. He didn't have any. Said it was bad for my health. Said it could give me bronchitis, emphysema, and it could damage my unborn child. I told him I wasn't pregnant. He asked if I wanted to be and laughed. He didn't have his stooge with him so the laugh just bounced around the car embarrassingly and soon died out.

## 323

'Business or pleasure sir?'

'Desperation,' said John Heron.

## 322

Michael Davies grabbed Rose the cleaner.

'You been drinking?' she asked.

'No,' he said.

'You smell like it.'

'I smell like lots of things.'

'You smell like you've been drinking.'

'Where did you get that tape you gave me?'

Rose said she'd been asked to put *Your Too Can Fly* in her bin.

Michael asked who gave it to her.

Rose said an old man.

Michael asked for more details.

Rose said that was all she could remember.

Michael cursed.

Rose thought it a very imaginative curse.

Michael said his life was turning to shit.

Rose said never mind. She said if he wanted to know more about the tape he should ask Angela. Angela worked at the check-in. Angela saw everything.

Michael ran to departures.

'Put on some cologne,' Rose shouted after him.

## 321

The car with me inside stopped outside a small house in a part of the city I didn't recognise. The driver got out and knocked on the door. Two people emerged. Both women. They got into the car and smiled nervously at me. I smiled back.

'OK, ladies?' asked the driver.

We all nodded.

He drove on.

'You're well wrapped up,' I said.

They smiled.

## 320

Michael stared at Angela's name badge.

He said, 'Do I know you?'

Angela said, 'Table tennis, broken car, Sinatra, six degrees of separation.'

She asked him how he was.

Michael said bad, but better for seeing her. He asked her how the table tennis was going.

Angela said she'd quit because a life in air travel sounded glamorous.

Michael apologised.

She said he had made his job sound like the choreographing of a ballet. As if he'd found a profundity which she'd failed to find in the exchange of plastic compound balls.

Michael again apologised. Said if it made her feel any better, there was a profundity in his job but it was a disgusting one. He said he must have been talking himself up.

Angela said it didn't matter. She said after she'd dropped him off that time, she'd driven straight to an incinerator plant and thrown her bat into a skip. The plant converted waste to electricity and she hoped that it would provide enough juice to power a runway light for a second or two. Help a plane home.

Ahh, said Michael.


## 319

Cody, sweaty from the drive, pulled up outside the coroner's office and entered. She was lucky, she was told, just in time, the office was about to close.

Cody asked for Kirsten's inquest tape. The assistant fetched it but mentioned that it was marked for the attention of Kirstien's long lost sister.

'That's OK,' said Cody, 'That's me.' It was a lie too far.

'I'm afraid I can't authorise this, you have to have a special interest to listen to the tape.'

'I do have a special interest.'

'What is it?'

'I want it.'

'That's not a special enough interest.'

'I really want it.'

'That still won't do.'

Cody didn't have time for this. She called the woman an administrative bitch.

The assistant took offence and told Cody that that sort of talk would get her ejected from the building. Cody told her to fuck herself, grabbed the tape out of her hands and ran like the wind.

## 318

Samuel Thorn went to Phoenix TV and got stuck in the lift.

## 317

Michael leaned against Angela's desk.

'Did Rose the cleaner mention anything about an audio tape yesterday?'

'Yes, but I didn't listen to it.'

'Why not?'

'I was too busy.'

'Did you happen to see who had thrown it away?'

'An old man.'

'Anything else?'

Angela didn't mind him looking at her provocative name badge.

Angela described Ronald Henderson. Said he was with a woman called Emma Heron who came back later having lost Ronald in front of a train, and her shoe somewhere else.

Michael asked Angela if she knew who'd win The Derby. Angela laughed.

Michael said Emma Heron sounded like the woman he nearly ran over in an underpass.

Angela laughed again but thought as a flirtatious line it wasn't up to some of his earlier ones.

## 316

The driver stopped by the side of the road and told me and the two other women to get out. We were led across a patch of grass until we came to a perimeter fence. He told us all to keep low as he snipped the wire.

I said I'd be Steve McQueen and who did everyone else want to be. No one replied. Perhaps they hadn't seen the film. I was told to keep my mouth shut.

## 315

Graham Johansson ordered gin in a bar in Manhattan. He would be flying SA 109 in barely three hours so he really shouldn't be drinking.

## 314

Cody Jameson jumped back into her stolen car and drove away. She headed for the M40. She planned to drive back to Birmingham and listen to the inquest tape on the way. The car had a good stereo. Speakers in every door. She'd get every sniff and whimper.

## 313

'Ronald Henderson's answermachine is full,' said PC Queely's opposite number in Edinburgh. 'The machine only allows a maximum of three minutes per message. So he's filled up the tape with fifteen three-minute messages.'

'What does he say?'

'It's a confession.'

'Could you play it to me?'

'Over the phone?'

## 312

The coroner's assistant told herself she wasn't an administrative bitch. She had rent to pay. Very high rent. She had to do her job well. Be keen. Get in early. Work weekends. Stay smart and attractive. Hide her asthma. Get felt up on the tube. Put off breeding till she earned enough. Buy tissues to remove the black snot. Keep her windows shut. Look at pictures of the seaside...

## 311

Samuel Thorn was rescued from the lift by the *Graft* casting woman.

'I'm sorry,' she said. 'I thought it'd stopped doing that.'

'It's because of me,' said Samuel, gloomily.

'We aren't going to be letting anyone know about *Graft* until tomorrow so...'

'I'm not here about that,' said Sam. 'I was wondering if you still had the unedited tapes from *Tunnel Vision?*'

'Oh.' Her eyes flicked towards a door marked Edit 2.

There Sam found the work experience girl playing with cross-fades.

'This is Jenny,' said the casting woman.

'Hi,' said Jenny. 'Sorry you didn't get the part.'

'Don't say that, Jenny. We aren't letting people know until tomorrow.'

'I thought you were great but—'

'Yes, thank you, Jenny,' said the casting woman.

'Bit of bad karma what with your track record—'

'Jenny's been learning how to edit,' said the casting woman quickly.

'And she's learning on *Tunnel Vision* footage?' said Sam.

'Well...'

'I thought they still had plans for it.'

'Oh...'

'I've put together the whole series,' offered Jenny. 'The last three don't make much sense and involve a lot of flashbacks, like the last Pink Panther film, but with imagination I think it works. I think we could broadcast it.'

'I don't think so, Jenny.'

There was an awkward pause all round.

'So I guess you know the footage pretty well, then?' said Sam.


## 310

Cody slipped the inquest tape into the stereo.

The coroner opened proceedings by introducing himself and giving a general note about the purpose of the inquest.

Cody skipped ahead.

The production assistant who'd discovered Kirsten Henderson was giving testimony. She sounded young, still rather upset by the whole affair. She said she'd been asked to pick Kirsten up for that day's filming at eight o'clock in the morning but that Kirsten hadn't answered the door despite quite hard knocking. She tried ringing her phone but she hadn't answered. The production assistant had become so concerned that she called the hotel manager.

The hotel manager had opened Kirsten's door and the discovery had been made...


## 309

*Tunnel Vision* footage.

Two shot. Sam with Kirsten Henderson. Waiting for the cue.

Director: 'OK, stand by everyone. Actors ready?'

Kirsten: 'Yes.'

Sam: 'Yes.'

Clapperboard in.

Clapperboard boy: '*Tunnel Vision* Ep. Two scene five, take two.'

Snap.

Director: 'And ... action.'

Small pause.

Sam: 'Well, I guess one thing's certain.'

Kirsten: 'What?'

Sam: 'Gives new meaning to the phrase the shit hits the fan.'

Kirsten: Laughs.

Small pause.

Director: 'OK and good, not bad, sound OK?'

Sound man: 'Yep.'

Director: 'OK, cut.'

## 308

PC Queely listened to Ronald Henderson's confession. Played through a Dictaphone down the telephone wires.

Pip. 'Concealment is impossible. You can try and cover your tracks but it'll always slip out some way or another. Someone's always recorded you, watched you, documented you. You can never keep things hidden away. Never try it. It's futile. A stowaway, how stupid is that? A stewardess on a crusade. Can't ... I was supposed to be a bloody doctor. I was supposed to cure people. You ever been to China? Anyone here been to China? <muffled voices responding, one male one female> No? No one been? It's a piece of piss these days, you can get package holidays to ride your bloody bikes along the Great Wall, eat in bloody McDonald's ...' beep beep.

## 307

Cody. Eighty miles an hour. Volume up high.

... Kirsten was discovered in the bath. Full to the brim with water. She had drowned herself.

Initially the police thought it must have been an accident, or worse. After all, indoor drowning? It seemed unlikely...

## 306

Director: '...OK, so we've got that one in the bag, I want to do one more, just to give us another option. Mark it.'

Clapperboard in.

Clapperboard boy: '*Tunnel Vision* Ep. Two scene five, take three.'

Director: 'Hang on. Actually, Kirsten, rather than laugh, could you look a bit disgusted?'

Kirsten: 'Disgusted?'

Director: 'Yeah, you know, like he's just stepped over the mark, might be a bit funnier.'

Kirsten: 'OK.'

Director: 'That OK with you, Sam?'

Sam: 'Sure.'

Director: 'OK then.'

Cameraman: 'Still rolling.'

Director: 'Mark it.'

Clapperboard in.

Clapperboard boy: '*Tunnel Vision* Ep. Two scene five, take three.'

Snap.

Director: 'Action.'

Small pause.

Sam: 'Well, I guess one thing's certain.'

Kirsten: 'What?'

Sam: 'Gives new meaning to the phrase the shit hits the fan.'

Kirsten: Pulls disgusted face.

Small pause.

Director: 'Good. I think that works, that might be better actually. OK, let's get a close up on that, Kirsten's face.'

Another voice: 'Kirsten, just quickly, Ali Bronski rang, she's in London tonight and wants you to ring her to meet if you get the chance.'

Kirsten: 'Right, thanks.'

Cameraman: 'Do you want me to cut this?'

Director: 'What? Oh yes, cut.'

## 305

Pip. '…I'm changing my will. I'm doing it now. I bought a kit from a stationers. Do-it-yourself wills. Cost me a fiver. I used to have a proper one. Drawn up by a solicitor and I left everything to Kirsten. No point now is there. That was money down the toilet. I'm writing it out now in this taxi cab. I don't have much and the executor shall be Emma <muffled 'What's your second name?' Muffled reply, 'Heron.' 'Like the bird?' 'Yes.'> Shall be Emma Heron. Emma here's a morgue attendant. You're at home with dead people, aren't you? Actually, perhaps you aren't the best person, I don't think you're long for this world, are you, Emma? How about you, cabby? Fancy it? No? Does anyone here believe in God? Emma? <muffled 'No.'> How about you driver? <muffled reply, indiscernible> So I guess no one here has any idea whether I'm going to a better place? I understand God has a problem with suicide. You wouldn't push me in front of a train, would you, Emma? I mean it might give me a better chance <muffled 'No.'> How about you, driver? <muffled 'No.'>'

Beep beep.

## 304

…Following an analysis of the contents of Kirsten's stomach during the autopsy, Kirsten, confirmed the coroner, had taken enough sleeping pills to knock herself comprehensively unconscious, and then, before the pills took effect, she switched on the bath taps to a slow stream, lay in the bath with her head resting on the bottom and her legs draped over the end and waited to fall asleep…

## 303

Kirsten, time coded, alive and well, big smile. A funny little squeal when she yawned. Said 'Bless you,' if anyone sneezed. Dark eyes.

Samuel Thorn wondered who Ali Bronski was.

## 302

Pip. '... it's an organised business too, the stowaway racket. There's people out there who, for a premium rate, will show you to the undercarriage, wrap you up warm, and give you a blindfold for the journey. You can go club class too. You get bloody peanuts and earplugs. I could have done it myself, an old man. One call to Michael Davies and it's a one-way trip to freedom via Hypothermia Air. That kind of luxury wasn't around twenty years ago. I should have gone to China now, would've been much easier. Mind you, I wouldn't've got Lin impregnated now, no sap left, dried up. Bloody good thing too. The world is a better place without Henderson spawn running around the place. <muffled protest 'Don't be too hard on yourself'> Well, what am I supposed to think? <muffled query, male voice> Yes, here's fine, keep the change <'Too much'> Well, I don't bloody need it, do I?...' Beep beep.

## 301

... By the time the water covered Kirsten's head, the pills had done their trick and the police could detect no sign of violence or forced entry or a thrashing struggle in the bathroom.

The overflow prevented the bathroom from being flooded and the dead Kirsten was not discovered until the following day. The coroner noted, mainly for the benefit of Mr Henderson who was present at the inquest, that Kirsten would have suffered only temporarily...

## 300

Pip. '... Lin's trouble was that she didn't have any patience, I'm saying patience here, not patients, though she had patients too once. She couldn't wait. I consider patience the most important virtue. Alongside honesty and chastity. What do you think Emma? <'I think impatience can sometimes be a good thing too'> Well, you have your own view. Why don't you buy us both a coffee? <'I'm going to leave you to it'. Sound of Ronald being kissed> Good luck to you too, my dear. <small pause> I'm looking at the clock and the goods train is coming in three minutes' time. Waiting for a train is so tedious, isn't it? Perhaps I could read another exciting chapter of *Tales of a Stewardess*. I could read about the thrill of serving cocktails to film stars, or clearing up the sick of diplomats. I can hardly wait for *More Tales of a Stewardess*. Can't wait for the chapter about killing people's wives. I actually can't wait for that as the train will be here in two minutes thirty seconds, two minutes twenty-five seconds…'

## 299

The coroner called Alison Bronski.

Miss Bronski had a good strong voice. The coroner sounded smitten.

Miss Bronski had been the last person to see Kirsten alive.

Miss Bronski said that she had gone to see Kirsten to retrieve a collection of blackbox tapes which Kirsten had stolen from Dan Bronski, her father, while at a party at his house at some point during the previous year.

'Did you know why she had stolen these tapes?'

Ali said she had been looking for a recording of AF 266, the flight which she had discovered her mother had been on. She had listened over and over to AF 266 and Kirsten had told her that she had detected a knocking which, in Kirsten's mind, was the knocking of her mother banging ferociously on the undercarriage.

'It was the sound of a lost parent. Faint. Muffled. Meaningless. Perhaps just a glitch in the tape. But the only real sound she'd ever heard. She played it to me. I couldn't hear it but I told her that I could.'

## 298

Graham Johansson told Kirsten that he could hear it too. She'd tracked him down from flight records, written to him at the airline and her letter had made its circuitous journey to his home address. He arrived at her hotel room before Ali and she gave him gin and headphones and played him AF 266. Could he hear thumping? He asked her to play it again. Kirsten watched him with such hopeful intensity that Graham said yes, it was possible that there was a thumping which could be from someone banging the undercarriage. She thanked him. She asked him if the thump thump thump was Morse code. Graham couldn't say. She told him that when he had walked down the aisle of AF 266, saying nice things to the passengers, asking how everyone was, he'd have walked over her mother. Graham said that was true. He said was there anything else he could do for her. She said no, she had another guest coming.

## 297

'What happened after that, Miss Bronski?'

'She said she wanted to be alone so I took the tapes and I left.'

'That was all?'

Pause.

'That was all?'

Pause.

'Yes.'

## 296

'...My wish is to be cremated <muffled approaching roar> and I want the ashes pissed on by a dog and flushed down the toilet of some big polluting jumbo by a stewardess who fucks a co-pilot while she does it <roar intensifies> and I want the ashes to mix with the puke and shit and then freeze into an ugly lump <Ronald has to shout> and then drop onto a fucking cruise ship sailing the Atlantic where it'll smash through the casino killing someone who thinks that their luck has changed, someone who thinks they've hit the fucking jackpot, someone who thinks their life is fine and dandy, someone who calls herself Cody Jameson! Tales of a fucking Stewardess. DON'T THINK I DON'T KNOW WHO YOU ARE! <loud bang, screech, crackle> beep beep.

## 295

...

## 294

...

## 293

...Hmm...

## 292

Graham Johansson ordered another gin.

Kirsten had had dozens of tapes, and she knew them all, almost off by heart. If you gave her two seconds of any of them she could tell you the flight.

'Oh Christ, get me another bag': TransGlobe 18, outbreak of food poisoning.

'Goddammit, I can't see!': Greenways 343, man burst into the cabin and seized the controls.

'What reading have we got for—': Jerwood Air 987, clipped a mountaintop.

Graham asked her if she had Chicago '87 and she said of course. It was one of her favourites. And she played it to him.

'Jesus. I don't know what to say.'

That was the first time he heard it.

Kirsten said, 'Isn't that beautiful? It's the only female voice on here.'

Graham said it was his wife, and he started to shake violently. Kirsten gave him brandy. Then she emptied the mini fridge.

She said he'd taken it pretty well. He said it was the most terrible thing he'd heard in his entire life.

Kirsten said it was better than thump thump thump.

Graham said, but not as good as 'Graham, oh Graham!'

## 291

PC Queely contacted the airport and requested that Michael Davies be brought in for questioning. He was surprised to find that Cody Jameson really was the last thing on Ronald Henderson's mind as he jumped, although the pushy woman who'd rung him up probably expected a better dedication.

## 290

The ex-government agent sat at his table in the diner and wept. He rang up the pharmaceutical CEO but got the answerphone.

'Boris Vlamenkov, that's who did it, Where's my ten grand?'

Two minutes later he rang again.

'Asif Khan, there's another name. The price is now twenty grand.'

And again.

'Mister fucking Kermit the Frog. He bombed your shitty car. Give me some money. A million. I want a million so I can drive Ali Bronski around in a big car and look at her legs.'

The waitress gave him the bill. The ex-government agent bolted for the door, the waitress's curses ringing after him.

## 289

Penny Lock asked Ali Bronski to guest on her show.

'As Activist 345?'

'No, as yourself. You're a counsellor, aren't you?'

'I don't think I'm a very good one.'

## 288

Happy birthday to you. Happy birthday to you. Happy birthday, dear Taaaaam-mmmmyyyy. Happy birthday to you.

'Too kind,' said Tamy, smiling.

## 287

Penny Lock introduced Ali Bronski to Tamy.

Tamy shook her hand and said it's always interesting to have a professional therapist on the show and said how much she was looking forward to her contributions.

Tamy said it was her birthday.

'Happy birthday,' said Ali.

'Thank you,' said Tamy.

Tamy asked Ali if, in a break, she could have a quick word with her about her father who was putting his stressful career as a pharmaceutical giant before his family.

Ali told Tamy to get addicted to sleeping pills. That would elicit both attention and guilt.

Tamy said, 'Um. Thanks,' and showed her into the studio.

That day's Penny Lock Phone-In subject was 'Where are you?' Missing persons.

Penny had a small studio but it was light and airy. A heavily sound-proofed window gave a spectacular view of the Hudson River. On the wall was a whiteboard with the words 'Don't forget to plug the Christmas special' written in black marker. There was a big swivel chair, executive style, on which Penny sat.

She had a console, similar to the one Dr Chekov used to fly the *Starship Enterprise*. Low tech. Big buttons. From here she played jingles. There was a microphone on an adjustable stand. Like an Anglepoise lamp. The day's papers were piled on an adjoining table. Tamy had bought them all and found the bomb attempt on her father's car in all but the *National Enquirer*. Tamy was eight times described as '…with one daughter'.

The guest chair was a bit raggedy. Guests with sharp keys in their pockets had bobbled and torn it.

Ali's microphone had a green foam covering which had a small hole in it, as if someone had bitten it.

The clock was analogue not digital.

Tamy was behind a screen. She offered callers to Penny via a monitor.

'Have you ever been in a radio studio before?' asked Penny.

'Yes,' said Ali.

Penny was hoping that she'd say no and feel more overwhelmed by the glamour of the situation.

## 286

The ex-government agent ran four blocks them vomited half-digested pancakes, croissants, egg, bacon, coffee, French toast, hash browns and orange juice in the doorway of a department store. It poured out of him. Seemed to go on for ever.

## 285

Penny waited for the cue.

## 284

Check-in Angela thought she was on to a good thing. Michael Davies was chatting to her in a way which, through her observation of airport courtship rituals, suggested there was some future in the relationship despite the wedding ring and despite him smelling strongly of drink and cigarettes and describing his life as having 'turned to shit'.

Then two policemen approached and Michael jumped like a startled faun. He ran. He ran much faster than Angela would have believed a man of his bulk could manage. The police were taken by surprise too and it took them a second or two to react. They gave chase.

Angela watched them disappear through glass doors. Watched the public watch them disappear through glass doors.

Another one gets away, thought Angela philosophically.

## 283

Me and my two compadres were taken through the wire and led around the perimeter of the runway complex and then hidden behind some cargo containers. Our guide told us to keep down and wait for someone to get us.

We sat huddled together and waited.

I tuned in my radio quietly. It was Penny Lock time. It was time to hear a comforting voice. Penny always said that things would work out just fine.

## 282

Edward the Fireman lay on the ground. A woman came up to him and asked him if he needed any help.

'Do I remind you of anyone?' he asked her.

'No, I don't think so.'

'Che Guavera?'

'No.'

'Lenin?'

'No.'

'Any revolutionary of any sort?'

'I don't think so.'

'How about Frank Sinatra? Do I remind you of him?'

'Not really.'

'I don't mean facially, I mean internally.'

'I couldn't say.'

'Have you ever seen your own liver?'

The woman walked away.

'Take a look!' he shouted. 'You could learn a lot!'

Edward sat up a bit. The news was trailing the Penny Lock show and that seemed to give him some strength.

## 281

In a bar in Manhattan, the barman topped up Graham Johansson's drink and turned up the radio. His customers always drank more when Penny Lock was on. The tall Dane was certainly doing his bit.

## 280

Ali Bronski asked Penny Lock if she'd ever talked a suicide down from a tall building on her show before. Penny said no. Ali said that mobile phones rather liberated the form as the caller no longer had to be confined to a stable location. It removed a level of domesticity. Ali offered to be that caller. She could do a good jumper. Empire State Building. She'd guarantee not to jump.

Penny said she would be happier if Ali just stick to being the guest.

'How should I introduce you?'

'Could you call me Dr Frankburg?' said Ali. She thought her own name would be mud if she gave a bad show. Frankburg was a pro. Frankburg gave her confidence.

Penny had a good radio voice. Sing songy. Ali wondered if she should have a radio voice too. Maybe she should try to imitate the real Dr Frankburg. She remembered back to that day in Boston in the toilet cubicles. Birmingham, she thought. Very sympathetic.

## 279

The pharmaceutical CEO picked up his messages. Boris Vlamenkov, Asif Khan, Mister fucking Kermit the Frog. The ex-government agent wanted a million to drive Ali Bronski around in a big car and look at her legs.

The CEO rang him back.

'You're not getting a single cent.'

'Piec...'

Click.


## 278

Ali could hear news being read. Penny cleared her throat.

A jingle was played. Penny Lock's name was transposed into an A minor seventh chord and she was in with her opening.

'It's Wednesday, it's two o'clock, it's the afternoon show, I'm Penny, how are you doing? Today,' small pause, 'Where Are You?'

Jingle.


## 277

Clara Redlake drove fast and tuned in. She hummed along to the jingle. Catchy. The nearer she got to New York the stronger the signal became.


## 276

'Are you looking for someone? Someone you love? Have you been looking long? Why did they go? Have you recently reunited with someone you thought you'd lost? We need to hear your stories. With me in the studio is Dr Frankburg...'

'Good afternoon,' said Ali, thick Birmingham accent.

No, that sounded awful. She would drop it. She couldn't really pull it off. Penny shook her head at her, Ali's microphone wasn't live yet.

'...a highly respected therapist from the UK who's going to be giving expert comment throughout the show. If you have anything to tell us, the number to ring...'

Some people sang the number.


## 275

Edward the Fireman sang along. Almost in tune. Perhaps he did have Sinatra's heart. He took some painkillers and waited for Penny and the anaesthetic to take effect.

'First up we have Jean from Maine. What have you got to say, Jean?'

'Hi, Penny. Hello, Dr Frankburg.'

'Hello, Jean.'

'What's up, Jean?'

'My mother has gone missing.'

'That's terrible, Jean,' said Penny.

'Well, yes it is, I'm awful cut up about it.'

'How old is she, Jean?'

'Well now, let me think. I guess she must be getting on for a hundred and eighteen now.'

'One hundred and eighteen?' said Penny. 'That's pretty old. When did she go missing?'

'Ninety-three years ago this spring.'

'Um...'

'I was born and she disappeared from the hospital.'

'I see.'

'I've been looking and looking but I haven't found her yet.'

'Right, well, Jean—'

'She has dark black hair and a little mole, like a beauty spot, on her left cheek, and she has perfect straight white teeth and red lipstick.'

'I think—'

'And she's wearing a blue dress, a maternity dress, which will now be hanging a bit loose on her.'

'Dr Frankburg, do you have any—?'

'And I'm afraid to say it, but she isn't wearing a wedding ring, not even an engagement ring. I feel like I'm betraying her but you need the description to be accurate, otherwise you might get all sorts of false alarms.'

'Indeed.'

'And I don't want false alarms knocking on my door.'

'Who would? Um—'

'I don't want to be getting my hopes up, you see.'

'Are you ninety-three years old, Jean?' said Penny.

'I'll be ninety-three in spring.'

'Have you ever considered the possibility that your mother may have passed away?'

A terrible pause.

'Jean?'

'What do you mean?' Jean's quivering reply.

'Well, I'm saying, after all these years—'

'Do you know something?' almost whispered.

'No, I haven't got any firm facts, but I'm just thinking, one hundred and eighteen. I mean, that's pretty old...'

'Oh, my lord.'

'As I said, um, Dr Frankburg have you got anything to say?'

'Jean,' said Ali, 'is your mother very beautiful?'

'Oh yes, yes she is.'

'Sparkling eyes, cheerful laugh?'

'That's her, yes, that's the one.'

'Soft hands, gentle manner?'

'You know her, you've got her right off.'

'Then I do know where she is, she's in Paris.'

'Paris? How grand.'

'She was taken there after you were born in order to join her real family, an aristocratic family. She sent for you but the papers went missing. She's spent her whole life trying to find you but without success. She's very ill now, Jean.'

'Oh dear lord.'

'But she's been sending messages to every radio station in the land in the hope you'll ring up, and here you are ringing in at last. Do you want me to read it?'

'Oh yes, please.'

'It says, "Should this message ever reach the ears of my beloved lost daughter, Jean, let her be sure that I have loved her and thought of her every single day of my life". That's what it says, Jean.'

'Is there a signature?' Jean's voice was broken with emotion.

'It's a bit smudged with tears, Jean, I can make out an "M", can I?'

'It'll be an "N", she was called Nell.'

'Nell, that's it. "All my love, Nell".'

A sob.

'Thank you.'

'Our pleasure, thanks for your call. Let's go to line five.'

Penny gave the gesture to Tamy which meant 'no more of those please'.

## 273

'Hi, Jean, this is Tamy, Penny's producer, you're off air now, thanks for your contribution, Penny appreciated it. Can I remind you that any contribution made today remains in the copyright of Fix Broadcasting Corporation, KKRC and all subsidiaries.'

'Could you send me the note?' asked Jean.

'Um ... OK.'

## 272

Clara Redlake was surprised to hear the Penny Lock Phone-In claim they had a Dr Frankburg in the studio, a highly respected therapist from the UK, as Dr Frankburg was sounding neither Welsh nor male.

## 271

Edward the Fireman felt his heart lurch, and because it lurched he became convinced it was his own.

He had cried only twice in his life. Once when he burned Beth alive. And once on the radio. Apart from those two times nothing had run over his cheeks. Clara Redlake had tried to wring tears out of him, many times, but none would come. Not even when the wind blew coldly into them. Perhaps there was something wrong with his eyes. Perhaps he didn't have tear ducts.

But he'd cried on the Penny Lock show. He'd cried when Activist 345 had told him how important it was to have a cause in life. How important it was to live by your principles. To live a conscionable life. To make the world a better place.

He'd cried because SOMEONE AGREED WITH HIM.

Every thing he did after that moment, every act, every conversation was carried out as if Activist 345 was watching him, approving him. If he did a good thing, she saw it. If he did a bad thing, she missed it.

He let out a cry and started hobbling towards the radio station. He wondered why she was pretending to be a doctor. Perhaps it was all part of a BIG PLAN.

## 270

Dan Bronski and John Heron left departures and got in a taxi.

Beth Davies breathed the air. Perhaps she was sniffing me out. Or perhaps now she'd left her husband's airspace, the air smelt different. 3,000 miles away and smelling 3,000 times better. She wondered what the air smelt like in Australia. Or the moon.

She joined Dan and John in the cab and thought perhaps she didn't need the driver to sing 'Don't Fence Me In'.

'The Hotel Monumental. Eighteenth Street,' said Dan.

Coincidentally, the driver sang 'Don't Fence Me In' anyway.

## 269

The next caller. Line six.

'Emma?'

Penny Lock gave frantic 'I know this person' signs to her producer.

Tamy ignored her.

## 268

Tamy didn't see Penny's sign as she was writing out a note for Jean from Maine.

'Should this message ever reach the ears of my beloved lost daughter, Jean, let her be sure that I have loved her and thought of her every single day of my life'. Tamy squeezed a tear onto the page, just for authenticity.

## 267

'What's up, Emma?' asked Ali Bronski.

'... Penny, I needed to send out <hiss> a message.'

'Is this caller a friend of yours?' asked Ali.

'Where are you, Emma?' asked Penny.

'...don't...exactly...'

Tamy finished the note and tried to get a clearer line.

'Why are you calling?' asked Penny.

Crackling. Breaking up.

'Emma, I thought you'd gone home.'

'<more hiss> at the airport.'

'It's a very bad line, Emma.'

'This is for Graham... I'm there... if you're listening Graham, I need...'

More break up.

Penny gave her producer the cut off sign. Emma was cut off.

'We seem to have lost our caller, don't know what happened there, we'll try to get her back for you. In the meantime...'

## 266

Beth opened the taxi window to get a better view of the Brooklyn Bridge.

Gephyrophobia, fear of crossing bridges. She didn't feel it. She crossed gephyrophobia off her list.

## 265

'Turn that up!' shouted John. He wrapped loudly on the taxi's glass.

'Hey, don't do that, OK? I'm trying to drive here.'

'Turn up the radio!'

'What's the matter, John?' said Dan.

'That's Emma on the radio.' He banged again. 'Turn up the bloody radio!'

'John, calm down.'

'Don't hit the goddamn glass, man. Jesus.'

'Stop the car.'

'Get a grip on yourself for crying out loud.'

'Take me to where the radio station is. Hey, you in there.'

'Stop banging the goddamn glass!'

'Jesus, what is this stuff? Bullet-proofed? Why's it bullet-proofed? What kind of country is this?'

'OK, that's it.' The taxi pulled over. 'Get the fuck outa my cab.'

'No, wait, you don't understand.'

'I understand that you're insane. Now get out.'

'Take it easy, will you,' said Dan. 'He's lost his wife, he's very upset. Come on, just take us to the Monumental, he'll calm down.'

'Where's the radio station?' asked John.

'John, we'll go to the station, OK? Just don't bang on the glass, it's unnerving the driver.'

The KKRC 'Your Station' jingle played.

John heard it and screamed at the driver. The driver got out of the cab pulled John, Dan and Beth out and threw their luggage by the side of the road. John tried to listen to the radio but was hit powerfully in the face by the cab driver.

The driver then drove quickly away.

John lay on the ground and sung the radio station's number. It had a catchy jingle which was how he remembered it. He'd been taught the alphabet in the same way.

John asked Dan to help him up.

Beth looked over the bridge.


## 264

Sitting in a bar in Manhattan, Graham Johansson asked the barman if he wouldn't mind turning the radio down.

'Sure, it's not a good one today. Not like "Fight the Good Fight". Did you hear that one? That was great radio. Tried to ring in myself, some of my customers ran out the bar, others started drinking like there was no tomorrow. I guess it's 'cos of where the bar is.'

Graham nodded. Financial district. Full of brokers. He must have walked miles.


## 263

The taxi driver sucked his knuckles and muttered to himself. Another fare gone. Perhaps he'd overreacted. He blamed the stress of the job.

## 262

Graham Johansson left the bar and flagged down a cab and told it to take him to the airport.

'You going on holiday?'

'No.'

'Business trip?'

'No.'

'You a pilot?' asked the taxi driver.

'Yes.'

Man, he smelt of booze, thought the driver.

## 261

Clara Redlake called in for petrol. She didn't want to stay away from the radio so she got a man to fill her up. She ignored his leers at the suggestive comment and didn't tip him.

## 260

The ex-government agent got in a cab and told it to take him north. He couldn't walk any more. He'd go back to where those two quiet cooking women were and sleep till noon. He smelt of sick.

## 259

Edward the Fireman wondered what Activist 345 had up her sleeve on this occasion. She was taking a big risk so he guessed the target must be a pretty big one. He listened out for explosions.

Edward realised he was near some big financial institutions and so thought it might be a good idea to move on. Just in case. He didn't relish getting caught up in an explosion caused by the organisation to which he'd pledged his, albeit unasked for, allegiance.

An old man helped him to his feet and asked him if he'd been shot. Edward said no and advised the man to head towards a politically unprovocative part of town. The old man asked where that might be. Edward said good point.

## 258

Some commercials played on the Penny Lock show.

Insurance. A web design company. A discount electrical retailer…

## 257

Edward limped and dripped blood. Activist 345 would certainly need some back-up. Moral support at the very least. He winced in pain and hoped that she wouldn't be requiring any physical assistance, or rough stuff.

## 256

Penny hurried into Tamy's booth to see if Emma was still on the line.

'No, I cut her off,' said the producer.

'I said get her off the air, not cut the call altogether.'

'You gave me the sign.' Tamy gave the finger across the throat sign.

'Yes, that's "off air" not "hang up",' said Penny.

'I thought this was "off air".' Tamy gave a thumbs down.

'No, that's "find me a better caller".'

'No, this is "find me a better caller".' Tamy waggled her finger in a circular motion.

'That isn't anything, I've never done that.'

'Well, you've never used it, I know, but I thought it was because I always got you good callers.'

'That is seriously in question, Tamy. Anyway, this is irrelevant, the point is I need to speak to Emma and I can't. Did she say anything else before you cut her?'

'No.'

Penny gave a grunt of frustration and returned to her console.

## 255

Johansson's cab sped to the airport. He asked the cab driver if he was afraid of flying. The cab driver said he didn't used to be, but he was feeling edgy about it now. Johansson said planes could fly themselves. Pilots just babysat. The cab driver asked if auto pilots got drunk. Johansson said they should try it.

## 254

...feminine hygiene products, eat all you can buffets. And then back to the show.

## 253

'Next caller,' said Penny. The show hadn't really caught fire yet.

'You had a caller on earlier called Emma. I think it was my wife.'

'John?'

'Yes. Did she say where she was?'

'What makes you think she was your wife John?' said Ali.

'Who's this?' said John.

'That was our guest therapist, John, Dr Frankburg.'

'Hello, doctor.'

'Hello, John.'

'I recognised my wife's voice,' said John.

'That's not really proof, though, is it?' said Ali.

'What?'

'True,' said Penny, 'although I recognised her voice as well.'

'But she's not your wife, is she?' said Ali.

'No.'

Small pause.

'What point are you making?' said Penny.

'Hey,' shouted John. 'Was it Emma or wasn't it?'

'It's a bit if a bad line John. Where are you ringing from?'

'I'm on... where am I?' John turned to Dan.

Dan was sitting morosely on his suitcase.

'Brooklyn Bridge.'

'I'm on Brooklyn Bridge. Where was Emma ringing from?'

'She didn't say,' said Penny.

'Did you hear the whole call, John? Because she didn't mention anything about a husband,' said Ali.

'Didn't she?'

'No.'

'Right.'

'Have you two had a bust-up, John?' asked Penny.

'I don't know.'

'She mentioned a guy called Graham,' said Ali.

'Graham?'

'Is that your middle name?'

'No.'

'I think she was talking about my Graham,' said Penny.

'Really?' said Ali. 'That's interesting.'

'I don't see what's interesting about it,' said Penny.

'Well, she didn't mention anyone called John.'

'Well, whether she did or she didn't...' said John.

<muffled in the background: 'Beth!'>

'What was that, John?'

'Oh Jesus.'

'What's the matter, John?'

'Um sorry, I've got to go. I think my friend is about to jump off the Brooklyn Bridge.'

'You're kidding?' said Ali.


## 252

Beth Davies looked down. It was getting dark and the water was disappearing below. Turning black. There was a chill in the air.

It was important to think of loved ones at times like this so she tried to think of some. But it was hard to think of them as loved ones when they'd burnt you and melted you up.

She'd kept quiet though. Beth never squealed. Although she screamed a bit.

She thought of Michael. Michael hadn't seen the scars, or pretended not to, but then he'd only seen me. He'd just been looking at genes or something, and not her.


## 251

'Perhaps Dr Frankburg could talk her down,' said Tamy.

Penny gave her a stare. Tamy was only allowed to go live in exceptional circumstances.

'I couldn't absolutely guarantee...' said Ali.

'I think we have to go to the news,' said Penny anxiously.

'This could be the fucking news,' said Ali.

Penny looked over at Tamy. Did she bleep that out? That could get her fined.

## 250

Did Activist 345 say 'fucking'? Edward the Fireman wished he was taping the programme. The hefty dose of lidocaine had frozen his entire left side. It made him walk very strangely but he was making good progress now.

## 249

'What's your friend's name, John?' said Ali.

'It's Beth.'

'OK. I'm... I'm going to get you to ask her a series of questions. OK?'

'Hang on,' said John. 'I don't think she can hear me.'

'Can you put her on the line?'

<muffled: Beth, do you want to talk to the radio?>

Pause.

'She didn't answer me,' said John.

'Just give her the phone then. Can you do that?'

<muffled: I'm going to give you this phone, Beth. OK?>

## 248

Rustling. Sound of the wind blowing. Traffic noises.

Penny filled. 'Of course the Brooklyn Bridge was first opened to traffic in eighteen eighty-five and is approximately sixteen hundred feet long... um... As far as I can remember the bridge is painted in Rawlins Red which is manufactured, I believe, in Rawlins, Wyoming, although to me it's always been a sort of beige colour...'

## 247

'Hello?'

'Am I speaking to Beth?'

'Yes.'

'This is Dr Frankburg,' said Ali.

## 246

There was my sister on the airwaves. Like a voice in a photo. I held up the radio to my two comrades behind the cargo crates.

'My sister,' I mouthed at them. They motioned for me to turn the thing off, someone would hear.

I hadn't heard her voice for over twenty years. Strange to hear it now. I wondered if our voices sounded similar. I thought she must have chosen to come to New York for a reason. I mean, of all the destinations in the world. Kind of prodigal. Properly prodigal too. The Romans called victims wholly consumed by fire *prodigae hostiae*. A lot of the school's Latin textbooks perished. I hope Beth got a chance to read them before they went up.

I wondered if she had a message for me. Perhaps some forgiveness, or a little hello. To me and maybe Edward too. Perhaps she would say hi to us over the radio. I'd always wanted that to happen.

## 245

Edward the Fireman heard her too and thought her diction was very clear. Edward wanted to tell her that he did good now. He put out fires. Well, used to.

## 244

'Do you know how much traffic crosses the Brooklyn Bridge each day, Beth?' said Ali.

'No.'

'About two thousand pedestrians, fifteen hundred bikes, and about one hundred and fifty thousand vehicles.'

'I didn't know that.'

'How many of those people think about jumping in?'

'I'm not...'

'All of them.'

'Really?'

'That's right, Beth. Each one of those people have the same thoughts you do.'

'How do you know that?'

'I'll prove it to you. I don't know what the audience demographic is for this show...'

Penny wanted to leap in, she knew exactly.

'...but a whole load are drivers coming home from work. Taxi drivers, too, with passengers inside.'

Beth believed that.

'So I want to say to all those listening, if you've ever thought of jumping into the Hudson, or thought of self-slaughter generally, then sound your horn now.'

On the bridge car horns rang out. Trucks, taxis, sedans, two-seaters. Beyond the bridge wafting across the river the faint chorus of trumpets produced a fanfare of subtle harmonics. Distorted by mist and air.

## 243

Johansson's cabby asked him if she should honk too. Johansson said why not.

## 242

The cabby driving the ex-government agent asked him if he should honk. The ex-agent told him to about-turn and drive back to the city. The voice belonging to Ali Bronski was currently broadcasting from the offices of KKRC and the ex-government agent thought he might still be able to pull things round.

The taxi driver honked anyway. Honked like there was no tomorrow.

## 241

'You hear that?' said Ali.

'Yes,' said Beth.

'That's how I know. That's the cry of a city in anguish...'

Penny frowned, she wouldn't have put it that way. This was supposed to be a life-affirming show. She had advertisers to consider.

'...but of all those who say they've thought of it, do you know how many actually jump in?' said Ali.

Beth didn't answer. The phone went dead.

'Hello? Beth?'

Nothing.

'Beth?'

Ali and Penny looked over to Tamy. Tamy pushed buttons.

'Has she jumped?' asked Penny.

'Beth?'

'Tamy, have we lost her?'

Tamy said yes.

Penny thought talk of a city in anguish must have pushed her over the edge.

'Well, listeners, we seem to have lost Beth there...'

## 240

Car horns honked again. Louder than before.

## 239

The pharmaceutical CEO had put his car into a valet service to get the bacon and coffee cleared off the seats. He was now stuck in a cab in traffic and, hearing the horns, wondered if his company headquarters had been blown up. He asked his driver to put on the Penny Lock Phone-In. He'd make it up to Tamy by saying he'd heard her show that day and thought she'd produced it very well. He'd tell her she really did a first-rate job. He'd take her out to breakfast tomorrow. He made some reservations.

## 238

I pressed the radio to my ear. Did Beth say anything? Request a record at the last?

Edward stopped too. Wondering whether to run to the river.

Beth had jumped into the lake once. In his mind, Beth's hair was on fire and she was trying to douse herself. That hadn't happened though. She'd jumped into the lake on another occasion, years later. He'd fished her out. She screamed at him and told him to leave her alone. She jumped in again and Edward had fished her out again. She told him to piss off home. He stayed by the side of the lake, though, and pulled her out four more times until Beth was too exhausted to jump any more. He took her home and hid all the sharp things.

Beth told him not to interfere in her projects ever again.

He was glad she wouldn't get mad at him this time. He was too far away from the Hudson to help.


## 237

Beth handed the phone back to Dan. His batteries had gone dead.

Dan Bronski took Beth Davies's hand and asked her if she saw any boats on the river.

'What?' said Beth, shouting over the noise of car horns.

Dan said it didn't matter.

Beth said she wasn't really going to do anything, she was just looking.

Dan said he knew.

'So doesn't your phone work now?' asked John.

'No.'

John abandoned them and ran across the bridge. He could get a cab to KKRC from the other side.


## 236

Line six. 'Yeah she jumped, I reckon.'

Line four. 'I don't think she did. I think the doctor did an excellent job.'

Line three. 'I think if she didn't jump, she should've done, she sounded whiney.'

Line eight. 'My uncle died whilst constructing the bridge, he was hit by a girder.'

Line ten. 'Perhaps the car horns startled her, some are pretty loud.'

'If you're OK Beth, call us back. We're on air until five. Let's take a break.'

Ali Bronski nodded and crossed her fingers and toes.


## 235

Life insurance, Burrito Palisade, Dial-a-cab . . .

## 234

Edward despised himself for making a crappy bomb which didn't blow up and didn't mess up the skin of the pharmaceutical CEO and didn't disfigure him so much it made him want to jump into the Hudson River. He pictured the Brooklyn Bridge in his head and he fantasised about the CEO jumping off it and he realised that it was jumping off the bridge would take some doing and if Beth had managed it then she was a resourceful woman who was a credit to the Wiltshire family.

He wished he had enough money to get a cab to KKRC. He wasn't thinking straight and walking really wasn't helping him order his thoughts.

## 233

...Flick clothing for that snappy look around town, wine and dine at Serento's. Now back to the show.

## 232

'I'd just like to quickly say happy birthday to my producer Tamy who's forty today.'

'Thirty'.

'Sorry thirty. What did I say?'

## 231

The pharmaceutical CEO said, 'That's my daughter,' to the taxi driver.

'Penny Lock?'

'No, Tamy.'

'Oh,' said the driver, disappointed.

## 230

'We have a Clara Redlake on line eight. Hi Clara, what's your story?'

'I'd like to say that Dr Frankburg is a fake.'

## 229

Dan Bronski flagged down a cab and took Beth to the Hotel Monumental.

'Are you listening to this?' said the cab driver. 'I honked my horn, I'm telling you. I honked it like there was no tomorrow.'

Dan told him to keep his eyes on the road.


## 228

Clara said it was irresponsible for a radio station to parade fakers and charlatans. Where were 'Frankburg's' qualifications? Her credentials? If a station was going to offer advice to vulnerable people the least they should do is make sure they used qualified professionals. She wasn't surprised this Beth had jumped.

She was cut off.

Although Ali agreed with her.


## 227

'Line five.'

'This is Stephanie Wiltshire. That was my sister Beth you were talking to. If she hasn't jumped I'd just like to say to her that I'm sorry for everything and I'm trying to do the right thing now.'

Click.

I always wanted to be on the radio.


## 226

Edward the Fireman heard me. He doubted my ability to do the right thing. Only Edward could do the right thing and thought I was stealing his thunder. He thought the Wiltshire sisters were getting too much airtime.


## 225

Beth heard me. The cabby turned the radio off in disgust, said it was easy for the broad to say that now.

Beth agreed with him.


## 224

John Heron's cab pulled up outside KKRC. John didn't have enough money to pay him. He entertained the cabby with his collapsible wand instead. The cabby laughed and let him off $3.50. John always knew he shouldn't have abandoned magic.

## 223

Beth and Dan's cab dropped them at the door of the Hotel Monumental. Dan checked them in. Beth requested a room with a view. The receptionist said they all had views, it depended on what sort you wanted. Beth said just put her high up.

## 222

The receptionist had mentioned to the manager that a female customer had told her that morning that her nights would never be as comfortable again. The manager thought about putting the quote on the Monumental's printed notepaper.

## 221

Line sixteen. 'I'd like to agree with the caller who said that Dr Frankburg was a fake. I've got *You Too Can Fly* and so has my sister and the voice on that is nothing like the one you've got in the studio.'

'I've got a cold,' said Ali.

## 220

Clara called the real Dr Frankburg from her car phone.

'Who?' said Frankburg.

'Clara Redlake.'

Frankburg nearly dropped the receiver.

'Oh God, um,' Frankburg coughed. 'Hold on, I'll just put you through to him.'

He held his head away from the receiver and shouted, 'Dr Frankburg there's a call for you!' Then in a muffled Welsh voice he shouted, as if from another room, 'Hang on a minute.' Then paused and thought about what to do.

'Hello?' he said in his normal voice. 'Um, Dr Frankburg is in with a client at the moment, can I help? I'm his assistant.'

'Didn't you just shout at him?'

'Well, yes, but I forgot that he was otherwise engaged. Can I pass on a message?'

'I thought I heard him shouting back.'

'Yes, true, he did shout back.'

'Won't that have been a bit distracting for his client?'

'No, not really, I don't think it's a serious case, probably just a whiner.'

'A what?'

'Nothing. Can I get him to call you back?'

'I wanted to alert him to the fact that there is someone on the air in the States at the moment who is claiming to be Dr Frankburg from England.'

'What?'

'Giving therapeutic advice on a talk show. She's pretty good actually.'

'She?'

'She.'

'The bitch.'

'What?'

'Sorry, yes, I'll certainly get Dr Frankburg to call you. I think I can hear him coming out now, in fact, so it'll only be a few minutes I should think. If that's all right.'

'Fine.'

She gave her number.

'Um, Dr Frankburg is still suffering from tonsillitis so don't be surprised if he's a bit croaky and not particularly Welsh.'

'Still? That was two years ago.'

'Well, it's a stubborn bug. Nice to talk to you.'

Frankburg put down the phone then immediately picked it up and dialled Clara's number.

'Clara?' rasped Frankburg.

'Yes.'

'Dr Frankburg here. Sorry about my assistant, he's new.'

'You sound terrible.'

'Yes, it still gets me now and then.'

'Perhaps shouting down from your consulting room strained it.'

'Yes, yes, probably did.'

'I was saying to your assistant, it must have alarmed your client.'

'Oh, I wasn't really in with a client, it was more a meeting, an informal meeting with friends. My assistant gets confused from time to time.'

'He sounded rather old to be an assistant.'

'Well, not that old, middle-aged. He's changing careers, he's been in prison.'

'I see.'

'Well, not prison exactly, more a prisoner.'

'What sort of prisoner?'

'Um, prisoner of conscience...'

'A political prisoner?'

'Um, yes.'

'My God, how awful, I'd like to talk to him.'

'Well, he's still a bit traumatised, I wouldn't bring it up if I were you.'

'Where was he in prison?'

'Chile.'

'Really? He didn't sound Chilean.'

'No, well he went to school here in England, and then sort of went over and sort of protested against, um...'

'Pinochet?'

'That's the one. Anyway, he's back now, but he doesn't want to talk to anyone about it, not even me and I'm a therapist after all. Ha! Look, do we have to talk about him? I thought you mentioned something about a radio show.'

'Are you sure you're up to speaking?'

'Yes... the radio... actually I might just get a glass of water.'

'Look, it's not important. It's the Penny Lock Phone-In.' She sang out the number.

'What?' said Frankburg. He could hardly speak. Psychosomatic failure of the larynx.

Clara finished the call. Those British bugs must be ferocious.

## 219

John Heron asked reception if he could have a word with Penny during a commercial break. It was OK, he said, he was a personal friend. His wife had just been staying with her, they all went way back.

Reception told him to take a seat.

## 218

Edward the Fireman burst into reception and tried to get his breath back. He asked if he could have a word with 'Dr Frankburg' during a commercial break. It was OK, he said, he was a personal friend, they'd wept together many times.

Reception told him to take a seat next to John Heron.

## 217

'I'm afraid I can't hear you,' said Tamy, thinking she may have a pervert on her hands. Not that that necessarily precluded participation in the show, but it was better if they were perverts with good diction.

'Put me <croak> on to the so-called Dr Frankburg <cough>.'

'You're very hard to hear.'

'I am the real Dr Frankburg. Please <rasp> put me <cough> onto the so-called...'

'I can't put you on to the show if we can't hear you. It makes for frustrating radio.'

'...get a lozenge...'

'This is ridiculous. Call back when you're better.'

Tamy cut off Dr Frankburg and made way for a Siamese twin from New Jersey.

## 216

'Hello,' said John Heron.

'Hello,' said Edward.

## 215

Frankburg sucked a lozenge furiously and rang Samuel Thorn's agent to get Samuel Thorn's number. He had to plead with her which was difficult under the circumstances but she gave it out when he promised that Sam could do *Five Steps to Defeating Anxiety*, Planned for the spring. She said Sam's rates were much higher now as he was on the brink of a serious TV-drama profile.

## 214

'Well, that's an extraordinary story, caller, but technically that doesn't make you a Siamese twin. Still, all of us here at KKRC hope you find her and thank you for calling. OK, we're going to the news now, but we'll be back soon so keep those calls coming.'

Penny flicked a switch and the news kicked in. They bought it in from somewhere else. A guy with a commanding and authoritative voice read it from a studio in a bunker somewhere.

'Oof,' said Penny.

Tamy gave the thumbs up. OK so far.

## 213

'Hello?'

'Mr Thorn, it's Dr Frankburg here.'

'My God, what's the matter with your voice?'

'I've strained it.'

'You want to use your diaphragm more.'

'It's more a nervous thing.'

'What do you want?'

Samuel was sitting in front of the TV screen looking at a freeze frame of Kirsten. The people at Phoenix productions had tried to make him leave but Sam asked them for a few more minutes. They'd said sure and looked at the clock. It was getting kind of late. Seeing him hang around was unnerving them and the casting woman had called the producer and told him she was finding Sam a bit creepy. Sam had deduced that the footage he was watching was from Kirsten's last day on this earth.

'There's a radio show currently airing in New York where someone is claiming to be me, Dr Frankburg.'

'Right,' said Sam.

'And I was wondering if you would come round to my office and denounce the fake Dr Frankburg on air.'

'Why?'

'Why? Because she's a fake.'

'Why can't you do it?'

'Listen to me. I'm struggling as it is. Besides, I've got a big stack of *You Too Can Fly* fans in America, they'll expect something a bit more, I don't know, Welsh.'

'Won't it be one fake denouncing another?'

'Well, yes, it does seem that way, but...'

'I don't know.'

'Oh come on.'

'Do you know the story of Jonah and the whale?'

'What? Yes.'

'I'm not a lucky man Mr Frankburg.'

'It's Dr Frank—'

'I don't think you want me on your side.'

'I'm not asking for much, it's just this Ali Bronski woman, she's—'

'Who?'

'Ali Bronski. She's done this before, taken my fucking glory – sorry to swear.'

'No, that's fine.'

'Taken my fucking glory for herself. Radio. I've never been on the bloody radio. The bloody cow. Well, it's not just that, it's a matter of principle. She could be doing untold damage. I've got a market to protect.'

Sam had rewound.

Voice: 'Kirsten, just quickly, Ali Bronski rang, she's in London tonight and wants you to ring her to meet if you get the chance.' Kirsten: 'Right, thanks.'

'Where are you?' asked Sam.

Frankburg croaked out a few directions.


## 212

Emma Heron sat in a café at the airport and waited.

Though her eyes were green they were also bloodshot. She'd been in the airport all day. Her husband John had passed within a hundred metres of her when he arrived but she'd been in Foot Boutique buying shoes. They didn't have her size but she bought them anyway. What was a little pinching in the grand scheme of things?

## 211

Cody Jameson hared up the M40. She listened to the inquest tapes again. She found a part where Ronald Henderson talked about his daughter Kirsten. He spoke of her movingly, emotionally, how her death had been the single most devastating event in his life and that was up against some stiff competition. It brought tears to Cody's eyes.

The coroner said that a note had been found. The note was passed to the coroner who asked if Ronald wanted to keep it. Ronald said yes he would.

'Read it out then!' shouted Cody.

She thought she heard the sound of a piece of paper being unfolded and passed around.

'Read it out!'

Beautiful words. She thought she heard a few little sighs, a few little murmurs of grief.

'Read the damn thing!'

No one said anything though. Cody thumped the steering wheel.

Cody tossed the tapes out of the window in frustration.

The magnetic tape unspooled and the wind carried it upwards and westwards and draped it over some Oxfordshire trees.

## 210

Emma Heron looked up at every pilot. None of them were Graham Johansson. They all looked too contented...

## 209

Miles opened the Wellington Arms for the evening.

The doorman arrived promptly. Dressed smartly.

'Some help you were last night,' Miles complained.

'What?'

'I said some help. There was chaos in there, where were you?'

'Watching.'

'Well, next time, don't watch, assist.'

'There'll be a next time, will there?'

'Not if I can help it.'

'I think there should be a next time. I think there should be a next time each week.'

'Comedy nights are over. The Wellington Arms is to be a blood-free venue. Be advised.'

The doorman grunted. Perhaps he could pitch a comedy idea to the Pig and Parrot.

## 208

... and Graham Johansson wasn't contented. She knew that. He'd told her that he had been thinking about death.

Emma said good for you.

Johansson said that that wasn't the reaction he had been expecting.

Emma asked what reaction had he been expecting?

He said shocked concern, like everyone else.

Emma said that by the end of August, nineteen forty-five, approximately four thousand Japanese soldiers had crashed their planes.

He said he wasn't planning on crashing his...

Emma said her favourite kamikaze letter said, 'It is an honour to be able to give my life in defence of beautiful and lofty things.'

Graham had said there was nothing beautiful or lofty in what he...

Emma said death could be about tradition. About spirituality.

He agreed but—

She said there were places where death wasn't seen in this way and told him that the Wellington Arms was one such place.

He said, a pub?

She said a plane overshooting the runway would hit the Wellington Arms squarely in the face.

He said she'd missed his point.

Emma said she wanted to die in a tragedy. You were remembered better. There was a vanity in death, wasn't there?

Johansson had said he wasn't prepared to put the lives of—

She said the whole plane would, at some level, want to die.

He said he doubted that.

She said all the people on the plane would be going to the same destination, they'd go to the same bars, they'd visit the same clubs, the same museums, the same restaurants, they'd eat the same food, they'd sleep with the same people. They all went because they all wanted the same thing. It happened all the time.

He said she was talking about package holidays and that was quite different.

Only in your head, she said. She asked him what his next flight was.

He said SA 841. Emma said good, she was booked on that flight, they'd go down together.

Johansson said he wasn't about to... He asked her why she didn't take pills, or jump off a building.

She said, 'Haven't you been listening?'

## 207

Emma had sat on SA 841 and hoped it would be the last journey she'd ever take. A kamikaze passenger. She'd read that kamikaze pilots wore a new uniform on their flights, so she'd bought a new top and new pair of trainers.

She spoke to the person in the seat next to her, an elderly gentleman called Ronald Henderson, about death. She asked him if he'd ever thought of suicide and he said oh yes, many times. She clapped her hands and wanted to go into the cockpit and assure Graham that his passengers all had the same aspirations.

Emma told Ronald Henderson that the pilot was a personal friend who was going to crash them all into the Wellington Arms and Ronald should think of some appropriate last words to utter. Ronald thought it was unlikely, pilots were very well-adjusted. Emma said this one wasn't. Said this was a suicide flight.

Ronald said he felt sorry for the other passengers. Emma said he shouldn't feel that way. She said if you talked to anyone long enough they'll tell you they think about dying. She said that people weren't afraid of dying, they were afraid of wanting to die. The two were often confused.

## 206

Then a voice had come over the cabin PA. Emma had been looking forward to this part, it would be the voice of God, she thought. But no. It was the voice of someone called Andrew.

'This is your captain speaking. I would like to welcome you blah blah blah.'

Johansson had changed his shifts.

Emma was disappointed.

Ronald was disappointed.

SA 841 landed with barely a bump.

Ronald said he wanted to die on public transport so they took a taxi to the train station. She didn't want to push him but she would watch if he wanted. He said no. He would feel self-conscious.

Emma understood. She left him there and took the taxi to the Wellington Arms just in time to see John blow his head off for a great big gag.

She left the Wellington and tried to get herself run over in an underpass but the driver was too good.

## 205

The splitter Johansson. Dishonourable Johansson. She'd rung Penny's flat.

Sobbing.

'Pick up, you bastard, I know you're there.'

More sobbing.

'I'm coming back. I'm coming back, OK? Stay where you are. Don't fucking move.'

She kicked the telephone box. Her trainer flew off.

'Bloody bloody stupid…'

More sobs.

'Why is this happening? Penny, don't let him leave.'

Pip pip pip pip…

## 204

Emma wondered if Graham could be persuaded to ditch in the Atlantic. It was a big ocean, there was always room for one more. She hoped he'd heard the radio broadcast. Hoped he'd fly her into oblivion.

## 203

Cody fantasised about listening to her own inquest tapes. She imagined the coroner calling Roger Frankburg and Roger Frankburg taking the stand and in a faltering and broken voice tell the court how much he loved his little Lily, how the world was indeed a cruel one to take away one so bright, so loving and so perfect. She imagined the tape picking up sobbing in the courtroom, noses being blown, perhaps even someone breaking down and being led out of the room.

Who would do that though? In the three years as Cody Jameson she'd made some new friends but they knew her as Cody, they wouldn't turn up to an inquest of someone called Lily. They probably didn't know any Lilys.

Her old friends might not remember her well enough to cry sufficiently.

Samuel Thorn might put on a good show though. Perhaps he could be the one being led out, choked with sobs.

## 202

Cody's phone rang. It was PC Queely saying that she had been right. Cody Jameson had been the last thing on Ronald Henderson's mind before he jumped in front of the train. He'd left a message on his answerphone. Cody asked PC Queely to play her the tape. He said it was a bit upsetting. She said she didn't mind.

'...my wish is to be cremated <muffled approaching roar> and I want the ashes pissed on by a dog and flushed down the toilet of some big polluting jumbo by a stewardess who fucks a co-pilot while she does it <roar intensifies> and I want the ashes to mix with the puke and shit and then freeze into an ugly lump <Ronald has to shout> and then dropped onto a fucking cruise ship sailing the Atlantic where it'll smash through the casino killing someone who thinks that their luck has changed, someone who thinks they've hit the fucking jackpot, someone who thinks their life is fine and dandy, someone calling themselves Cody Jameson! Tales of a fucking Stewardess. DON'T THINK I DON'T KNOW WHO YOU ARE!' <loud bang, screech, crackle> beep beep.

## 201

Cody didn't want to be remembered that way. She wondered what she'd done to deserve that and couldn't remember, so she wondered what I'd done to deserve that. She decided it must be something pretty awful.

'That's not so good,' she said.

'No,' said PC Queely.

'You must think I'm a pretty terrible person.'

'I don't have an opinion one way or the other.'

She decided to stop being Cody Jameson. It wasn't really working out. She'd go back to being Lily Frankburg. Lily Frankburg would get a better dedication. Despite everything, she didn't think anyone would want a frozen lump of piss and shit to land on Lily Frankburg.

Lily Frankburg thanked PC Queely and hung up.

She reached the Birmingham turn-off and so she decided to drive home.

## 200

Michael Davis thought he'd lost the police. He had a quick car. They were too slow. Weren't expecting him to run. He wasn't expecting to run either. He was sick in the back. The sweat was popping out over his brow and his hands were clammy. He rang up every contact he knew and told them he was quitting all stowaway operations until further notice. He'd had enough. The heat was on and running made him puke. He didn't get through to the American team. They had their phones switched off. He tried playing Sinatra but found, to his irritation, that he'd stolen a tape by an artiste called Sinita and it wasn't doing the trick at all.

## 199

Graham Johansson arrived at the airport. He checked in, booked in and was going through his flight procedures in the cockpit of SA 109.

'You all right?' asked his co-pilot.

Johansson nodded.

## 198

John Heron was being escorted through KKRC's building towards Penny Lock's studio. It was still the news break. Penny OK'd him. She was reluctant at first but

Ali had pointed out to her that he would know what happened to Beth on the bridge. Penny liked to update her listeners and told reception to show him up right away. Edward followed. Reception thought they were together.

## 197

I was shown into the wheel housing. From apartment to undercarriage was a very slick operation. There was even a little ladder to help me over the wheels. I was surprised that Michael could be associated with such an effective outfit. I would've thought he'd have bodged it. I asked what I was supposed to do with the duck tape. The guy shrugged. 'Tie up a duck?' How was that for service? A little joke even under these circumstances.

## 196

Michael stopped outside a telephone box. He didn't think he'd been followed but accepted he wouldn't have a clue one way or the other.

He dialled a number in the US and finally persuaded a man to tell him the names of that night's SmuggleAir passengers. All passengers were paid up and aboard.

When he heard 'Stephanie Wiltshire', Michael kicked the telephone box till the glass smashed.

Yobbo, thought a passer-by.

## 195

Emma heard the last call for flight SA 109 to Birmingham. She picked up her bag and posted the envelope containing her hair and nail cuttings to the morgue. It was easier if she thought she was already dead. She made her way to the gate. Hobbling on her silly shoes.

## 194

John asked the production assistant if he could do some magic on the radio. She told him it probably wouldn't come across too well.

Did either of them want to check in their coats? John said yes, the other guy said no. Even though he was sweating.

## 193

As the news played, Penny and Tamy were drinking Tamy's birthday bubbly in the corridor. Someone popped a little indoor firework and gave Tamy a birthday kiss. Penny and Tamy thought the newsreader was an arsehole, they'd both met him once, he sounded great on air but when he wasn't following a script, Jeez, he could bore you to—

'John, hi, how are you? Nice to see you. I meant to say it was lovely having Emma to stay. This is Tamy, it's her birthday.'

'Happy birthday.'

## 192

Beth had chosen the highest vacant room at the Hotel Monumental.

The windows opened a bit but not enough to jump out of, even if she wanted to. The hotel had been jumped out of many times in the 1980s so it changed the design of all its windows. But Beth didn't want to jump out anyway. She just wanted to look at the view.

'What do you think of fire, Dan?' she asked.

'Hot.'

'Someone said of the burning monk Quang Duc that the symbolism of fire was more profound than the heat of the fire.'

'Sounds like someone who's never been burnt.'

'You're right there.'

## 191

The ex-government agent looked at the metre on the taxi.

'Are we nearly there?'

The taxi driver only spoke Twi.

'How much is this going to cost me?' said the ex-agent.

The taxi driver didn't fully understand but he recognised the signs of a non-payer so he pulled over and gestured to the ex-agent to get out.

'What? Why?'

The taxi driver said something offensive in Twi.

The ex-agent waved his expired ID at him.

It didn't wash.

## 190

John followed Penny into the studio where he was introduced to Ali Bronski.

Edward the Fireman held back and then followed Tamy into the producer's booth and when she asked him what he was doing he told her to take a seat and not to get alarmed by the gun in his hand.

Tamy said Oh.

Then OK.

Then she sat down.

He asked Tamy if the woman sitting behind the green microphone was 'Dr Frankburg'. Tamy said she was. Edward the Fireman asked Tamy if she thought Dr Frankburg was beautiful? Tamy said it depended on your taste. Edward the Fireman said he thought she was very beautiful. Tamy said she agreed and asked if he was going to shoot Dr Frankburg. Edward the Fireman said God no. Never. Tamy asked who he was going to shoot. He said he didn't know. He was just here as back-up.

He asked if 'Dr Frankburg' could see him through the dividing window. Tamy said yes they could if they looked over. He said that was good, he thought it might be one-way glass.

## 189

'And finally, a woman of ninety-three has been reunited with her one hundred and eighteen-year-old mother according to reporter Arty Greenson. What have you got for us, Arty?'

'I'm here at the Mary Jane Rest Home in upstate New York and with me is Nell Smithson, the one hundred and eighteen-year-old mother of Jean Smithson who, if you were listening earlier…'

## 188

The controller of KKRC had a pang of conscience at yet another faked story. Still, it was the good news station. And it could happen.

## 187

Graham Johansson said a few words to the passengers. Some nervous flyers who usually liked hearing the captain speak found themselves growing uneasier but couldn't put their finger on why.

Emma Heron in 34A smiled and told the person next to her that they were in for a great trip.

The person nodded. He wasn't convinced, he'd heard some bad things about Birmingham.

Graham Johansson waited for clearance and then took off.

## 186

Deafening.

Pitch black but for the occasional flashing light.

Runway hurtling beneath.

Wind swirling through me.

The terrifying pneumatic whine of the hydraulics, pushing, contracting. Vast wheels gathering themselves around me.

Burning hot from friction, penning me in, breathing choking rubber fumes into my lungs.

Scrambling away from the monumental mechanism.

Screams merging with the engine wail.

Muffled by the closing undercarriage.

A continuous roar. Darkness.

I endured it. I deserved it.

Up and over the Hudson, circling, wishing I could look down.

Radio transmitting but no sound coming.

## 185

'...a case of new time for the old timers. Back to Penny Lock.'

## 184

Green light.

Pause. Too long.

The controller frowned. Thought the Tamy kid had probably hit the wrong button. Tipsy on birthday champagne. Bad bad. Looked amateurish.

## 183

<small cough>

'Listeners. Um, welcome back. I... I have to describe a situation to you. Behind my producer's window is Tamy. My producer. With her is a young gentleman of average height. White. Who has a gun to her head.'

## 182

Some taxi drivers shunted each other.

## 181

The controller's jaw sagged open.

## 180

The wind had blown my eyes shut and had frozen the tears so that my lids wouldn't open. I was glad of that though.

## 179

Edward felt his heart beating hard and fast. All his organs felt jumpy.

## 178

'Can she hear me in there?' asked Edward.

Tamy flicked a switch and nodded.

'Hi,' said my brother.

'Hello,' said Penny Lock.

'Hello,' said Ali Bronski.

'You remember me, right?'

No.

'Yes.'

He smiled.

'You sound great,' said my brother.

'Well. Thanks,' said Ali.

## 177

He'd locked himself and Tamy inside. Tamy wished she hadn't left the keys in the lock. Her father had arranged basic self-defence classes for her, but they didn't start till tomorrow.

## 176

'Shall I switch to some more news?' said Penny.

'No,' said my brother. 'Am I broadcasting now?'

Tamy said if she flicked another switch then the producer's booth would go live.

'OK, good, do it.'

Tamy went live.

'OK? Am I on air?'

'You're on.'

'Good. Hello, everyone.'

He paused.

'Say hello, Tamy.'

'Hello,' said Tamy.

## 175

Clara Redlake recognised Edward's voice and she slowed down to help her think.

This could either be a very good thing or a very bad thing for her.

She thought she ought to ring the station. Talk him out of trouble. She knew him best. Knew what his buttons were. God only knew what 'Frankburg' would say to him.

## 174

'Do you want to introduce yourself?' asked Penny.

'In a minute. Can I say this is going to be a great day?'

'Um . . . yes.'

'This is going to be a great day.'

'OK. Good,' said Penny.

'That was good,' said Ali.

'Well, I truly believe it's going to be a great day,' said Edward. 'Don't you?'

'Yes, I'm sure it'll work out very well,' said Ali.

'OK. I'm right here for you.'

'Well, thank you.'

'My pleasure.'

'You've got a natural radio voice. Hasn't he got a natural radio voice, Penny?'

'Um. Yes.'

'See? Penny agrees with me about your natural radio voice.'

'Thank you.'

There was a pause.

'Do you want to introduce yourself now?' said Penny.

'Yes. My name is Activist 346 of TWA, the Third World Army.'

He winked at Ali.

Penny clicked. 'Fight the Good Fight.'

Ali clicked. Her weeping fake fireman.

Tamy clicked and regretted putting him through that time. She'd been given a raise following the show but it didn't seem worth it now.


## 173

I would've clicked too but I couldn't hear my radio over the noise of the aeroplane. And I was too scared to think of it. Scared scared scared.


## 172

Clara wondered if someone had made a Taking Hostages tape. Or if her ex-fireman was doing other experiments on the sly. If so then she reckoned there was some competition out there.


## 171

'What's your name?' asked Penny Lock.

'You don't need to know my name.'

'I thought it might be nice for the listeners to know your name.'

'Nice? What do you mean nice?'

'Well, it's nice to know people's names.'

'What's nice about it?'

'It's just nice.'

'Nice. Jeez.'

'Names is for tombstones, isn't it, Edward?' said Ali.

'Yeah,' said my brother, smiling.

'We know Dr Frankburg's name,' said Penny.

'Sure we do,' said my brother winking again.

'So what's yours?'

'You don't need to know my fucking name.'

Tamy instinctively went for the mute switch.

'Stay still, what are you doing?'

'Sorry,' said Tamy. 'I didn't think. I have to blank out swearing. Station policy.'

'Don't touch anything. Leave the switches alone.'

'I'm sorry.'


## 170

John stared at the guy with the gun in his hand. Saw how alive his eyes were. How quick and twitchy his movements were. How he kept switching the gun from hand to hand to wipe the sweat off his palms and onto his coat. John thought he should do that too, in his act, switch the gun from hand to hand. And sweat more.

'What do you think we should do?' asked John in a whisper.

'Tell the magic guy to shut up,' said my brother.

'Sorry,' said John.

'Why are you here anyway?'

'This is John, he's looking for his wife.'

'Hello, we met in the lobby...' said John.

'You're English?'

'Yes.'

'Does your wife work here?'

'No.'

'Then why are you looking for her here?'

'She rang in.'

'She rang in from somewhere else, right?'

'Yes.'

'So why are you looking for her here?'

'Um…'

'John was ringing the show about his missing wife but got cut off when his friend jumped off the Brooklyn Bridge.'

'She didn't jump,' said John.

'Didn't she?' said Penny.

'Beth didn't jump?' said my brother.

'No.'

'That's good,' said Ali.

'That's good,' said Penny.

'Did you stop her from jumping?' asked my brother.

'No, she just decided not to,' said John.

'That's good because she wouldn't have thanked you if you'd tried to stop her.'

'I didn't.'

'That's good.'

## 169

The KKRC's controller wished they would spice the dialogue up a bit. He thought the 'fucking' from before was good. He could let a few of those go fine.

## 168

The pharmaceutical CEO dialled the ex-agent with trembling hands.

'Are you listening to the Penny Lock Phone-In show?'

'I was but I got kicked out of my cab. Anyway, you're a piece of shit. I don't talk to pieces of shit. Unless they're giving me ten thousand dollars, in which case—'

'Tamy's got a gun to her head.'

'Good.'

'What? You arsehole.'

'You're the arsehole.'

'My daughter's got a gun to her head you arsehole.'

'Perhaps the pilot flipped.'

'He's not a fucking pilot.'

'How do you know?'

'I want the best man on the job. Pull some strings. Get some sharpshoot-ers down there.'

'You want the pilot shot?'

'Stop calling him a pilot.'

'You want Kermit the frog shot?'

'You son of a bitch.'

'Where's my money.'

'You fucking arsehole.'

Click.

The ex-agent flagged down another cab. The driver responded to his ID without question and drove like the wind.


## 167

Samuel Thorn arrived at Dr Frankburg's house. They shook hands. Sam said 'Good evening' as he did so and Frankburg felt vibrations in his fingers. The voice really was very resonant, especially up close.


## 166

'This is dead air,' said my brother. 'We should play a record.'

'What would you like?' said Penny.

'I don't know. Something by Frank Sinatra.'

'Well, sure, but that's usually Tamy's job, she does that kind of thing.'

'Who's Tamy?'

'She's the woman who's head you have a gun to.'

'Right. Sorry, I forgot. Hi Tamy.'

'Hi.'

'Today is her birthday,' said Penny.

'Many happy returns,' said Edward.

'Thank you.'

'Have you got any Frank Sinatra?'

'Yes, but I'd have to go into the store to get it.'

'Where's the store?'

'Next door.'

'I guess we'll leave it then.'

'I guess so.'

'My analyst tried to tell me I was Frank Sinatra,' said Edward.

'Really?' said Ali. 'Sounds like a bit of a quack analyst.'

'Yeah, that's what I think.'


## 165

Clara was outraged. That was a total misinterpretation of what she was trying to do.


## 164

Another radio station had noticed what was happening at KKRC Your Station and was broadcasting it as news. KKRC was confused about the copyright issues here and they put some lawyers on to it.


## 163

The pharmaceutical CEO called the terrorist squad. Did they know his daughter was being held hostage by someone calling himself the TWA?

The airline?

'No, not the fucking airline, the people who tried to blow up his car. Thought there was a remote possibility the man was a pilot.'

'A what?'

'No, scratch that, he's not a pilot.'

They said the matter was in hand.

He said he'd have thought they'd have been more vigilant what with the bomb incident the day before. He wondered where his taxes went.

## 162

Samuel Thorn told Dr Frankburg that he was called the Albatross at school. Frankburg asked him if it was because he was good at golf. Sam said of course not and looked terribly disappointed in Frankburg. Frankburg apologised. Said he was a bit het up.

## 161

'Do a trick then. Yeah? Magic guy? Can you do a trick?'

'Well.'

'Come on, something with cards.'

'Well.'

'Come on.'

'Is everyone happy to see a trick?' asked John.

'Sure,' said Penny.

Ali nodded.

## 160

Ali was looking into Tamy's eyes. Tamy was looking back at Ali with the clearly communicated request to do something about this situation.

Ali tried to tell her that when it came down to it, she didn't know what to do at all, and all of them were consequently just going to have to hope for the best.

## 159

'OK.'

John took out a pack of cards and started shuffling them. 'I'm shuffling the cards.'

Sound of shuffling. John's hands were trembling. A card dropped on the floor. John picked it up.

'Sorry,' he said, 'bit rusty.'

## 158

The KKRC controller had tried magic on the radio before. It sucked.

## 157

'Now I'm spreading them into a fan.'

Small pause.

'Now I'm asking a volunteer to pick one out.'

Pause.

'I volunteer,' said Penny.

'OK, Penny's our volunteer and she's picking a card. But don't show it to me, Penny.'

Small pause.

'She's picked one. Now look at it.'

'OK.'

'Memorise it.'

'OK.'

'Now show it to, um, Activist 34... Sorry, I've forgotten your, um...'

'346.'

'Sorry. Activist 346.'

'OK.'

'I see it,' said Edward.

'Good, now put it back.'

'OK,' said Penny.

'Now I'm shuffling the pack again.'

Sound of shuffling.

Edward thought something by Frank Sinatra would perhaps have been more entertaining.

## 156

Ali said, 'Are you bleeding?'

'Yes, I am,' said Edward.

'What happened?'

'I wanted to see my liver.'

'I see. And did you see it?'

'Yeah. It looked pretty good but I couldn't say for sure if it was mine.'

'Did you touch it?'

'Yeah.'

'What happened?'

'I passed out.'

'I guess it was yours then.'


## 155

'Now... I'm... sorry, does anyone want to see this trick? Because it's fine to stop. I think I may have made a mistake anyway.'

'No, carry on,' said Edward.

John flourished a three of hearts. 'Was that your card?' he asked.

'No,' said Penny.

'Oh.'

There was a pause.

'Sorry.'

'What happens now?' asked Penny.

'Shall I have another stab at it?' asked John.

'I think we'll leave the magic now,' said Edward.

'Good idea,' said Penny.


## 154

Samuel Thorn got on the phone and was told that there was a crisis at KKRC and could he call back later? Samuel said he knew the true identity of the Dr Frankburg they had in the studio and demanded to be put on to the show.

The station said they'd call him back and hung up.

'What happened?' asked Dr Frankburg.

'They cut me off.'

'Outrageous. Try them again.'

Samuel dialled again.


## 153

Dan poured from a whisky bottle. He and Beth drank out of toothbrush glasses. They toasted Beth's top ten phobias.

To hypnophobia: fear of sleep. Clink. To athazagoraphobia: fear of being forgotten. Clink. To dementophobia: fear of insanity. Clink. To illyngophobia: fear

of vertigo. Clink. To dystychiphobia: fear of accidents. Clink. To anuptaphobia: fear
of staying single. Clink. To mastigophobia: fear of punishment. Clink. To mnemo-
phobia: fear of memories. Clink. To onomatophobia: fear of hearing a certain
word. Clink. To optophobia: fear of opening one's eyes. Clink.

## 152

'Don't you think we would get a bit further if you let my producer go?' asked
Penny.

'I think we'd get less far,' he replied.

John had to agree with him there, even if it was Tamy's birthday. From his
own experience, the guy with the gun was the guy calling the shots.

'What is it you want?' said Penny.

'I'm here as back-up,' said Edward, looking at Ali.

'Back up for what?' asked Penny.

My brother winked at Ali.

'Why does he keep winking at you?' said John.

'Tell the magic guy to shut up,' said Edward.

'Sorry,' said John.

'The magic guy doesn't speak from now on.'

'OK.'

'No more words from Mr Magic.'

'None coming.'

## 151

Someone at KKRC had rung the police. Squad cars had sealed the street. The
police advised the controller of KKRC to stop broadcasting.

The controller of KKRC watched the listening figures climb and climb and
said that the guy with the gun was calling the shots and the guy with the gun
wanted to stay on air so stay on the air they would.

## 150

Five o'clock came. Penny's time slot was over. The next DJ started whining and
muttering about contracts. The controller told him to can it. He'd never get

figures like Penny was getting. In fact he was fired. The DJ stormed out. Then stormed back in again, assuming the controller was joking.

## 149

The KKRC receptionist was sobbing in the toilets. Wishing with all her heart that she could turn the clock back and be more vigilant about who she let in to see Penny Lock. If anything happened to her then she'd never forgive herself. She looked at herself in the mirror, wiped away her mascara and tried to see the glamour in the situation.

## 148

The ex-government agent arrived at the radio station.

He flashed his ID and told the officer in charge that he was the negotiator. The police said they hadn't called a negotiator yet as no demands had been issued. The ex-government agent said he was here anyway. Stand aside.

## 147

'This is quite a day for the TWA,' said my brother.

'Quite a day indeed,' said Ali.

'Perhaps a landmark day?'

'Well perhaps.'

'How has the struggle been?'

'Fine.'

'I heard you on the radio and I came straight down.'

'So I see.'

'Is this helping?'

'Well...'

'Just tell me how you want to play it and I'm right there.'

'OK, thanks.'

'My pleasure. You're the boss.'

'I see. I was wondering if maybe you'd like to hand the gun over?'

'Hand it over? To you?'

'If you like.'

'Do you want to shoot someone?'

'I wouldn't say "want" exactly.'

'Forced to out of necessity?'

'Something like that perhaps.'

'Is it going to be the magic guy?'

'Hey?' said the magic guy.

'Is he the target?' said Edward.

'No.'

'Have you ever fired a gun before?' asked Edward.

'No,' said Ali.

'I think I'd better keep hold of it then, for now.'

## 146

Dan said he didn't have any phobias.

Beth pressed him.

Dan said OK, if pushed he hated poems. But he couldn't call it a phobia.

'Metrophobia,' said Beth. 'Next one.'

'Fear of philosophy,' said Dan.

'Philosophobia.'

'Fear of God.'

'Theophobia.'

'Fear of looking up.'

'Anablephobia.'

'Fear of stars and celestial space.'

'Astrophobia.'

'Fear of persons with amputations.'

'Apotemnophobia.'

'Fear of imaginary crime.'

'Peccatophobia.'

'Fear of clowns.'

'Coulrophobia.'

'Fear of heaven.'

'Uranophobia.'

'Fear of dreams.'

'Oneirophobia.'

'Are these real?' asked Dan.

Beth shrugged. 'Why are you afraid of dreams?' she asked.

'I don't have them. Or I don't remember them. I think when they do come they'll be terrible.'

'Don't you remember any?'

'No.'

Beth said she dreamt all the time.

Dan asked her to describe some of them.

Beth said no. She said she didn't do that. Telling someone a dream was like telling them a bad story.

Dan was secretly glad. But he didn't want to be secretive so he said he was glad out loud.

Beth was glad too. If he'd actually wanted to hear her dreams she'd have gone off him a bit.


## 145

'I wish I knew your name,' said Ali. 'It's very hard to speak to you like this.'

'Do you think it's a good idea to say our names over the air?'

'Well, it makes it easier to talk together.'

'Is that what today's about? Are we talking? I thought there might be action.'

'Well, there might be action too.'

Penny looked alarmed. She didn't think Ali should be encouraging him to take action.

'You can call me Edward.'

'Edward? Really?'

'Do you like it?'

'It's very...'

'Dignified?'

'Dignified. Yes.'

'Activist Edward.'

'It's very catchy.'

## 144

The police chief handed over operations to the ex-government agent reluctantly. This was always happening, dammit. He didn't know why he couldn't be allowed to take control of these situations himself. The ex-government agent told him not to be a whinging piece of shit. The police chief's jaw bunched up in anger and humiliation.

'How do I speak to Penny Lock?' asked the ex-government agent.

He was shown into an adjoining studio and talked through the talkback system.

'OK then,' he said. 'I'll take if from here.'

The ex-government agent hoped that cocksucking pharmaceutical CEO was still tuned in.

## 143

Lily Frankburg was glad her 'Lily Forever' tattoo was still visible, though a bit red and scuffed. She regretted having '100% Cody' tattooed on her belly but figured her father might pay for laser surgery.

Lily sat in her stolen car outside Dr Frankburg's house and smoked a cigarette. She rang my telephone to tell me that I was on my own now and that she'd had enough of being Cody Jameson. She was going to give Lily Frankburg another shot. If there was to be a *More Tales of a Stewardess* , I had to write it myself.

My phone didn't pick up her incoming signal. It was undergoing far too many atmospheric disturbances. Much like its owner.

## 142

A voice came through Penny's headphones.

'Miss Lock, this is the negotiator, I'm here to help you out of this little crisis.'

Penny jumped a little at hearing the voice.

'Don't acknowledge me as it would be better if our friend believed you were speaking for yourself. You'll find you can say yes and no to me without opening your mouth and arousing suspicion. For yes you can make a "Hmmm" sound.'

Penny Hmmmed.

'For no you can make a Mm-mm sound.'

Penny Mm-mmed.

'Good. This will be our system. It seems that the station as well as the hostage taker is keen to keep broadcasting and for the time being I'm happy with that if you are.'

'Hmmm'.

'What are you doing?' said Edward.

'I'm just humming,' said Penny.

'Why?'

'It's good for keeping the spirits up.'

'Is it?'

'Sure.'

'I've never found that.'

'You should try it.'

'My spirits are already up.'

'Well, good. Good for you.'


## 141

Samuel Thorn's call was connected to KKRC. He was put on hold. The negotiator was told that there was a guy ringing from England claiming to know the real identity of Dr Frankburg. The negotiator told KKRC to keep him on the line.

Samuel told Dr Frankburg that he was in and was on hold. Frankburg gave him the thumbs up.


## 140

John Heron asked if this would be a good time to make a quick announcement to his wife.

The negotiator told Penny to ask Edward.

'What do you think?' asked Penny.

'What do you think?' Edward asked Ali.

'What do you think?' Ali asked Edward.

'If he's quick,' said Edward.

Over the radio waves. Reaching maybe a hundred miles. Many of them over the sea. John leaned into Penny's microphone and said: 'This is a message to Emma Heron from your husband John. If you can hear this please ring KKRC—'

'No, not KKRC,' said Penny. 'Now isn't a good time.'

'Oh, no, ring home. Leave a message for me at home.'

## 139

Emma was miles in the air. The radio waves caught up with the plane but bounced back off it.

Emma felt stifled with heat and lack of air but as the plane soared, her eyes caught sight of the lights of the city and her mind told her that it was a magnificent view and she must have been half asleep not to have noticed it before. And there were other views like this to be seen. And sounds to be heard, and smells to be smelt.

She wondered if she should tell Graham Johansson to take a look out the window too.

## 138

KKRC was getting so many calls that the police had told them to shut down the phone lines.

'Can we keep this one?' asked a call minder. 'She says she's the hostage taker's analyst, a Miss Clara Redlake.'

The ex-government agent nodded.

Clara was put on hold with Sam. All other calls were directed somewhere else.

## 137

Penny flicked the wrong button. The KKRC jingle blared out.

'KKRC is Your Station twenty-four seven, it's Penny Looooock'.

'What the hell is that?' said Edward.

'Sorry, pressed the wrong button.'

'No one press anything.'

## 136

The negotiator spoke in Penny's ear.

'We have a caller here who claims Dr Frankburg here is a fake.'

'Hmmm.'

'I think we should put him on as it might be a good idea for the hostage taker to feel his ally is undermined.'

Penny didn't think that was such a good idea at all. 'Hmm mmm hmm?'

'I don't recognise that Ms Lock.'

'Mm mm'.

'Are you saying no?'

'Hmmm.'

There was a pause.

'What are you singing, Penny?' asked Edward.

'Um…'

'You should sing something you know the words to.'

A few clicks were heard. Then Sam's powerful Welsh voices boomed into the studio.

'Hello?'

Everyone jumped.

'Hello?'

'Who the fucking hell is this?' said my brother.

Penny recovered. 'This is just a caller, Edward. This is a phone-in. There must be some calls getting through.'

'Hello?' said Sam Thorn.


## 135

The real Frankburg wished Sam would stop saying hello. Made him sound stupid.


## 134

Clara Redlake, driving with the phone clamped to her ear and the radio blasting, heard the powerful Welsh voice surging through the airwaves. 'Ataboy,' she said. Those British lozenges must be pretty damn good.

## 133

Lily Frankburg walked up to her father's house and cupped her hands round her face to look in through the window., She saw big Samuel Thorn on the phone and her father beside him, leaping up and down like an excited child.

## 132

'This is the real Dr Frankburg,' said Sam.

The real Dr Frankburg put both thumbs up at Sam again. Sam smiled and gave the thumbs up back.

'All right,' said twelve per cent of Manhattan taxi drivers.

## 131

Beth said that the practice of suttee required a woman to follow her deceased husband to his funeral pyre. Dan said he knew. Beth said it might not be so bad second time around as the job was half finished already. Dan asked if she was scarred all over. Beth took off some clothes.

Dan sat on the edge of the bed and watched her.

'I think I'd like to take everything off,' said Beth.

Dan nodded.

And so Beth stood before Dan and let Dan look at her. And she turned round and to the side and to the front again. And Dan's eyes filled with tears and so did Beth's.

'Late in life,' said Beth, 'Monsieur Chabert the fire king made and sold an alleged cure for the White Plague. He raised and dashed many hopes. He was a faker and a quack. If he'd really gone into an oven he'd have burnt to a crisp.'

Dan agreed.

Dan said he'd like to dance. Beth said she'd like to too. And she put on a dressing gown and they pushed the bed against the wall and put the chairs and table on it to give them room.

Dan put his hands round Beth's waist. She put her arms round his neck. They stayed still till their breathing was in time.

'What sort of dancing would you like to do?' said Dan.

'It'll depend on the music.'

Dan reached over and switched on the radio.

## 130

'Is there a so-called Dr Frankburg in the studio?' asked Samuel.

'Yes,' said Ali.

Samuel paused slightly for effect.

'Aren't you really Ali Bronski?' asked Samuel.

'Yes,' said Ali.

Pause.

'Oh.'

## 129

'Oh,' said the station controller, hoping for more of a struggle.

## 128

'Oh,' said Clara Redlake. She was disappointed Ali Bronski had caved in so easily. She switched the phone to the other ear. She was still on hold. A voice thanked her for being patient.

## 127

'What's she saying?' Frankburg asked Samuel Thorn. 'What's she saying?'

## 126

'Who is this?' asked Ali Bronski.

'This is the real Dr Frankburg, ringing from Birmingham, England.'

'Really? You don't sound like him.'

'Of course I sound like him. Surely you've heard my tape *You Too Can Fly?*'

'Then you must be Samuel Thorn.'

Pause.

'Are you Samuel Thorn?'

Pause.

'Oh,' said Samuel.

Pause.

'Yes,' said Samuel.

## 125

Frankburg hopped up and down and asked what was happening.

## 124

Clara scrabbled around in her glove compartment for her copy of *You Too Can Fly*.

## 123

'Why has this caller been put through?' asked Edward. 'Why are we taking calls?'

'I don't know,' said Tamy. Tamy usually got to select the callers. She wondered who was in charge. Probably that upstart receptionist, she'd been angling for more responsibility.

'We're in a bit of a crisis situation here, caller, have you got anything constructive you'd like to say?' said Penny.

## 122

Tamy wanted to look into the eyes of the bleeding man beside her. Tamy thought she had nice eyes. She thought if he saw her eyes he would find it harder to do anything bad to her. Especially on her birthday.

## 121

'Can I ask Ali Bronski about something else?' asked Samuel Thorn.

'Yes,' said Ali Bronski.

'Were you with Kirsten Henderson when she died?'

'Oh.'

## 120

There was a pause in the studio.

## 119

Someone tried to enter cab 3345. '*Koh. Me pawocheo*,' said the driver; he was listening to the radio.

## 118

The ex-government agent told Penny that though the conversation had moved on to death, she shouldn't feel worried and that as far as he was concerned, he thought it was all going fine.

Penny didn't think it was going fine. 'So John, where did you learn magic?' she said.

## 117

Ali Bronski's eyes lost focus. And in that moment Ali Bronski is in a hotel in Islington and her eyes are filling. She is sitting by the side of a bath and stroking Kirsten's hair as the bath fills and she is making a silly little joke about rubber ducks and Kirsten is laughing a little bit and gripping Ali's hand and Ali is saying that perhaps Kirsten should put on an eye mask so that it's nice and dark and Kirsten is saying that she would rather keep her eyes open until hey close of their own accord and Ali is saying that's OK whatever she wants and she's thinking of a song to sing but nothing is coming so she just hums a bit but that seems OK and Kirsten starts to go a bit sluggish and she says to her that she's glad that Ali isn't an old friend and Ali is saying she is too, otherwise it would be a much worse moment than it is, although secretly Ali is thinking that this is as bad as it can possibly get…

## 116

'What's the matter?' asked Edward.

And Ali hasn't answered.

'It's just you're on the inquest tape,' said Samuel Thorn.

'Oh…'

'And some video tape of the sitcom she was in.'

'Oh…'

'What's the matter?' asked Edward.

'And I wanted to know…'

'Ali?' said Penny.

## 115

Tamy's father wanted to know what the hell was going on. Why weren't there stormtroopers all over the station.

## 114

Dan and Beth stopped dancing and just listened. Dan said he'd been trying to find his daughter and here she was. He only had to tune in.

He said she sounded very upset and Beth said she had a lovely voice. Dan said she got it from her mother. Beth said she thought she got it from Dan. Dan said thank you. And Beth asked if she should turn the radio off and Dan said just keep it going for a little bit.

## 113

'What do you want me to do?' asked Edward.

'I wanted to know what Kristen's last words were?' said Samuel.

'Oh…'

'Do you know?'

'Shall I cut him off?' asked Penny.

'Yes,' said Edward.

'Yes,' said John.

'No,' said the negotiator.

'Which?' asked Penny.

'Do you know what her last words were?' asked Samuel.

## 112

'My head is hurting,' said Tamy.

'Shut up,' said Edward.

'Ali?' said Sam.

## 111

Tamy's father burst into KKRC and demanded to know why the doors hadn't been smashed down and tear gas pumped through the air conditioning.

## 110

Frankburg wrote furiously on a piece of paper 'What are you doing?' and held it up to Samuel.

## 109

'Did she mention me?' asked Samuel.

Ali said, 'No.'

'Are you sure?' said Samuel.

'Cut him off,' said Edward. He thought Activist 345 was going to cry and if she did then he would too and he didn't think it was the time for crying.

'Did she mention me?' said Samuel again.

Ali said, 'No.'

## 108

John shuffled a pack of cards nervously. He wondered if he could diffuse the situation with another trick. Or his collapsible wand.

## 107

Ali is keeping Kirsten's head under the water and Ali is crying and crying and Kirsten has got her eyes closed but suddenly and without warning they open and they look at Ali and they look eye to eye and Ali doesn't know what to do but Kirsten has told her to keep her head under, no matter what, she's made her promise and so she has to keep it under even though Kirsten's hands are flapping a bit and her fingers are wiggling a bit and Ali is crying as she holds Kirsten under and Ali was crying now, the tears wouldn't stop now.

## 106

My brother Edward watched her and wanted to know what she wanted him to do.

'What's the plan here?' he asked and everyone wanted to know that too.

## 105

'Kirsten's last words were "I've changed my mind",' said Ali.

'What?' said Samuel.

Penny thought Ali should speak up. She should get a bit closer to the microphone.

'Kirsten said, "I've changed my mind",' said Ali, and the tears dribbled onto the green foam mike cover and John shuffled his cards and Penny bit her lip and Edward bled.

## 104

The ex-government agent told Penny that Tamy's father had entered the building and told her to mention the fact, so Penny did.

'Tamy's dad's arrived,' said Penny.

'Don't say that,' said Tamy. She didn't want that.

'You could try telling everyone that Tamy's father is a piece of shit,' said the ex-agent.

Penny thought she must have misheard.

'He's a worthless fucking piece of back-stabbing shit.'

Everyone near the ex-government agent wondered what kind of negotiation technique this was. The chief of police wanted to have a closer look at his ID.

'What's the plan?' asked Edward.

## 103

'What did she mean "I've changed my mind"',' asked Samuel.

'She'd changed her mind,' said Ali.

'About what?' said Samuel.

'Tamy, your dad's entered the building,' said Penny. 'And he's a piece of shit.'

'He's a what?' asked Edward.

'A worthless fucking piece of back-stabbing shit,' said Penny.

'I wouldn't have said "worthless"',' said Tamy.

'What do you want me to do?' said Edward. It didn't get through so he shouted it. 'What do you want me to do!'

## 102

Clara Redlake was put through.

'Hi, Edward,' said Clara. They put her on with Samuel. There were voices all over the room.

'Why is she speaking?' said my brother. 'Why has this woman been put on to the air? Why is her voice in here?'

'Don't be like that, Edward,' said Clara Redlake.

'She'd changed her mind about dying,' said Ali.

'She was in the bath, though,' said Samuel 'She died in a bath.'

'This is getting...' said Penny.

'She wanted me to...' said Ali.

'Just keep calm, Penny,' said the ex-agent. 'You're doing fine.'

'Mm-mm.'

'Put the gun down, Edward,' said Clara.

'I was holding her under,' said Ali.


## 101

The police didn't think it was a good idea for Tamy's dad to get involved at the sharp end but the ex-government agent instructed them to let Tamy's dad bang on Tamy's door.

'Tamy!'

The chief of police grabbed the ex-agent's ID.

'Why is this a good idea?' asked Penny.


## 100

Bang bang bang!

'Who the fuck's that?' asked Edward.

'You were what?' asked Samuel.

'Kirsten asked me to hold her under,' said Ali.

'Don't bang on the door, Dad,' said Tamy.

'Tamy!'

'What's the plan here?' said Edward. 'Tell me what to do!'

'Tell him who he is,' said the ex-government agent.

The chief of police realised he'd made a bad decision.

'Shall we stop the calls now?' said John. 'I don't think we should have any more calls coming through.'

'Tell the gun guy who Tamy's piece of shit dad is,' said the ex-government agent.

'Why is that a good idea?' asked Penny.

'What do you want me to do?' asked Edward. He was losing a lot of blood. The room had started to swim.

'Get this man out!' shouted the chief of police.

'Just tell him,' said the ex-government agent.

'Why?'

'Tell him!' The ex-government agent was manhandled out of the room, headphones flicking off his head as he went.

'Tamy's dad runs a pharmaceutical company,' said Penny.

'Don't tell him that!' said Tamy.

'Try to picture a field of wheat Edward,' said Clara.

It clicked for Edward.

Click.

Click.

Tamy was the target.

Click. Very clever. He wanted to tell Ali he loved her.

'Tamy! Tamy!' Thump thump thump.

Edward shot Tamy through the head.


## 99

BANG!


## 98

I love you. Not heard over the noise.


## 97

John rethinks his act. He'd got the effect badly wrong. He snaps his collapsible wand.


## 96

Penny screams.


## 95

Clara says, 'Oh goodness!' drops the phone and loses control of the car.

## 94

Blood covers Tamy's window.

## 93

The police help Tamy's dad smash down the door. He rushes in with a bellow and a howl.

## 92

Samuel Thorn gets cut off. 'Hello?'

## 91

Dr Frankburg asks Samuel how it went.

## 90

Tamy's dad jumps at Edward. Gas is sprayed into the room. Another shot goes off and smashes the window before hitting Ali in the chest.

　　'Oh,' said Ali. 'Oh.'

## 89

Another shot goes off and hits the studio's whiteboard, 'Don't forget to plug the Christmas Special.'

　　Penny ducks under the table.

## 88

Edward sees Ali go down but everything is fuzzy now. He is aware of bodies all over him. The gun goes off again and the bullet goes through Tamy's dad. Tamy's dad thinks he's been punched. Not for long, though.

## 87

Forty per cent of Manhattan's taxis are stationary.

## 86

'You piece of shit!' shouts the ex-government agent, hoping it'll be the last thing the CEO hears.

## 85

My brother Edward feels that too much blood has left his body and he slips away. He uses his last reserves to say, 'Why weep you! Did you think I should live for ever?' But no one is weeping and no one thinks he will live for ever and Tamy's microphone has been flicked off and no one hears it anyway.

## 84

John is sick on the floor.

## 83

Samuel Thorn tells Dr Frankburg he didn't think it went terribly well.

## 82

Graham Johansson hits a pocket of turbulence and the plane drops violently. The co-pilot gasps, a stewardess breaks an ankle.

## 81

Emma in 34A drops through the turbulence and thinks of blue skies and green water and hot sun and pink shells and bright stars and the northern lights and waterfalls and cliffs and breaking waves and bluebells in the woods…

## 80

The KKRC controller tries to think of an appropriate jingle to play.

## 79

Clara fumbles for her phone and her car clips a truck and spins off the road. The car turns over and over and dented chassis hits Clara's head and it hits it so hard that she won't live any more and her brain flickers out a little thought about lobsters hissing in a pan and perhaps she shouldn't eat them any more and then she dies.

The truck driver pulls over and runs to the car. Clara Redlake is suspended upside down, held by her seat belt, and her car is telling her in a pleasant and non judgemental way: Your oil pressure is low. Ping. Your oil pressure is low. Ping…

## 78

And the plane drops down.

## 77

Dan hears shots ring out and he hold on to Beth and waits for a voice to say 'I'm all right.'

Beth hears Edward ruin someone else's life and she holds Dan tight. She reaches back and finds some music. Another station. Tommy Tempo's Nite Moods Orchestra. Plenty of soft woodwind and saxophone. Tommy of old. Tommy on form.

She keeps a tight hold on Dan. She strokes his hair.

Through his tears Dan tells Beth he loves her.

## 76

And Graham Johansson pulls on the controls and fights the plane and rides the currents and thinks of his wife and takes a deep breath and he hangs in the air and it's up or down and he thinks of down and he thinks of crashing down and he thinks of hitting the ground and he thinks of a ball of flames bouncing down the runway and being chased by fire engines and he thinks of firemen gripping their axes tightly and ground staff gripping their binoculars tightly and news teams gripping their cameras tightly and onlookers gripping each other tightly…

## 75

And Lily Frankburg knocks on the window of her father's house.

## 74

And Graham Johansson thinks of up, he thinks of a gentle breeze, and he brings the plane up. And Graham Johansson levels. And the co-pilot pats him on the shoulder. And Graham keeps flying.

## 73

And Michael Davies drives out to the place under the approach path for New York flights. He parks his car then tramps across an open field to where he believes the undercarriage of my plane will open. And he stands and he looks up at the stars and he breathes the air and stands in the dew and he waits and he holds his arms out, he holds his arms out wide, ready to catch me if I fall out.

## 72

And there is a breath. And static on the radio.

## 71

And I have been sick and the sick has frozen.

## 70

And when the signal clears it will bring news of other stories, and KKRC won't be the story anymore, the skyline will be the story...

## 69

And I may be dead. But I'm still counting...

## 68

...

## 67

...

## 66

...And if I am dead then it's been a gentle death. And I deserved worse...

## 65

...and the journey's been repeated though repetition is impossible...

## 64

...and there's you.

I am trying to picture you. Are you a man or a woman? Are you young or old? Are you attractive? Do you have facial hair? Do you have blue eyes or brown? Do you have a scar? Do you have responsibilities? Do you hate me or like me? Have you no opinion on the matter? Are you in bed now? Warm? On a chair? Cold? Ill? Are you on a train? A plane? Inside? Outside? Is your life a good thing or a bad thing? Are there times when you've been ashamed of yourself? Times when you wished there was someone watching? Do you have difficulty sleeping? Do you breathe easily? Are you loved? Do you have valuable possessions? Are your ears pierced? Do you wear make-up? Do you like popular music? Do you recognise birdsong? Can you hear traffic? Do your clothes fit well? Are you getting fat? Have you ever thought of taking up squash? Or table tennis? Is your job fulfilling? Do you have a job? Do you frame photographs? Have you ever been under general anaesthetic? When did you last faint? Have you ever puked in public? Do you feel your own pulse now and then? Are your teeth straight? Do you check the colour of your piss? Are your parents alive? Would you recognise your own belly button?

## 63

...It has been six hours...

## 62

...my watch still works and my ears have been popping...

## 61

...popping or bursting. I would guess that we have been losing height.

## 60

...

## 59

...Do you know what I should have done? I should have tied myself on. With rope. Or duck tape.

## 58

...

## 57

...My fingers have no strength. I can't make a fist.

## 56

...There's a tear on my cheek. I could lick it. See if it's solid, but my teeth are glued together and my tongue is swollen. I think there is liquid on my neck. I can shout now. I'm doing it. Mm-mm-mm-mm! I can't hear this. Not even in my own head. Not even a buzzing.

## 55

...Mm-mm-mmmm!

## 54

...And now there's movement. Suction and whirlwinds. Wrenching and trembling. What a bird. Pistons and judders and contractions and openings. Perhaps we're hatching an egg.

Lights. Lights below. And tiny things. A wood. A road. A pattern.

## 53

...I'm the egg and out I tumble.

## 52

...over and over.

## 51

...Be elegant. Be a diver...

## 50

...A double pike and a triple salchow and a flapping in the wind...

## 49

...and no parachute.

## 48

...But time enough to think of landing.

## 47

...Let me land on a haystack.

## 46

On a bush.

## 45

In a field.

## 44

Something soft.

## 43

...Where is he? Michael Davies. Always waiting. Standing with his arms outstretched ready to catch me.

## 42

Here I come.

## 41

Can't see him.

## 40

Break the fall Michael. Bend your knees.

## 39

...What shall I say now? What have others said?

## 38

Kirsten: I've changed my mind.

## 37

Ronald: DON'T THINK I DON'T KNOW WHO YOU ARE!

## 36

Tamy: Don't tell him that!

## 35

Tamy's father: Tamy! Tamy!

## 34

Edward: Why weep you! Did you think I should live for ever?

## 33

Ali Bronski: Oh, oh.

## 32

Clara Redlake: Oh goodness!

## 31

And for me? As I fall...

## 30

## 29

...down...

## 28

...

**27**

...down...

**26**

...

**25**

...I need...

**24**

...

**23**

...a ripcord to pull...

**22**

...

**21**

...or a fast-rising current...

**20**

...

**19**

...to keep me afloat...

**18**

...

**17**

...but I'm not buoyant...

**16**

...

**15**

...so let me be found by a little explorer...

**14**

...who'll arrange my arms and legs

**13**

...neatly...

**12**

...and tidy my

**11**

...hair...

**10**

...and pat my

**9**

...head...

**8**

...and sing me a

**7**

...song...

**6**

...

**5**

…and now…

**4**

…here it comes…

**3**

…

**2**

…

**1**

…catch

## Acknowledgements

Jim North. Derek Nisbet. Talking Birds. Bill Massey. Sarah Keen. Simon Trewin. Sarah Ballard. My family.

# Characters

John Heron. Unfunny John. Comic.

Emma Heron. His wife. Morgue Attendant.

Penny Lock. Talk Show Host.

Graham Johansson. Pilot.

Samuel Thorn. Actor. Wooden.

Cody Jameson. Writer. Real name Lily Frankburg.

Dr Frankburg. Father. Self-Help Therapist.

Dan Bronski. Air Crash Investigator.

Ali Bronski. Daughter. Counterfeit Therapist.

Stephanie Wiltshire. Ex-stewardess. Speaking to you.

Edward Wiltshire. Ex-fireman. Shouting at you.

Beth Davies. Nee Wiltshire. Sister. Aerophobe.

Michael Davies. Husband. Air Traffic Controller.

The Pharmaceutical CEO.

Tamy. His Daughter.

The Ex-Government Agent. No Gun.

Miles. Nightclub Owner.

Clara Redlake. Therapist. Eye Catcher.

Kirsten Henderson. Dead actress.

Ronald Henderson. Dead father.